D0531808

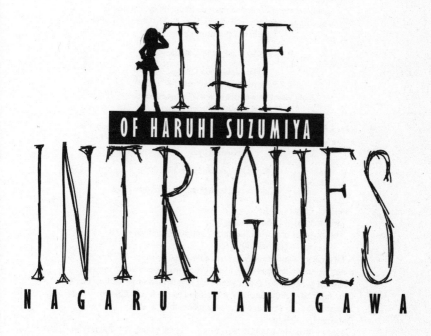

THE INTRIGUES
OF HARUHI SUZUMIYA

NAGARU TANIGAWA

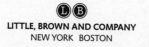

LITTLE, BROWN AND COMPANY
NEW YORK   BOSTON

Yen
Press

Suzumiya Haruhi No Inbou copyright © Nagaru TANIGAWA 2005
Illustration by Noizi Ito

First published in Japan in 2005 by Kadokawa Shoten Co., LTD., Tokyo.
English hardcover/paperback translation rights arranged with
Kadokawa Shoten Co., LTD., Tokyo, through
Tuttle-Mori Agency, Inc., Tokyo.

English translation by Paul Starr

Little, Brown and Company

Hachette Book Group
237 Park Avenue, New York, NY 10017
Visit our website at www.lb-teens.com
www.jointhesosbrigade.com

Little, Brown and Company is a division of Hachette Book Group, Inc.
The Little, Brown name and logo are trademarks of Hachette Book
Group, Inc.

First U.S. Edition: June 2012

Library of Congress Cataloging-in-Publication Data

Tanigawa, Nagaru.
  [Suzumiya Haruhi no inbo. English]
  The intrigues of Haruhi Suzumiya / Nagaru Tanigawa. — 1st U.S. ed.
     p. cm. — (Haruhi ; 7)
  Summary: "Kyon is ready to start a new year with the SOS Brigade,
a club whose leader is Haruhi, a girl who doesn't realize that she's a
powerful goddess. But then Kyon gets a visit from his friend Mikuru...
from eight days in the future! Kyon, guided by the future Mikuru,
attempts to stop a terrible future from becoming a reality" —
Provided by publisher.
  ISBN 978-0-316-03895-9 (hardback) — ISBN 978-0-316-03896-6
(paperback)
  [1. Supernatural—Fiction. 2. Clubs—Fiction. 3. Time travel—
Fiction. 4. Japan—Fiction.] I. Title.
  PZ7.T16139Int 2012
  [Fic]—dc23
                                                   2011042551

          HC: 10 9 8 7 6 5 4 3 2 1
          PB: 10 9 8 7 6 5 4 3 2 1

                      RRD-C

            Printed in the United States of America

THE

OF HARUHI SUZUMIYA

INTRIGUES

NAGARU TANIGAWA

First released in Japan in 2003, *The Melancholy of Haruhi Suzumiya* quickly established itself as a publishing phenomenon, drawing much of its inspiration from Japanese pop culture and Japanese comics in particular. With this foundation, the original publication of each book in the Haruhi series included several black-and-white spot illustrations as well as a four-page color insert—all of which are faithfully reproduced here to preserve the authenticity of the first-ever English edition.

PROLOGUE

Haruhi Suzumiya was behaving herself.

Neither melancholy nor sighing, and in point of fact not even seeming bored, she had of late been strangely quiet—and that inexplicable calmness worried me.

I'm not, of course, talking about a physical quietness, much less an emotional one. For one thing, Haruhi doesn't have the self-doubt it would take to alter her already formed personality, and even if she did, that would probably wind up turning into a different kind of pain in the ass for me, so I had no intention of attempting to remedy that situation—but in any case, it was like the color of her aura as it might show up in Kirlian photography had dimmed from red to a kind of orange.

Among her classmates, there was only one or maybe two at the outside who would have noticed the change. I can tell you with certainty who one of them was: me. She'd sat directly behind me ever since we started high school, and I see even more of her after school, so nobody's in a better position to notice such changes. And while she may seem calmer at the moment, her gaze that challenges all of creation is still there, as well as her action potential, tireless until satisfied.

She'd only managed to get second place in the school-wide hyakunin isshu poetry memorization competition late last month, but this month she'd won the school marathon—incidentally, it was Nagato who won the hyakunin isshu; she placed second in the marathon. Excelling in fields both literary and martial with their one-two finishes, the SOS Brigade chief and the resident bookworm had the entire school (including me) wondering just what the brigade was up to.

If there was one thing I was sure I understood, based on my experiences thus far, it was that when Haruhi got like this, she was without a doubt formulating some sort of evil scheme. And once she'd hit upon it, her face would light up with a smile, as surely as the sun rises.

I can't remember any instances of that not happening. Have there been any? Were there any sections in the history book within my mind where Haruhi had stayed calm and constant?

The worst storms are always portended by a fleeting calm. It has ever been thus.

So, then—

It is early February, the final stage of winter's coldest period.

The last year, with all its insanity, is now more than a month gone. If it felt as if time had passed especially quickly, it was probably due to January being full of activities surrounding New Year's.

Here I'd like to turn back time for a moment. I had no idea what Haruhi may have been planning, but I had my own business to come to terms with. February might seem too early to be already looking back on the year, but I've decided to tell the story of something I had to do—no, something I *wanted* to do.

During the whole thing, I had a single notion running through my head.

Finish what's been left undone, as quickly as you can.

Although it was during the winter break trip that I made up my mind to do this, I needed some time before I could put it into action.

2

This story starts on the second day of January, in front of the same train station we always use.

...

...

...

The winter vacation affair that had us stranded in the middle of a blizzard and trapped within a mysterious mansion ended on the second of January, with the return of the SOS Brigade from its "training camp" deep in the mountains.

"Whew, we're home!"

Haruhi greeted our little suburb, narrowing her eyes at the setting sun.

"It's always relaxing to be home. Snowy mountains are nice and all, but nothing beats the smell of home, even if it is a little musty."

Having taken a different route, the Tamaru brothers, along with Mori and Arakawa, were no longer with us. Thus the only ones collecting their luggage at the small, homey train station were Haruhi and Tsuruya with their tireless superalloy constitutions, Asahina (to whom my sister clung possessively), and the expressionless-as-always Nagato, along with Koizumi (who wore a tired, resigned smile) and me, holding Shamisen the cat in a carrier. I had the feeling that it was still plenty of people.

"So, that's all for today." Haruhi's face was content. "Everybody make sure to rest up. We're hitting the neighborhood shrines and temples for hatsumoude tomorrow, got it? Meet here at nine AM. Oh, Tsuruya—do you have any plans?"

You have to admire the kind of vitality that lets someone make plans to go back out the day after returning home from a trip, especially for something like a New Year's temple visit, but unfortunately, ordinary humans—take me, for example—aren't powered by internal perpetual motion machines. Tsuruya seemed to have a capacity to match Haruhi as she replied, though.

"Sorry! I'm heading to Switzerland tomorrow! I'll bring back

souvenirs, so toss a little extra in the offering boxes for me, okay?"
Tsuruya dug some small change out of her wallet and handed it to
Asahina, continuing, "Here, a New Year's present!" She gave some
to my little sister too. "Bye-bye! See you next semester!"

She smiled and waved as she left the station. She seemed totally
relaxed; it was enough to make me want to ask her parents just
how they raised a daughter like that, just for my own future
reference.

Haruhi kept waving until the older girl's relentless smile disappeared behind an apartment building. "Well, then, shall we all
head home? Take care, everybody! The club trip isn't over until
you make it home!"

If anything else happened, I doubted Koizumi or I would be
able to handle it, but surely nothing weird would happen in the
time it would take us to return to our homes from the train
station.

I looked at Nagato. The affliction she'd suffered in the mystery house had vanished, and she'd returned to her normal,
impossible-to-read state of expressionlessness—but just as I was
noting this, her eyes moved slightly, and her gaze met mine. I
don't think the tiny nod I perceived from her was an illusion.

I then looked to Asahina. She'd been largely oblivious during
the entire trip; her cluelessness had spilled over into uncertainty
during the mystery house episode, but in retrospect that may
have been for the best. She would have a much larger role to play
starting now. I looked at her meaningfully, but unfortunately she
missed my signals completely, instead playing happily with my
sister as though they were the same age.

"Okay, see you all tomorrow! Make sure you grab your New
Year's money—there're gonna be stalls lined up all around the
shrines and temples."

Once Haruhi had said her piece, I left her and Asahina and
boarded the bus, dragging my sister and Shamisen (in his cat
carrier) on board with me.

"Bye, Mikuru!"

As I hauled my recalcitrant sister back to the bus seat, Asahina waved repeatedly with one hand, her other tightly clenched. I really didn't feel like waving, although Haruhi or Koizumi probably would've yelled a loud "Bye-bye!"

A few minutes after we returned home and I'd gotten Shamisen and my sister out of my hair, I called the two brigade members of whom I'd just taken my leave.

Why?

Because there was something I'd deeply regretted leaving undone before the year's end, and I wanted to fix that as soon as possible. I didn't want to break out in a cold sweat because of my own laziness like that ever again, and while part of me wanted to go back and teach my self of late last year a lesson or two, I needed to go back a little further. Thanks to Nagato's and Koizumi's efforts, we'd managed to avoid the worst-case scenario at the mysterious lodge, but there was no guarantee we wouldn't wind up in a similar situation again—in fact, it seemed unavoidable. I'd hesitated to take action during the trip, reasoning that it would cause trouble, but now that the club members had gone their separate ways, I would dither no further. I'd had plenty of time to make up my mind during the game-playing and mystery-solving at Tsuruya's villa.

I had to go. I had to go with Nagato and Asahina back to that day.

Yes—back to the morning of December eighteenth.

Without taking any time to recover from the exhaustion of the winter trip, I first called Asahina. She sounded a bit surprised to be receiving a phone call from someone with whom she'd parted ways so recently.

"Oh, Kyon—what is it?"

"There's somewhere I want you to go with me. Immediately, if possible."

"Wha...? Where?"

"December eighteenth of last year."

She sounded confused and taken aback. "Wh-what do you mean—?"

"I want you to take Nagato and me back in time. The three of us have to go back two weeks."

"What? No, my TP—I mean, I can't just change time whenever I want to. It takes thorough investigation and the permission of a lot of people!"

I was willing to bet she'd have no trouble getting that permission. My mind filled with an image of Asahina the Elder, winking at me and blowing me a kiss.

"Asahina, please contact your superiors or whatever they are immediately. Tell them I want to return to the morning of December eighteenth with you and Nagato."

Maybe thanks to my overconfident tone, Asahina's little sounds of hesitation that leaked through the phone's receiver fell silent. "W-wait just a moment."

Oh, I waited. I was fascinated to know just how one communicated with the future, but all I could hear was the quiet sound of Asahina's breathing. After no more than ten seconds of that background music—

"I don't believe it..." Her voice sounded dazed. "I've received permission. But...why? Why so easily?"

It was because the future now rested on my shoulders—but I didn't want to have a long conversation about it, so I just said, "Let's meet at Nagato's apartment. You can be there in half an hour, right?"

"Oh—wait. Let me have an hour. I want to confirm things again, and also I would rather just...meet in front of Nagato's apartment building."

I readily agreed, then after taking a moment to grin privately at

Asahina's surprise, I straightened and turned serious again. The time period I was proposing to revisit was not one that inspired a pleasant smile. I knew that better than anybody else.

The next person I planned to contact would probably have understood everything without my saying a word, but better safe than sorry. I picked up the phone again.

An hour later—

I'd arrived early, having gotten excited and sprinted over on my bike. I had been waiting at the entrance to Nagato's luxurious apartment building for fifteen minutes, stomping my feet to stave off the cold. Finally a fluffy-looking silhouette approached. Either she hadn't thought to change clothes or hadn't had time—although to be fair, neither had I.

"Kyon." Asahina looked at me, full of wonderment. "I just don't understand it. Why was your request so easily granted? Not just that—I was *ordered* to go with you and Nagato. When I asked for details, it was totally classified. And...I was instructed to do everything you tell me to do. Why?"

"I'll explain. In Nagato's room," I said, punching the code for Nagato's room into the panel in the entryway, then pushing the buzzer. The response was quick.

"..."

"It's me."

"Come in."

I passed right through the now-unlocked door—whoops, couldn't forget about Asahina. She still seemed pretty dumbfounded by all of this, and she took a moment to catch up with me. She had the same timid demeanor she always had when she came here. It was as though her nervous face were surrounded by question marks there in the elevator.

Nagato opening the door and letting us into her apartment didn't do anything to change Asahina's expression.

Nagato seemed unhurried. Despite being back at her house, she'd changed into her school uniform. The fact that it made me feel so at ease wasn't because I have a school uniform fetish, but rather because I knew she would understand my situation.

Earlier, I'd lost consciousness as I watched a short-haired figure in a school uniform holding a knife. Given what we were about to do, it would probably be hard for my past self to see her in any other outfit. I doubt I would mistake Nagato for anybody else, but the uniform had really become her trademark.

"..."

She wordlessly indicated that we should sit in the living room as she went into the kitchen to prepare tea.

I took the opportunity to relate to Asahina the details of the adventure before last.

"I don't believe it..." Asahina murmured, her eyes wide and round. "History was completely changed, and I didn't notice a thing..."

Her shock was understandable. The only one with an accurate memory during those three days was me, and without Nagato's hint and the other Haruhi's unhesitating action, I wouldn't have been able to do anything about it.

"A global alteration of space-time and direct intervention from the future... for both of those things to happen at the same time, it's..." Asahina's voice quivered as her gaze swam around the spartan room. There were three cups of tea now on the table in the living room. Nagato had made it for us, but Asahina was so stunned as she listened to my explanation (and Nagato's occasional "Yes") that she hadn't touched her cup, and it was growing cool.

"..."

Diagonally across from me, Nagato regarded Asahina, then looked questioningly at me before looking again at Asahina.

I had a pretty good idea of what Nagato wanted to say. What I'd explained to Asahina was that errors had accumulated in Naga-to's system, causing her to rewrite the world on December eigh-teenth, but that using her escape program I'd been able to successfully travel back in time, to the day of Tanabata four years earlier. There, I'd enlisted the aid of pre-buggy Nagato to make it back to December eighteenth, but there I'd had the misfortune to encounter Ryoko Asakura, who'd mortally wounded me—but just before I lost consciousness, I'd seen Nagato and Asahina, along with myself, presumably having traveled back from the future to set things right. Nagato might have some things to add to this incomprehensible explanation.

And that wasn't even the whole story. I hadn't said anything about the fact that the elder Asahina had waited for me there, four years in the past. I wasn't at all certain it was something I should mention. It was obvious that the elder Asahina was keep-ing her younger counterpart deliberately in the dark about all this. The younger Asahina was still in regular contact with the future, so if it were that important for her to know something, I'd leave it to her superiors to clue her in. I didn't know anything about their information exchange system, but I could make an educated guess based on things she'd said. "When I asked for details, it was totally classified," she'd said earlier.

Asahina didn't know. Knowledge was being deliberately kept from her.

I had no idea why that was. But it was obvious to me. It had occurred to me several times that she was awfully careless for a time traveler. The August where we nearly got stuck in an infinite time loop, and the strange house that suddenly appeared in the middle of a blizzard—at the very least, she could've given us some kind of futuristic warning so we could've avoided the trou-ble those two incidents had caused. Why hadn't she?

I had an idea why.

Asahina the Elder *had* to know everything. Her former self—that is to say, the current Asahina—had to go through all these experiences. Anything that let us avoid them would change her own history. Perhaps she had no choice but to experience these things, just as Nagato could predict her own malfunction but in the end could do nothing to avoid it.

But it made me feel truly sorry for the current Asahina. She'd endured even more moments of shock throughout her SOS Brigade experiences than I had. I was even starting to be suspicious of her real purpose in this time period. If they just needed to surveil Haruhi, wouldn't a simple spy camera have sufficed?

There had to be something else—something not even this Asahina knows, but that her older self *does* know...

A freeze-dried voice addressed me as I was deep in thought.

"I have a favor to ask of you."

I was happy to listen to anything Nagato would ask of me.

"I want you not to say anything to my self in that time."

Not even "Hey" or "Hi?" I wanted to know.

"If possible, no."

In Nagato's stoic eyes was visible a rare expressiveness. Her black pupils entreated me, and I would have sooner agreed to scoop the moon's reflection out of a pond than I would have refused her.

"Okay. If you say so, I'll try not to."

The artlessly short head of hair nodded slowly.

It fell to Nagato to explain the fine details of the space-time manipulation, and Asahina would be the one to faithfully carry them out. I'm sorry, but I didn't care how powerful Koizumi's Agency was—they were no match for this alliance of alien and time traveler. Although I have no idea if they ever plan on fighting.

The three of us—Nagato, Asahina, and I—went to the entryway to put on our shoes, our shoulders bumping into one another's as we jostled in the tight space. Last month, when I'd traveled back in time with Asahina the Elder, we'd forgotten our shoes. The lesson had not been wasted on me. Thanks to Nagato's personality, the older Asahina's high heels were still here, four years later, but we couldn't very well return them to the current Asahina, so I said nothing.

"Um, what time on December eighteenth last year was it again?"

In response to the question, Nagato gave the answer down to the second, at which Asahina nodded.

"Okay, here we go. Kyon, close your eyes."

And then—

Time shifted. No matter how many times I experienced it, it felt the same way—a dizziness that brings me to the edge of nausea. Though my eyes were closed, there was a light flashing, and an indescribably uncomfortable feeling of falling backward, of loss of spatial orientation. The equilibrium of both my body and mind was gone; it was like going around a roller coaster dozens of times in a row, and just when my sense of balance was on the verge of collapse—

The soles of my feet registered contact with the ground. Gravity reasserted its hold on my thankful body.

"We're here," Nagato said, almost whispering. I opened my eyes.

And was immediately shocked.

I saw myself standing directly in front of the school gates.

Recall, if you will: the last time I time-jumped to this particular December eighteenth, I'd come from the Tanabata of four years previous, having made the jump with Asahina the Elder at past-Nagato's behest. From the cover of darkness I'd watched the present Nagato change the world, and then I'd stepped into the light.

And we'd just now landed smack in the middle of that scene.

The other me was now saying something to Nagato, who'd finished changing both the world and herself. I could also see the back of Asahina the Elder, who was wearing the jacket I'd lent her. This was dangerous—this was too close.

"Don't worry," my Nagato said in a monotone. "They cannot see us. I've erected a light-and-sound isolation field."

I supposed that meant that from the perspective of past-me, older-Asahina, and glasses-Nagato, the three of us were silent, transparent beings. Maybe the reason Nagato hadn't bitten us this time was because she was personally present.

Asahina blinked rapidly. "Um...who is that woman? She seems like an adult, but why is she here?"

We could only see Asahina the Elder from behind, after all. It wasn't surprising that Asahina couldn't recognize the woman, and to simply infer that the person was actually an older version of her required an even greater mental leap. Just as I was agonizing over whether to tell her, my thoughts were obliterated by what happened next. Though I knew it was coming, watching it from outside still gave me goose bumps.

A dark form bolted out of the shadows. Just after it swept past us, I realized it was Ryoko Asakura, lunging toward my other self, about to slam into him—no, she *did* slam into him. Hard, and holding a knife at her waist.

Asahina the Elder cried out as my useless other self was stabbed. Just as I remembered being.

"Unggh—"

It definitely looked painful. I hadn't noticed it at the time, but Asakura was twisting the knife back and forth. She was murderous—she was really trying to kill me. Asakura the corrupted backup was guilty of attempted murder.

"I" collapsed to the ground.

"Wha...aah! Kyon!" Asahina called out, and started to run to my other self, but she soon collided with an invisible barrier. "Ow—" she cried, looking up. In the moment, she must have forgotten that I was still right beside her. All she could see was the collapsed "me" across the way. I felt both grateful and not.

"Nagato!" Asahina shouted.

In response, Nagato nodded softly. "Dissolving barrier...now."

Asahina ran out as Nagato herself began to move—more swiftly than the night wind. Nagato was upon Asakura a moment later, grabbing Asakura's upheld knife blade with her hand. Asakura's cry, a mix of shock and hatred, reached my ears as I reached myself. *Geez—I look terrible.*

Asahina the Younger clung tearfully to "my" collapsed body. It was nice that she was worried about me and all, but if she kept shaking me like that, she was just going to make me die faster.

Luckily, she was kneeling and desperately calling out to me so fervently that she forgot all about the other woman. It was enough to make me want to thank her.

The silent Asahina the Elder looked up from where her gaze had been to regard me.

"So you came."

I was still a bit late, though—not in terms of time, but mentally.

"...Wha...?" The voice was Nagato, exactly as I'd remembered her. It pained my heart to see her there—still wearing glasses, having fallen as she'd stumbled back, her expression one of shock. Her dark eyes moved from my other self's collapsed form, to Asakura, to her school uniform–clad doppelganger, then finally to me.

"Wh...why...?"

I had promised Nagato. Which meant I could say nothing to *this* Nagato, the one who had just rewritten the world. There was only one thing I could do, one thing to say.

I picked up the needle gun that the Nagato from three years ago had made, then looked down at myself. I opened my mouth to say the line I remembered hearing. I was pretty sure I got it right, and even if I didn't, I was sure a bit of deviation would be allowed. My other self's barely open eyes finally closed completely, and his neck slumped sideways. It was a textbook loss of consciousness, good enough to make it look like I'd died—and if we didn't stop my bleeding soon, I really *would* die.

Now it was really my turn—even though starting then, I didn't know what was going to happen.

The first thing I looked at was my Nagato stopping Asakura.

"..."

The knife that Nagato held turned to sparkling dust. Asakura tried to jump back, but her feet held fast to the ground, as if stuck there. Nagato murmured in a quiet, rapid voice.

"No—Why? Isn't this—" Asakura's body began to shimmer. "Isn't this what you wished for? Why...even now..."

Asakura fell silent with the question on her lips, as the dissolution of the knife was followed by that of her own body, which finally crumbled and scattered. At the same time—

"Ah...uhh..."

Asahina the Younger had fallen prostrate over "my" body. With her closed eyes and her barely parted lips, she looked for all the world like she was sleeping. Asahina the Elder's hand lay softly on the nape of my lovely upperclassman's neck.

"I put her to sleep."

The adult Asahina stroked her younger self's head sadly.

"She mustn't learn that I am here. I had to make sure that wouldn't happen."

My Asahina breathed softly as she slept, her head pillowed on my unconscious self's slack arm.

"I have to stay a secret to her."

Asahina's sleeping face looked exactly like it had on that park bench at Tanabata three years ago. The reasoning was likewise the same—Asahina the Elder didn't want to reveal herself to her past self. Catching a glimpse of her from behind was one thing, but if we'd gotten close, the older Asahina's identity would've been obvious.

"..."

Nagato knelt on one knee, putting her hand to the spot on

"my" torso where I'd been knifed. That's obviously what saved me. In any case, the bleeding stopped, and "my" face looked a little less pallid. So it *had* been Nagato who'd healed my wound.

Nagato stood without ceremony, then held out her hand and spoke.

"Give it."

I silently handed her the gun. I hadn't been able to do anything with it, anyway. I just couldn't make myself do it. I didn't want to pull the trigger on any Nagato, at any time.

Nagato took the gun unconcernedly, then aimed it at her collapsed, glasses-wearing other self and pulled the trigger.

" … "

There was no sound, and I saw nothing miraculous fire from the gun, but—

" … "

Nagato (glasses) blinked, then got slowly to her feet. She stood there, ramrod-straight, very much like the Nagato I knew so well—not the girl who had given me the application form for her club, tugged hesitantly on my sleeve, and smiled shyly and faintly.

As though to confirm my thoughts, that Nagato smoothly removed her glasses, then after glancing to me with her own eyes, locked her emotionless gaze on her other self.

"Request synchronization."

The two Nagatos stared each other down. This incident included, I'd had several occasions to see my other self. My retinas had also been graced with the sight of both Asahina the Younger and Elder. But this was the first time I'd seen two of Nagato, and it was strangely moving. Magnificent, even.

"Request synchronization," the gunshot Nagato repeated. The Nagato holding the pistol responded immediately.

"Denied."

Even I thought this was weird—to say nothing of the Nagato who now held her glasses in her hand. Her eyebrows moved a millimeter. "Why?"

"I do not wish to."

I was stunned. Had Nagato ever so clearly expressed a preference? It wasn't an excuse. She had definitively and unambiguously spoken words of emotional refusal.

"..."

The other Nagato fell silent, as though in deep thought.

"..."

The night wind ruffled her hair.

The Nagato who had come back from the future with me spoke.

"You will reset the world changes you effected."

"Understood," said the other Nagato, but then continued on to say, "I cannot detect the existence of the Data Overmind."

"It is not here," replied my Nagato indifferently. "I am still connected to the Data Overmind in my own space-time. I will effect the reversion of changes."

"Understood," said past-Nagato.

"After the reversion," continued my Nagato, "take whatever actions you wish."

The newly repaired other Nagato looked to me, her head cocked ever so slightly. I was certain of the invisible information her expression revealed. Nobody understands Nagato's feelings the way I do.

This Nagato is *that* Nagato. The Nagato who appeared at the hospital that night—that is her. The one who made me so angry by claiming that her punishment was being debated.

I also understood why the Nagato who came from the future with me rejected synchronization. She doesn't want to tell her current self what action to take, when the time comes.

Why, you ask? It goes without saying.

Thank you—the words I heard from Nagato then are the answer.

"Kyon—" said Asahina the Elder to me, hesitantly, as I stood there, stock still. "Please, take care of her...of *me*."

She went to pick up her heavy-looking younger self, who was still deeply sleeping. I hurried over to lend a hand, and no sooner had she asked me for help than I'd gotten the lesser Asahina on my back, her warmth and softness just as I remembered it.

"A large-scale time-quake will soon occur."

Asahina the Elder hugged her shoulders, her face anxious. "This is a larger and more complicated space-time modification than the one that just happened. I don't think we'll be able to keep our eyes open this time."

If she said so, I believed it—but why would this be any different? I asked.

"The first change only changed the past and present. Now, in addition to that, we must take pains to restore time to its original flow. Think back. Where do you remember waking up?"

The evening of December twenty-first—I'd regained consciousness in the hospital.

"That's right. So we have to arrange things for that to come about."

My blazer still hanging over her shoulders, the barefoot older Asahina drew closer to me, looking somehow melancholy. She touched my shoulder, upon which Asahina the Younger still rested, then turned her head to regard Nagato. The Nagato who had come here with me now walked over to join us, the other remaining where she stood, and my collapsed other self still lying on the ground.

Asahina the Elder put her other hand on Nagato's shoulder. "If you please, Nagato."

Nagato nodded faintly, then looked at her other self, as if acknowledging that this would be their final parting. The other Nagato said nothing. I got the impression that she was lonely, which might have been my imagination, but I didn't worry about it. I remembered what I'd said—what my other self, still lying on the ground, would soon say. "Relax and come visit me in the hospital. And don't forget to tell your boss to drop dead."

"Close your eyes, Kyon," whispered Asahina the Elder. "We can't have you getting time-sick."

I took her advice and squeezed my eyes shut.

The next moment, I felt the world twist around me.

"Whoa—"

I'd experienced the weightless, spinning sensation many times, and while I felt like I was getting used to it, the magnitude of the spinning felt different this time. Previously, it had felt like an amusement park roller coaster, but this was like being inside a spaceship that was blasting randomly around and I'd forgotten to fasten my seat belt. But since gravity was not acting on my body, nor was I actually being spun around, this was simple dizziness. Though I wanted to see what was going on outside me, opening my eyes made the drunken feeling terrifyingly worse, so the only vision I had was the flashes of light that sparkled behind my closed eyes. I was very grateful for both the weight of Asahina the Younger on my back and her older counterpart's hand on my shoulder.

—And then, there was a piercing, dangerous flash of light that penetrated my closed eyelids.

Unable to resist the desire to see, I opened my eyes, and I understood the source of the flashing red light. Only emergency vehicles are allowed to have red lights that revolve like that.

It was...?

An ambulance was parked in front of the North High School entrance. Rubbernecking students looked on from a distance as emergency personnel carried someone out on a stretcher. Two forms walked alongside the stretcher as it moved, two forms whose names I'll never forget as long as I live. Haruhi looked pale and scared, and Asahina's face was streaked with tears as they followed the paramedics, with an unsmiling Koizumi trailing behind them.

The stretcher was immediately loaded into the ambulance, and Haruhi got in as well, after a short exchange with the paramedics. The flashing red lights and siren got bumped up a notch, and the ambulance started to move. Asahina covered her face as Koizumi had a serious conversation on his cell phone. Nagato was not there—but that was to be expected.

Some part of my body felt Asahina the Elder let out a sigh of relief.

"Now we can return to our own time, Kyon."

The scene faded out. I guessed that was the end of this particular bonus scene. I closed my eyes. It had been worth seeing—a fragment of three days of which I had no memory. That's right— Haruhi had claimed that it was the brigade chief's duty to be concerned about her brigade members.

The dizzy feeling started up again. I was desperate for some motion sickness medication—next time, I'd be sure to bring some.

"I'll aim for the time coordinates you came from. Be nice to me, won't you? It will take a while before I wake up. Hee hee, you can even kiss me, if you want."

Asahina the Elder's lingering, mischievous voice felt very distant.

And then—

When I opened my eyes, I was standing in Nagato's living room with Asahina on my back.

Nagato stood, facing me. "Sixty-two seconds have elapsed since we departed," she said, looking up at me. "We have returned."

To our own time.

I let out a deep breath and lowered Asahina to the floor. Her sleeping face was definitely a top candidate for Most Kissable, but I wasn't so naive as to take the other Asahina's words literally. Of course, were this not Nagato's living room, and were Nagato not currently observing me, I might've given in to sketchy behavior. Wait, no—I wouldn't. I wouldn't!

Taking my teacup off the table, I downed the remaining tea in one gulp. It had turned lukewarm before we'd started time traveling, but it was still awfully tasty. It was perfect, like having barley tea right after a bath—it was even a match for the tea Asahina brewed in the clubroom.

"Geez."

I felt like I'd finally sorted out all the trouble from the previous year. There was nothing more that needed doing. We'd changed the world back to what it needed to be and had gotten back from the club trip that had overlapped into the new year. All that remained was the first temple visit of the year. Oh, sure—Haruhi would probably come up with something strange, but until then I figured I'd be able to relax a bit.

Incidentally, the angelic time traveler didn't seem to be waking up. The method by which she'd been put to sleep was unclear, but her sleeping face looked as happy as Shamisen's did when he had a full belly and was curled up somewhere warm, so I was loath to wake her. I asked Nagato to get a futon ready for her in the guest room, then carried her there and tucked her in.

"Nagato—do me a favor and take care of her until she wakes up, okay?"

Nagato was certainly getting her fill of sleeping guests, but she looked at me and nodded.

I would've loved to stay until Asahina awoke, but to be honest I was utterly weary myself. If I didn't get home soon and ameliorate my exhaustion via a good bath and my own bed, there was no way I'd be able to be up tomorrow morning by nine, and I wanted to put an end to the evaporation of my wallet's limited resources. Five people's worth of New Year's cash would've been a crushing blow.

It would've been nice to crawl into a futon next to Asahina, like I'd done back when I'd slept through three years after Tanabata, and while I'm completely confident that I would've fallen immediately asleep upon putting head to pillow, I couldn't help but feel that nobody was asking for me to sleep there.

It was kind of nice that the time traveler was crashing at the alien's place.

"See you tomorrow."

"Understood."

Nagato saw me off with a gaze that put me at ease, her tranquil pupils fixing on me from behind her bangs.

"Good work today. Sorry we caused you so much trouble."

Asahina had done her part, but Nagato (and her counterpart in this apartment, at Tanabata four years ago) had put in the most effort.

"It's fine," she said, her expression unchanging. "I was the cause."

I watched the alien until the door closed. I had wondered if she would possibly smile, but unfortunately—or perhaps fortunately—her pale face and small frame were as impassive as ever. And yet you can thank my keen eyes for noticing that there was a hint of something different.

I rode my bike slowly home after leaving the apartment building, and I fell asleep immediately after falling down on my bed.

Somehow I got the feeling that the dreams I had in my exhausted sleep were really great ones, but thirty seconds after I woke up, I'd forgotten them entirely. But the lingering feeling told me everything.

I'm sure it was about an alien and a time traveler enjoying a pleasant tea together.

And so it was that just as I'd lowered Asahina off my shoulders, I'd planned to cast off my worries and enjoy a relatively peaceful January.

But a single problem remained.

Her sleeping face had been so lovely that it entirely slipped my mind—that precisely *because* the sleeping Asahina was asleep, from her perspective she'd seen and heard almost nothing of what Nagato, Asahina the Elder, and I had done that December eighteenth. As far as she knew, I'd suddenly told her that space-time had been altered, and, half disbelieving, she'd taken us back in time, only to see my other self be immediately struck down and be immediately rendered unconscious herself—and when she woke, she'd already be back in her own time.

As far as I was concerned, she'd fulfilled her role perfectly well, by doing something only she could do, but Asahina herself evidently didn't see it that way. Now that I thought about it, ever since the winter break had ended, she seemed to be constantly getting lost in thought.

This is all connected to the melancholy Sunday pseudo-date she'd asked me out on, where we'd barely saved the boy in glasses from a traffic accident. If I had to take a guess, I'd blame it on Asahina the Elder's policy of secrecy. While it was true that anyone who would make Asahina cry deserved a thorough pummeling, I wondered if I hadn't been more often the cause of her tears myself. Maybe I needed to get Haruhi to go to a boxing gym with me. A little bit of punching and getting punched might do me good, I thought.

In any case, the Sunday of tea shopping got me thinking about the future of the SOS Brigade, and it also succeeded in lifting Asahina's spirits. To be honest, I'm not sure how much she figured out, but we reached enough of an understanding that detailed explanations weren't necessary—at least, not to *this* Asahina.

Just as I don't mention the name John Smith to Haruhi, I'll never tell Asahina about the existence of her adult self. It's a trump card, only for emergencies.

And should the time come—

Well, I don't *want* that time to come.

...

...

...

* * *

As we enter February, our story returns to its beginning.

Toward the end of the school year, the mood around the school changes somehow—you start to see the seniors around less, for example. Most of them were now toiling in the depths of their college entrance exams, which makes the teachers' room a tense place to be. Come the year after next, I'll be a senior myself— that'll be me. If this year's senior class doesn't rouse themselves to beating the municipal high school's college acceptance rate, the principal is going to be pushing extra classes or mock exams that cancel the school anniversary, which will only serve to annoy me, since I'm still two years away from seniorhood.

Speaking of exams, it was about time for the diagnostic tests that the entering middle school students would take to get into special classes, of which my school had a couple. Koizumi's Class 9 specialized in science and math. I don't know whether it was the shadowy Agency backing him that got Koizumi into that class, or if it was just his own academic ability, but either way it was impressive for a transfer student to get in. I sure as hell didn't have any interest in a class whose main dish would be extra helpings of math and science.

In any case, I turned my attention away from the hell of college entrance exams into which I'd inevitably descend, purposefully avoiding the calendar in an effort to extend my few remaining days of life as a freshman, and once I got back from that fateful December eighteenth, carefully maintained my state of relaxation.

After all, I sure can't think of anything more dangerous than repairing space-time, and having successfully done so, surely I deserved some R&R. Nagato had returned to her usual self, Asahina's smile was back, and while something was up with Haruhi, she'd start making noise about it soon enough.

So there really shouldn't have been any problems at all, or at least I didn't want to think about them. But there was one person in the clubroom who selfishly insisted on making mountains out of molehills—the only one who, like Haruhi, had been left out of the loop, the esper whose powers were useless when it came to changing space-time—one Itsuki Koizumi, who said:

"You've repeatedly visited two separate mornings of December eighteenth."

Koizumi had enjoyed hearing about the time-travel incidents I'd been through ever since the episode at the snowy mountain mansion, pestering me to relate them to him like a kid begging his grandfather for another story. As an aspiring time traveler, he seemed to envy me. Taking the train back from Tsuruya's villa, he'd gone on and on about "Might you not find some way to take me back with you?" and "It should be fine so long as your past self doesn't see me," but it went without saying that I paid him no heed.

I was still deeply embarrassed about the whole Nagato thing, and although it was all over and settled, I still tended to prevaricate about it, but in the face of Koizumi's curiosity-borne persistence, and when just the two of us were in the clubroom, I finally told him the whole story.

And as I'd expected, he happily began his commentary.

"You see, it was the morning of December eighteenth when the malfunctioning Nagato changed the world into one where Suzumiya and I, and even Asahina, were all normal people. You spent three days in that world, then used Nagato's escape program to travel three—no, *four* years into the past. There you met the still-functioning Nagato and returned to the morning of December eighteenth."

That was all true. And incidentally, I've now been back to that morning yet again, I told him.

"I know. But think carefully now. Suppose we refer to the moment Nagato changed the world on the morning of December eighteenth as time x. When you returned to time x from Tanabata four years previous, it was no longer the same x."

What was he talking about? There was no way there could be more than one version of the same time, I told him.

"There can—in fact, there must. The reasoning is simple. If the time x where Nagato changed the world disappeared, then neither Suzumiya's disappearance nor her and my transformation into regular people would have happened. And were that the case, you would never have needed to travel into the past."

He was talking about a time paradox. I had plenty of first-hand experiences with those, I said.

"But a necessary precondition for returning this world to its previous state was you traveling into the past. If you hadn't, the world would have stayed changed. But you did go, and you did repair it. Otherwise, this timeline would not exist."

I glanced over at the door, hoping desperately that someone would come and interrupt this conversation.

"Let me use a diagram to explain. It might make it easier to understand."

Ever since the incident, Koizumi seemed to have gotten really into diagrams; he took an erasable pen and walked over to the whiteboard.

"Say this vertical line represents the flow of time from past to future." He stopped the line in the middle of the board, drawing a dot and labeling it with an x.

"This is the first time x. This is where Nagato changed the world that surrounded her, and where the time as it exists in your memory was created."

Koizumi resumed the movement of the pen, but he did not directly continue the line. Instead it curved to the right, eventually creating a circle that returned to point x. The diagram now looked like a morning glory sprout with one leaf plucked off.

"The circle is the history that you remember since December eighteenth. You used the escape program to travel back to the Tanabata four years earlier, then jumped back to the morning of December eighteenth. If Nagato had just been repaired at that moment, everything would have been fine, but that's not how it went."

Yeah, because Ryoko Asakura was there. But Asakura wasn't the only one there. There was also another version of me from the future, along with Asahina and Nagato, and we managed to put things right. From my perspective now, it had happened a month ago.

"Indeed. You saved yourself. And that"—Koizumi's pen started at x again, this time drawing a circle that looped to the left—"is this point, from which this world is now continuing. In Suzumiya's memory as in mine, you fell down the stairs on December eighteenth and were unconscious until the twenty-first. And a month later, you would travel back from this timeline to go save yourself."

Once he'd finished drawing the circle to the left of the line, Koizumi didn't stop. He then continued on past the x, extending the line up until it reached the top edge of the board, then setting the pen down. Koizumi then took a half step back from the board and regarded me carefully.

I quickly grasped the nature of the diagram. It looked like an eight turned sideways—the symbol for infinity—with a line exactly bisecting the point between the two loops. Point x was where all the lines met.

Even I, who'd long proclaimed my cowardice in the face of math and science, gradually began to understand what Koizumi was trying to explain.

The loop on the right was the time in my memory. After a lot of hassle, I'd returned to point x and met glasses-Nagato just as she was changing the world, then gotten stabbed by Asakura.

On the other hand, the loop on the left was time of which I had no memory. I'd been stabbed, lost consciousness, been taken to the hospital where I was in a bed for three days until waking up—all within that loop.

And both of those loops had their start at x.

"Which means that there are two points x," explained Koizumi. "There's point x, where the world was changed, and...let's call it x', where the change was undone," he said, looking contemplatively at his diagram. "Without x, there can be no x'. So x was not erased. You can probably think of them as being superimposed. Yes…one written atop the other. Just as old data is covered up by new data written atop it, x, along with the changed world that followed from it, was overwritten by x', but it hasn't disappeared completely. It's still there."

"I do not remotely understand," I said with nonchalance even as I recalled Asahina the Elder's words.

An even larger and more complex space-time-quake, she'd said.

"It's something like looking at a multilevel circuit board from above. There are points where the circuits appear to cross each other in two dimensions, but when you factor in the third dimension, you see they're on different levels. Things that appear to occupy the same space in two dimensions differ in depth."

I rubbed my temples. Koizumi was explaining all this, but I wondered what a time traveler would say. Or an alien.

"There is another possibility. May I explain?"

Given the circumstances, I'd listen to whatever the hell he wanted to say.

"The memory that you lack but which we have—the three days between December eighteenth, when you fell down the stairs, and December twenty-first, when you awoke—that may never have existed."

Did it matter one way or another? I'd been asleep either way, I said.

"Indeed, it's precisely as you say. Do you remember what I said earlier? We can't prove for certain that the entire universe wasn't created five minutes ago. You being rushed via ambulance and being comatose for three days may never have actually happened. It's possible that the time between your repair of December eighteenth and your awakening on December twenty-first didn't exist. Which would mean that Suzumiya's and my memory of those three days is completely fabricated, and we were made to hold them after the reconstruction on the night of the twenty-first."

I'd agreed to listen, but this was just ridiculous—but no, I couldn't claim that. It wasn't impossible. It was possible to rewrite an entire year—when considering that, these three days were small by comparison.

"Also, this is changing the subject, but we can now state the identity of the 'mystery girl' that Suzumiya saw."

Who was it? Who pushed me down the stairs?

"Nagato."

Now he was just talking nonsense. Hadn't Nagato been at the bottom of the stairs with everybody else at the time? They'd said I was at the tail end of the group, hadn't they?

"Yes, that's what we remember. Nagato didn't directly shove you from behind. However, she was the one who created the history wherein you'd been knocked unconscious. Suzumiya must have subconsciously realized that fact. Of course, she doesn't know Nagato was the culprit—in reality, the culprit wasn't there. And yet somehow Suzumiya sensed the fact that *someone* was behind all this."

Koizumi smiled brightly.

"That feeling of suspicion became the image of a girl pushing you. A phantom girl who never really existed."

You could hardly use intuition to explain away all that. If Nagato could change the world, she could certainly alter a few memories. Yet Haruhi had realized that something was amiss— that someone was doing something. Or had done something.

"It's just a theory. A hypothesis I created to answer your questions." The pleasant bastard sat down in a folding chair and spread his arms wide. "Practically speaking, I don't know the first thing about time construction and movement. But Asahina came from the future to accomplish something here. So this is my question: if you were in the position to travel into the past in order to avert a disaster, would you do it?"

I thought of Asahina the Elder on the night of Tanabata. Surrounded by a Haruhi and Koizumi who had gone to a different school, an Asahina who'd stayed in the calligraphy club, and a glasses-wearing Nagato, I'd pushed Enter on the computer and traveled back in time again. The version of myself, sitting on a bench at that park. The version of myself, helping a middle school–aged Haruhi draw pictures in the school courtyard.

If I had gone running up to my other self, what would've happened? If I'd told him everything that would happen—if I'd told him not to let Haruhi make a movie, not to cause Nagato constant trouble, if I'd spilled my guts to him.

All I could do was shrug my shoulders. "I have no idea."

When an opportunity like that comes up, your body moves on its own before you can think. I didn't really trust my brain, but my body knew what it should do. That had gotten me this far, and I figured I'd keep it up. Good luck, self.

"Still, though—I really don't think there'll be any more time travel. The whole reason for doing it is gone now."

"That's a shame. I had been hoping that you'd take me along next time."

I didn't care if his eyes looked as desperate as Shamisen's when he's hungry in the middle of the night. He could go ask Asahina. And not current Asahina, but Asahina the Elder. Not that I had any idea where or when she was. The only thing I could tell him was to make sure to bring motion sickness medication.

Koizumi shook his head resignedly and returned to the game of shogi he was playing against himself; my attention drifted back to the manga magazine I'd been reading, and silence returned to the room.

"Sorry to keep you waiting!"

Wham. The door slammed open, kicked, and the main ingredient in all this chaos entered. Haruhi the omnipotent smiled with pointless energy, a convenience store shopping bag in her hand, her skirt and hair fluttering attractively.

"The snack shop nearby didn't have this stuff, so I had to go all the way back down the hill. Whew, it's cold!"

Following soon after the brigade chief, who was now warming

her hands by the electric heater in the corner of the room, came Nagato and Asahina.

"..."

Nagato silently closed the door.

"Um, what do we do with this?" asked Asahina, her head cocked at a puzzled angle.

"Isn't it obvious? Don't you know what today is, Mikuru? I mean—did you buy this stuff without realizing it?"

"It's February third, but what...?"

"It's Setsubun! Setsubun!"

Haruhi produced a small packet from within the convenience store shopping bag.

"Honestly, you're just hopeless. Didn't you celebrate it when you were a kid? Today's Setsubun, and Setsubun equals bean-throwing and ehomaki-eating!"

It's true that ehomaki, or the practice of eating a whole piece of futomaki in an auspicious direction while contemplating one's hopes for the upcoming year, was, of course, an obscure local tradition, but our brigade chief was a fanatic about observing every obscure seasonal tradition she could. If you'd said we weren't the "Save the world by overloading it with fun Haruhi Suzumiya Brigade," but instead the "Save the world by celebrating every obscure seasonal event Brigade," you wouldn't have been wrong.

"What's that, a Bernoulli curve?"

Haruhi spied the diagram Koizumi had written on the whiteboard, suspiciously scrutinizing the path I'd taken through time as though it were a kid she thought she knew.

"No, it's not. What kind of calculation yielded this curve?" she asked.

"It's just a scribble," Koizumi said casually as he stood and used the eraser to clean the board. "I was just killing time. Pay it no mind."

Shyeah, right.

"Ah," replied Haruhi mildly, having decided it wasn't important. She tossed the convenience store bag to me. It landed in my hand with a rustle. There was a package of dried soybeans inside.

Today was Setsubun. And being Setsubun, there had to be bean-scattering—or so Haruhi had been thinking all through lunch, when she'd finally shouted in self-reproach: "I *knew* I was forgetting something! Setsubun!"

She'd probably realized it after seeing the sushi rolls in Taniguchi's lunch box. "Aw, c'mon," Taniguchi had said, bitter disappointment in his voice. "Is this it? No side dishes?"

"Just be happy somebody made you a lunch," I shot back, though in my heart I could not sympathize with the parent who'd pack a lunch like that; I agreed with the son. They could've at least cut the roll up before packing it, so that it wouldn't catch Haruhi's eye.

"We can't just celebrate foreign holidays. Local traditions have a right to get some respect, too. I mean otherwise it's just a waste! You're just missing out on the fun! People who lose track of their roots are just gonna wind up going down the wrong path!"

She was one to talk. Did she really think she was heading down the *right* path? From where I stood, it seemed like she was always just charging the wrong way down some random animal path, I said.

"What're you talking about? I walk the path of righteousness. I do that which must be done. I bet you forgot it was Setsubun today, Kyon. That's hard to forgive."

Even though she herself had also forgotten (or perhaps *because* of that), as soon as homeroom ended, Haruhi threw herself into preparations. If you can call them that—all she needed were beans and sushi rolls. She went to get them herself. Since I had been lucky enough to get a lecture from Mr. Okabe under the pretenses of academic counseling, and Koizumi had cleaning duty, she brought Nagato and Asahina along to help her carry things, and after school the three of them set off on their merry way. They had just now returned, which brought us to the present moment.

As far as the sushi rolls went, we could just eat those while facing the proper direction, but beans had to be thrown at something.

"So where do you propose to do the scattering?" I asked, opening the package and popping a bean into my mouth. It would've gone well with some tea. "It'll be a pain to clean up if we do it in the clubroom, not to mention a waste."

"We can do it anywhere," said Haruhi, eyes blazing. "Oh yeah, what about tossing them from the top floor hallway's windows down into the courtyard? That way the birds can just eat the beans and we won't have to do any cleaning up." She then added, "We've already got our good-fortune girls, so we've gotta do this up right." Apparently, no Setsubun is truly complete without good-fortune girls who dress up like shrine maidens and hand out good-luck charms.

The target of the SOS Brigade chief's Type-1a-supernova-strength gaze was Asahina, who was assiduously reading the text printed on the bag of beans, and Nagato, who had already seated herself at the table, absorbed in a detective novel with a disturbing-sounding title.

Ah, indeed.

If you were to hold a school-wide good-fortune-girl contest, the likely winner as well as the special judge's prize awardee were both sitting right here, and even setting that aside, they were perfectly suited to this sort of evil-spirit banishment, given that Asahina could pretend, and Nagato would actually do the banishing.

Haruhi tolerated no complaint as she dragged Asahina up to a hallway on the top floor of the school, the rest of us trailing behind them, whereupon we complied with the order to begin scattering—the three girls doing the actual scattering, with Koizumi and me in charge of keeping their bean scoops, and there was no question that for once Haruhi's direction was resulting in a good outcome for everyone involved.

At first, the students down in the courtyard had scattered like cockroaches fleeing insecticide, but soon groups of guys started to return to collect the beans that Asahina and Nagato had tossed down, milling about to and fro as they pursued the precious items. They were all of one mind in moving to dodge the shotgun blasts that resulted from Haruhi's overenthusiastic throwing.

"Oh, shoot," said Haruhi with genuine regret. "I should've had Mikuru dress like a shrine maiden—we could've made some money that way. Even a hundred yen a pop would've gotten us quite a bit, don't you think?"

If she'd dressed up like that and walked around the school, I had no doubt that Asahina would've become even more popular than she already was. But if only to keep my worries from multiplying any further, it was best to restrict her costumes to clubroom only.

"Um, g-good luck! In th-*there!* Good luck...*in!*"

I watched Asahina's eager bean-tossing and Nagato's completely silent rendition of the same, the vision of them performing the ritual while wearing shrine maiden outfits very clear in my mind.

"Five hundred yen a pop," I said gravely.

Incidentally, they were only shouting "Good luck in." As to why—

"Ever since I read *The Red Demon Who Cried*, I've always thought that if I ever did see a real demon, I'd want to be nice to it. I just bawled my eyes out when I read that story. The second I saw his sign, I totally would've gone right over to the Red Demon's house for tea and snacks." She was totally on the demons' side as she looked at me gravely. "Got that? If you ever run into the Blue Demon, you better be nice to him. Shutting the demons outside is prohibited! The SOS Brigade's doors are open to all, even non-humans!"

Although I had the premonition that if this half-baked inclusiveness continued, we'd soon end up with so much "luck" that eventually something would pop like an invisible balloon, I had to agree with Haruhi on the matter of the Blue Demon.

That might've been because as an impressionable kid, I'd cried over the story myself, or perhaps it was because in addition to scattering beans, Nagato was wearing a cheap demon mask on the side of her head. Nagato had been listening as she read the fairy tale Haruhi had mentioned, and had for some reason taken an interest in the paper demon mask, picking it up quietly and scanning it, laser-like, before putting it on her head.

I wondered if Haruhi's phrase "even non-humans" had somehow touched her heart.

After Asahina and Nagato's free bean-throwing performance ended, we all returned to the clubroom to wolf down our ehomaki. We looked up this year's lucky direction on the Internet, and Haruhi passed out the food.

"You can't say a word until you're done eating, got it? Okay, everybody stand up. Now, face that way, and—let's eat!"

The strange scene—all five of us lined up and facing the same direction, our mouths full as we silently ate chilled sushi rolls—continued for several minutes. Haruhi and Nagato finished first, roughly simultaneously, while Asahina held hers daintily in both hands like a small woodland creature. I fervently prayed that we wouldn't be having the same thing for dinner tonight.

The remaining beans were emptied into a bowl and ended up mostly in Haruhi's and my stomachs, along with some tea that Asahina kindly brewed, giving me a new appreciation for how full a person could wind up on Setsubun.

Surely this would return Haruhi's spirits to normal, but for some reason, the next day she was still subdued. As I said before,

the fact that remembering Setsubun had improved her mood so thoroughly proved that she wasn't seriously melancholy, but that only made me more worried about this subtle shift. It seemed I was the only one who'd noticed the change in Haruhi. It would've been one thing if minor characters like Taniguchi or Kunikida hadn't noticed, but apparently even the self-proclaimed Haruhi expert Koizumi hadn't detected it.

It was just weird.

While I couldn't get the thought out of my head, I also couldn't very well constantly pay attention to Haruhi's movements—because something more obviously strange had happened.

And unlike Haruhi's shift in mood, this one was a thing you could see with your own two eyes.

I'd just told Koizumi that I didn't anticipate there being any further time-travel episodes for a while, and I stuck to that. I wanted to avoid anything involving going back in time and changing things there. That isn't the kind of thing you should do over and over again—and *definitely* not when you don't know why you're doing it.

Whether or not my pathetic wish was heard, well—it wound up coming true anyway.

This time, it wasn't me who traveled through time. I didn't take a single step outside of my own present moment. And yet I still wound up getting sucked into another temporal disturbance.

The person in question appeared in the Literature Club's mop closet.

CHAPTER ONE

It happened one evening, a few days after Setsubun.

When I got to the clubroom and opened the door, all that greeted me was the chilly air and an empty room. Asahina wasn't there to greet me, nor was Nagato sitting silently at the corner of the table—and Haruhi was nowhere to be seen. Today was her day to talk to the guidance counselor, so right about now she was in the office with Mr. Okabe, freaking him out with her crazy ambitions. If someone had asked her what she wanted to be when she grew up, I had the feeling she would've said something crazy like "dictator" or "galactic president" with a completely straight face. And lest that actually happen, I fervently hoped that Mr. Okabe would put forth the effort to gently guide her onto a more reasonable path. Her personality was such that more forceful persuasion would cause her to be even less flexible than elements in the chromium group.

I put my bag on the table and turned on the electric space heater to warm up the chilly, lonely room. It took a while for the ancient heater to start radiating heat.

The only other sources of warmth would've been the steam coming off Asahina's kettle and the hot tea she brewed with it. I thought about how much I wanted to have some as I grabbed the nearest folding chair, when—

Clunk.

"What was that?"

It had come from the corner of the room. I reflexively looked in the direction of the sound, but the only thing there was the same tall steel object with which every classroom was furnished—namely, a broom closet. So far as I could trust my ears, the sound had come from within it.

I'd just convinced myself that it had just been the random shifting of a mop or broom, when—

Clunk.

The noise was softer this time.

"Cut it out," I murmured to myself.

Have you ever felt anything like this? Say your family's out, and you come home to an empty house, and even though you should be the only one there, you can't help feeling that you're not alone. You feel like there's some kind of movement behind the curtains, like someone is hiding there, and you want to pull them back to check, but you're scared of what you might find if you actually do, so you leave them alone—and it almost always turns out to be your imagination.

I was sure this was my imagination too. If it had happened when I was home alone instead of in the clubroom, I probably would've been too freaked out to open the door, but I was at school, and the sun hadn't even gone down yet. There was hardly anything to be nervous about.

I casually walked over to the broom closet, and with no particular expectations, I opened the door—and was immediately struck dumb.

"...Huh?"

Brooms, mops, and dustpans weren't the only things in the closet. I was so surprised that the shock forced itself out of my mouth, becoming a question. "...What the hell are you doing in there?"

The person to whom the obvious question was directed answered.

"Oh...Kyon." It was Asahina. An expression of relief flickered across her face. "So you waited for me? Oh, thank goodness. I was starting to worry about what I was going to do, but now I can relax. So, um...what should I do?"

"Wha?"

"Huh?" She looked up at me, blinking in surprise. "Umm... This is the right time, today, right? I'm certain you said this was the place..."

As the girl who'd apparently happily shut herself in a janitorial closet looked up at me uncertainly, a terrible premonition welled up within me, like smoke pouring from a factory smokestack in a growth economy.

"Asahina..."

What was going on here? Was she playing hide-and-seek in the broom closet? Surely not. Couldn't be.

The smoke of unease was beginning to well up in my chest, when—

Knock knock.

There came a knock on the clubroom door; both Asahina and I looked in its direction, startled. Just as I was about to open my mouth to ask a question—

"Oh—wait—no, don't—!"

Asahina grabbed my uniform's necktie, and I was pulled forward. She drew me farther into the broom closet, then reached out her hand and closed the steel door behind me.

What the *hell* was going on? What was all of this?

"Shhh, Kyon—be quiet. Don't make a sound."

Thanks to a sliver of light, I could just barely make out Asahina putting her index finger to her lips. Even if she hadn't said anything, I would've been speechless. I mean—just thinking about it.

Usually a person wouldn't be able to cram themselves into a broom closet. Even one occupant would exceed its capacity—but now there were *two* people inside, and not just any two people either. It was Asahina and me. Asahina, whose curves were generous enough to catch even Haruhi's eye. Obviously, given the circumstances, we wouldn't be able to avoid being pressed together, so pressed together we were. Even through the school uniform I could feel something soft and warm against the lower part of my chest.

Just as I was becoming lost in the sensation, I heard the sound of the clubroom door opening. Somehow, I didn't care. Asahina clung to me like someone trying to keep warm in a frigid mountain shack, holding her breath. I didn't know why, but she was. How was such happiness even possible?

Terrible premonition, my ass. The black smoke in my chest was transforming to crystal-clear ozone, beckoning me to a soothing paradise... No, words are unnecessary. I just wanted the moment to last forever.

But my intoxication was forcibly interrupted by the voice of the person who'd just entered the room.

"Huh? Nobody's here... but the heater's on. Oh, that's Kyon's bag. Maybe he went to the bathroom."

I looked down at Asahina, who still gripped my necktie. She looked up at me.

Next, I craned my neck around in an effort to look behind me. The sole source of light in the closet was a thin slit in its door. While humans cannot rotate their heads 180 degrees, I was about to catch a glimpse of the room out of the corner of my eye.

"...!" I was too shocked to voice my surprise.

There was Asahina.

Yes, it was *Asahina* who warmed her hands in front of the heater, humming to herself before she moved out of my line of sight, then reappeared having taken her maid outfit off its hanger. She then smoothly removed her school uniform's ribbon, hanging it neatly over the back of a folding chair, then undoing the buttons on her blouse as she began to remove it.

"...!" I continued with another stunned ellipsis.

Asahina laid her newly doffed top on the chair as well, then put her hands to the waist of her skirt—just as other hands touched my face.

"...!"

Holding my face between her two hands, *this* Asahina forced my head to turn back around and face her. Even in the dark of the closet, I could tell she was blushing furiously. Her lips moved.

"D-o-n-'t l-o-o-k."

I didn't have to do any lip-reading to know what she was trying to say, and realizing too late that I had already seen some untoward things, I hurriedly shut my mouth and reassessed the situation.

There were two Asahinas.

Now wait just a minute. If one of them had been Asahina the Elder, that much I could've understood. That sort of thing had happened several times, so her appearing again would hardly have been surprising.

But this was different. A perfectly matched set of identical Asahinas was now separated by a single flimsy steel door—one with her body pressed up against my own, and the other smack in the middle of changing into her maid uniform.

Both of them were the real Asahina. When it came to the ability to read Nagato's expressions or judge Asahina's authenticity, I prided myself on having a higher level of skill than anyone else. And if that skill could be trusted, then both of these girls were the genuine article. And two of the same person existing in the same space had to mean—

—time travel.

If I had to guess, it was probably the Asahina squeezed in the broom closet with me who was from a different time, one not far removed from the current time. The two of them were just too similar. Even identical twins would've been more different from each other.

But I was only able to consider it for a brief moment. Obviously, instinct precedes rational thought in such situations.

I mean, here in the closet Asahina was clinging to me, her eyes squeezed shut, and out there the sound Asahina's clothing made as she removed it was stimulating my imagination, and it was only a matter of time before my mind's defenses were completely overrun. Just as in the summer siege of Osaka Castle after the death of the great general Yukimura Sanada, there was nothing that could be done. It was just as impossible to tell me not to have any reaction in the face of this two-front psychological assault.

I felt lightheaded, as though some strange drug were working its way though my brain. *Somebody, do something!*

At this rate I was either going to wind up embracing Asahina the Nearer with all my might or jump out of the closet and scare to death the Asahina in the room mid–costume change.

The sound of the clubroom door opening again brought me back to myself.

"..."

Whoever it was seemed to be standing there without saying anything. The door didn't close.

"Oh, Nagato," I heard Asahina say in her clear voice. "Wait just a moment, and I'll put the tea on."

I craned my neck around again.

Through the door's slit I only caught the hem of her maid outfit's skirt as it whirled around. I was left to imagine the now-changed Asahina quickly lighting the portable burner.

"..."

I didn't hear any more sound from Nagato. While she's certainly capable of moving quietly, the door certainly cannot close without making noise, so I inferred that she was still standing at the room's entrance.

"Um…is something the matter?" came Asahina's uncertain voice. Again my imagination: Nagato held her bag in one hand, with the other holding the doorknob as she stared, I was certain, at the broom closet.

"…"

"Er—"

"We need to talk." Nagato's voice.

"Huh?" Asahina sounded surprised.

"Come with me."

"Wha—?" said Asahina, her surprise growing. "G-go where? I…wha…?"

"Anywhere, as long as it is not this room."

"B-but, what do you want to talk about…? Why can't we do it here?"

"We cannot speak here," said Nagato shortly.

"And…you really want to talk to *me*? Really?"

"Yes."

"Wha—? Wait, Nagato, don't—you don't have to drag me like that—!"

There were no further words. I heard Asahina's tottering footsteps, followed by the sound of the door closing. The two girls disappeared down the hallway beyond the door.

Thanks, Nagato.

I clattered out of the broom closet, its door slamming open; Asahina tumbled after me.

"Fwaa—!" On her knees, Asahina cried out in a voice that could've been either relief or total fatigue. "Gosh, what a shock!"

I doubted she was more shocked than I was. "Asahina," I said. "Just what is going on here? *When* did you come from?"

Asahina lifted her head up from its lowered position to look at me, blinking as she replied. "Huh? You don't know, Kyon?"

Know *what*, I wondered. Just what was it that I was supposed to know?

"I mean"—Asahina continued, her expression like a passenger aboard a sinking ocean liner who'd just gotten to a lifeboat only to discover that it had a hole in it—"you were the one who told me to go to this time, weren't you?"

Now wait just a minute.

I racked my brain. I had said something like that. Definitely. It was on January second, when I'd needed to return to December eighteenth the previous year. We'd gone back, then returned to our time.

But that had wrapped things up, hadn't it? At the very least, I had no memory of telling Asahina anything about a jump into the future. I hadn't even considered the notion.

Which meant...

The future. This Asahina had come from the future.

"When did you come from?"

"Uh..." Asahina went blank for a moment, then looked down and checked her wristwatch. "Um... A week and a day, so... four fifteen PM, eight days from now."

"For what reason?"

"I don't know."

She'd just up and admitted it.

"I really don't know," she continued. "I just did what you told me to do. And I want to ask you something: why are your requests always so quickly approved?"

Asahina pouted, looking a bit like Haruhi. It was cute, but this was no time to be thinking about things like that. I purposefully turned toward the clubroom door. "I told you to do this? The me of eight days from now did?"

"Yes. You seemed kind of nervous, and you told me that if I

44

went, I'd understand why. And you said to say 'Hi' to the you of the past."

What the hell had the eight-days-later-me been thinking?

I struggled to understand. What had he sent Asahina into the past to do? "Say 'Hi' to me?" That didn't tell me anything.

No, wait—something else was strange. This Asahina said she'd come from eight days in the future. Meanwhile, the Asahina who was wearing her maid outfit—the Asahina of *this* time—had been dragged away by Nagato.

So...what? There were two Asahinas. One was here in the clubroom. Nagato had taken the other one somewhere else in the school and hopefully wasn't giving her too hard of a time.

"She took me to the emergency stairs and said all kinds of strange things," said Asahina, cocking her head to one side. "Like how to use number theory to prove the existence of God, asking me how to conceptually refute that...or something. Nagato did all the talking, and I didn't understand a thing. What was that all about? Oh—" There Asahina cut herself off. "I see."

Just as Asahina seemed to figure things out, the Color Timer in my head began to flash an alarmed shade of red. At this rate, we were headed for big trouble.

As I silently prayed for Nagato's crazy-talk to drag on, I said, "Asahina, you didn't meet your future self anytime in the past week, right?"

"Er, no..." She shook her head meekly, looking flustered. In that case, we'd have to hurry.

I couldn't let this Asahina meet her counterpart.

Nagato had realized this. She'd sensed Asahina and me in the broom closet and had taken steps to buy us some time. The reason she'd dragged maid-Asahina out of the clubroom was to give this Asahina and me a chance to escape.

Haruhi and Koizumi would be here before long. SOS Brigade members were like salmon returning to spawn—they always came back to the same place. I should know; I was the same way.

And if Haruhi were to see the fissioned Asahinas, it wasn't hard for me to guess how likely it was that she'd buy the explanation that they were twins.

If I didn't get Asahina out of here and fast, I had the feeling things could turn ugly very soon.

"Asahina, let's go."

I grabbed my own bag, opened the door slightly, and checked the hallway. Nobody was there. I beckoned Asahina to come over, which she did, looking tremulously out into the hallway. The countdown had already begun. There were two conditions. One: not letting the two versions of Asahina meet each other, and two: not letting Haruhi witness two Asahinas in one place. I thought about putting her in some kind of disguise, but a glance at the hanger rack in the clubroom revealed nothing but costumes that would've stuck out, so I gave up on that idea. Fortunately this Asahina was wearing her school uniform. Like the saying goes: the best way to hide in a forest is to be a leaf.

I took Asahina's arm and hurried out of the room.

"You're sure you came from eight days in the future, right?" I asked as we strolled briskly along.

"Yes, because you told me to go back eight days, to three forty-five PM."

Asahina's stride was longer than usual as we descended the steps two at a time. I prayed that Mr. Okabe's lecturing of Haruhi would run long.

"So you know what's going to happen for the next week?"

We reached the bottom floor, and I hesitated for a moment before picking a route that took us across the courtyard. If we had taken the covered pathways back to the main school building, there was the possibility of a direct encounter with Haruhi, and this path would get us to the shoe lockers more quickly.

Breathing a bit heavily, Asahina answered: "I guess so..."

"So was there some incident that made you have to travel into the past?"

"No, it wasn't anything I could think of. You just dragged me over to that broom closet and pushed me in."

So I'd pushed her in and ordered her to go to this time, today. That was strange, even for me. What the hell had I been thinking? I should've come with her. I would've saved myself the trouble of figuring all this out.

We'd just made it to the shoe lockers without meeting anyone we knew when I suddenly stopped short.

"Where should we go?" I asked.

We obviously had to get away from the school, but I had no idea where to hide Asahina after that.

So what was I supposed to do? I couldn't very well do nothing and just have her return to eight days in the future, could I—? I asked.

"You can't," said Asahina, her upturned gaze sad. "I thought the same thing and asked about it, but they said no. The time when I'm allowed to go back is also classified, and I don't know it myself."

Which meant that this Asahina from eight days in the future had something she had to do today, or tomorrow, or soon. I'd just assume that much.

So?

So the number one thing I wanted to know was what that was. Why had my eight-days-later self sent her back without so much as a single note?

As I hurled curses at my future self, Asahina trotted over to the second-year students' shoe lockers, and just as I was changing from my school slippers into my sneakers—

"Asahina!" I hurriedly looked around for the time traveler's form. She was reaching up to her own shoe locker, which was located on a high row.

"Yes?" she replied, looking over her shoulder as she reached up. "What is it?"

I couldn't believe she was asking me that. "Those shoes belong to your past self! The one in *this* time!"

47

"Ah—r-right…" she said, closing the door to the locker. "If I put these on, then my other self would have a hard time getting home. And I don't remember my shoes going missing, so…"

That wasn't all. She would've put her own school shoes back in the locker, and then what would've happened? The other Asahina would come back, open the locker, and find shoes precisely identical to the ones she was already wearing already inside.

"R-right," said Asahina, flustered. "But, um, how am I going to get home?"

She'd just have to wear her school slippers, I thought. It might be a little embarrassing, but there was no other way. She couldn't very well borrow another student's shoes. And at the moment, I was more worried about *where* she was going to go home, rather than *how*.

I returned to my own shoe locker, opening it as my heart banged away in my chest.

And there, nostalgically enough, I found a message from the future.

"…Good job, Asahina. You're always prepared."

There atop my dirty, worn-out sneakers sat a fancy little envelope.

A cold wind stabbed at Asahina and me as we walked down the street, away from the school.

There was a scattering of other students from North High around, and I wondered if the feeling I had that they were all glancing at Asahina's strange state—carrying no school bag and wearing her school slippers—was just my imagination.

Asahina was to my right, her chestnut-brown hair swaying softly. Her expression was far from soft, though—it was as dark as the clouds before a snowstorm.

And there was no doubt my own face was hardly untroubled. After all, I'd been forced to flee the clubroom, and my skipping club activities (actually, it was a brigade, so brigade activities) without notice would put the Chief in a bad mood, and unless I thought of a funny enough excuse or a good enough reason, I'd become fodder for one of her special punishments.

Nevertheless, leaving Asahina alone was risky in several ways. Seeing her wander aimlessly under the freezing night sky would make anyone want to help her. But seeing as how there was no guarantee that such helpers would be persons of good repute, I would have to do it myself.

"I'm sorry," she said in an adorably sad voice. "Causing you trouble again, I—"

"No, not at all," I answered quickly before she could finish. "I'm the one who sent you here in the first place, right? Future me's the one at fault here."

He and Asahina the Elder both. For being our future selves, they sure weren't very nice to us. Did people from the future just hate the past, or what?

I grabbed the envelope I'd shoved into my pocket.

On the note, which had no indication of recipient or sender, there was simply written: Please take care of the Mikuru Asahina beside you.

That was all. I'd seen the careful handwriting before. The previous spring, I'd visited the clubroom during lunch in response to a similar missive, where I met the curvaceous form of Asahina the Elder before she told me where her mole was, in addition to more important hints. She was definitely the sender.

But still—even if I was supposed to "take care" of this Asahina, what did that mean? What could I do? Hadn't Asahina the Elder told me I could even kiss her, if I wanted to?

Incidentally, I'd already shown the letter to the Asahina who was right here. I didn't think there was anything wrong with that. She could understand what "Please take care of Mikuru Asahina" meant. If this message had been meant for my eyes only, that part would've said "me" instead of "Mikuru Asahina."

"What could this mean…?" murmured Asahina, as she held the letter, staring intently at it. She seemed not to realize that she was the one who would end up writing it.

She would probably gradually come to that realization, though. During the second visit to December eighteenth, she'd noticed a fourth person, someone besides me, Nagato, and Asakura. She'd been put immediately to sleep, but *because* she'd been put to sleep, she must have sensed the other woman's presence.

And the previous month, when I'd saved that kid in glasses from being hit by a minivan near Haruhi's house, and Asahina had been so depressed that I'd clumsily tried to cheer her up— surely she'd gotten some information from me then. I didn't know how much she'd figured out by now, but Koizumi was right: the members of the SOS Brigade were gradually changing.

According to Koizumi, the rate at which Haruhi created closed space was decreasing.

Also according to Koizumi, Nagato's alienness was lessening.

And Koizumi himself, he'd changed a bit too. *Isn't that right, Mister Lieutenant Brigade Chief?*

From what I could tell, although it was gradual, Haruhi was starting to engage with the people around her more. She'd been a substitute vocalist during the school festival, and when you compared activities like her game battle against the computer club and the winter training camp with her isolated state at the beginning of the year, she was like a different person now, smiling, happy, and able to reach mutual understandings with complete strangers.

—*If there are any aliens, time travelers, sliders, or espers, come join me!*

—*We're going to search for aliens, time travelers, and espers, and have fun with them!*

It was like she knew it had come true.

I wanted to think that all of these things were signs of her growth as a person.

As to my own growth, I had no idea.

*   *   *

A half hour later, it was into my own home that I wound up escorting Asahina.

"Oh, I see!" she said as she entered, taking off her shoes. "This is why you weren't in the clubroom today."

Her carefree voice had an admiring tone.

Since I couldn't very well let her go back to her own home, and in lieu of any better options, I'd asked if there were any other people from her era that she could possibly stay with.

"There might well be, but I haven't been informed of them," she told me, her face looking like a greyhound's right after a grueling dog race.

I'd had no choice but to invite her over. Asahina's sorrow was deep, and the situation was completely mystifying. I had no idea what was going to happen, and I didn't really want to know. And then, my sister, who had nothing to do with our current troubles, jumped out at Asahina.

"Hey, it's Mikuru!"

My sister had been trying to drag Shamisen the cat out from under my bed, but no sooner did we open the door to my room than she slammed into Asahina, causing the beautiful object of every male North High student's desire to stumble backward.

"S-sorry to disturb you!"

"Hey, wait—it's just Kyon and Mikuru? Where's Haruhi?"

My little sister looked up at Asahina with shining eyes before I grabbed the eleven-year-old fifth grader by her collar.

"Haruhi's still at school. And I told you not to go into my room uninvited."

I knew it was pointless no matter how many times I told her. Which meant finding hiding places for things I didn't want found was a huge pain.

"But Shami wouldn't come out!" My sister clung to Asahina's

skirt, giggling. "Where's Yuki? And Koizumi? And Tsuruya? Aren't they coming too?"

She tended to call everybody by the names she heard other people call them, which was obviously why she'd started calling me "Kyon." An elementary school kid with no concept of respect for her elders—that was my little sister. All I wanted was for somebody to call me "big brother" once in a while. Was that so much to ask?

"Oh! Is this a date? Hey—"

I kicked her out of my room and shut the door before she got any further.

"Well then," I said, sitting down and facing Asahina. "Can you give me an idea of what happens this week?"

"Hmm." Asahina puzzled over it. "Eight days ago...which would be today, I went back to the clubroom and noticed that the heater was on, even though nobody was in the room."

I'd seen that happen.

"And then when I was changing, Nagato came in, and then she took me over to the bottom of the emergency stairs."

I'd seen the first half of that.

"When I came back to the clubroom, your bag was gone, and Koizumi was there."

Which meant we'd escaped in the nick of time.

"About half an hour later, Suzumiya came."

Her guidance counseling must have run long. I needn't have worried about running into her, apparently.

"She seemed kind of angry."

Maybe she'd gotten into some kind of argument during counseling. There weren't exactly application forms for the kind of careers she probably had in mind. And if there were, I wanted one too.

"She just glared out the window with a scary look on her face and drank three cups of tea in a—oh!"

Asahina's eyes went wide, as though she'd caught a glimpse of a ghost in the corner of the room.

"Suzumiya realized you weren't there and…"

Realized?

"…And she called you—"

The instant Asahina said those words, my phone rang.

Crap.

When I really thought about it, what Asahina was talking about was prerecorded, but for me it was a live broadcast. I didn't have time to listen to her dithering recollections. I still hadn't come up with a good excuse for skipping out on the brigade meeting. I should've left my phone on vibrate. If I didn't answer, it would only seem more suspicious to Haruhi. But before I answered, I had to ask something.

"Asahina, do you remember if I answered?"

"Um, yes, it seemed like you did."

I guessed I'd better answer.

"Hello?"

"Where are you?" Haruhi's voice already sounded highly irritated. I answered truthfully.

"I'm at home in my room."

"What, you're ditching?"

"Something came up." Here's where I would have to start lying.

"What do you mean, 'something came up'?"

"Uh…" Just then, my eyes lit upon Shamisen crawling out from under my bed. "Y'know, Shamisen got sick, so I took him to the vet."

"*You* did?"

"Yeah, my sister's the only other one at home right now. She called me."

"Huh. What's he sick with?"

"Uh…alopecia areata. Y'know, fur loss."

Hearing my half-assed answer, for some reason Asahina clamped her hand over her mouth.

"Shamisen's losing his fur?"

"Yeah. The vet said it was stress-related, so he's resting at home now."

"Do cats even *have* stress problems? And doesn't Shamisen always 'rest at home'?"

"Well, yeah, but my sister messes around with him too much, apparently. So my room's been turned into a Shamisen preserve, and my sister's not allowed to come in."

"Huh." Whether or not she bought it, Haruhi sniffed and fell silent before continuing. "Are you with anybody else now?"

"..."

I took the phone away from my ear and stared at the call-time display on the screen.

How did she know? Asahina hadn't said a word and had even covered her mouth so as to avoid carelessly letting anything slip.

"No, nobody's here."

"Oh yeah? Something was weird about your voice, so I was sure somebody was there."

Her intuition was as sharp as ever.

"It's just Shamisen. You want to talk to him?"

"Not really. Just tell him I hope he gets better soon. Bye."

She hung up surprisingly briskly.

I tossed my cell phone onto the bed and looked at the calico cat as it rubbed up against Asahina's leg. I wondered where I should shave a circular patch of hair off the feline—if Haruhi decided to come visit him, God forbid, I'd be in trouble otherwise.

"So what did Haruhi do after that?"

Asahina made a face as she tried to remember, absentmindedly scratching Shamisen behind the ears. "Umm, we were in the room until after five o'clock, and then we all went home. Suzumiya...seemed kind of quiet. All she'd done in the clubroom was read some magazines..."

It seemed that even Asahina was starting to pick up on Haruhi's strangely subdued behavior lately.

I wondered about the others. Nagato had surely sensed it.

Drawn in by her scratching, Shamisen put his front paws on Asahina's skirted lap and purred. Asahina stroked his back as he occupied her lap.

"There wasn't anything really out of the ordinary...I'm sorry. I don't remember very well."

It couldn't be helped, I guessed. I wouldn't have been able to tell you about Koizumi's facial expressions a week ago, myself. If I'd been asked, all I could've said was that he seemed normal.

"Was there anything else? Tomorrow or the day after?"

Her eyes downcast, Asahina held the purring Shamisen's tail lightly. "How far ahead should I go?"

I told her to just give me my future schedule, and I'd do my best to make it happen just like she remembered.

"Um, well, the next day is a holiday, so we all go on a treasure hunt."

A treasure hunt? I asked.

"Yes. Suzumiya brings a treasure map, and we all go digging."

Digging? Seriously? I asked.

"Yes. Suzumiya got the map from Tsuruya. She said that when they were organizing things in the family storehouse, this weird map that one of her ancestors had drawn just popped up. Like"— Asahina fluttered her fingers like tiny fish swimming through the air—"A weird old map drawn in ink."

Tsuruya. She'd gone and given Haruhi another thing we'd all pay for. And really, digging for treasure? It wasn't like we were in a Heian-era archaeological dig. Where did we go digging, I wanted to know.

"The mountains." Asahina's answer was straightforward. "There's a mountain on Tsuruya's estate. The round one you can see from the road that goes down the hill on the way home from school."

Just thinking about it was exhausting. This wasn't *Onshu no Kanata*, and doing a bunch of exhausting excavation *after* climbing a mountain made about as much sense as going on a long hike to stave off the cold in this freezing February weather. I should say that it came as no surprise that Tsuruya's family owned their own mountain. Their villa had its own ski slope, so surely they had resources enough to furnish their home with a mountain or two.

I didn't even try to hide my sigh. "So did you even find a treasure?"

"Um...no."

She seemed to hesitate before answering but eventually shook her head. "There weren't any old treasure chests buried anywhere."

I shouldn't have asked. Despite it being a rare day off, I was going to have to waste the day playing treasure hunter while looking for a treasure we'd never find. There's nothing worse than knowing in advance your efforts are going to end in vain.

"Also, the day after that..."

More digging? I asked. We'd be better off just boring a hole in the Tsuruya family garden. Who knows what we'd find. A hot spring, maybe.

"No, on Saturday we—we did a city patrol."

Ah, *that*. The main activity of the SOS Brigade—wandering around town looking for mysterious phenomena. Now that she mentioned it, we hadn't done that in a while.

"Pff, not like there's two straight days' worth of stuff to do," I said.

"No...wait—yes, that's right." Asahina looked askance for some reason. "Since Monday was also a vacation day..."

I remembered as soon as she said it. Next Monday they were holding the special class entrance examinations, so students were excused from school.

"And did we find anything mysterious?" I asked, thinking that perhaps that was the reason Asahina had been sent back.

"No." She shook her head without hesitation. "It was the same as always. We drank some tea and ate some lunch..."

It was getting more and more puzzling. As far as I could tell, there was no reason for my future self to send Asahina into the past. I could maybe understand if she'd come from a year hence, or even a few months. But what difference could traveling into this week from next week make?

I watch Asahina vaguely as she fluffed Shamisen's belly fur, the cat having rolled over on its back.

Since we were only dealing with a week this time, there'd be no need to borrow Nagato's power, and we could still use her method. At last year's Tanabata, when Asahina and I had traveled to the Tanabata four years earlier, we'd been frozen in time for three years while we waited to return to our original time. I'd just apply that lesson here. I'd be able to return Asahina to her proper time frame just by keeping her out of sight for a week. There wouldn't be any need for cold sleep, and while she'd age a week in the meantime, I didn't think that would make much of a difference.

But in that case, what was the point? There had to be a reason for this—a reason for my eight-days-older self to send Asahina into the past, and a reason for Asahina the Elder to leave another handwritten message for me.

"How did I seem? Did I do or say anything strange?"

"Mmm…" Asahina only continued to pet the squishy furball that was Shamisen, his eyes by now having closed dazedly.

It was time for a different approach.

"Tell me, just what was the situation when my future self told you to travel back in time?"

"That much I remember perfectly, since from my perspective it happened today." Removing her hand from the cat, Asahina drew several horizontal lines in the air with her finger. "We were doing a fund-raiser in the courtyard. A lottery to sponsor the SOS Brigade."

What the hell was that? I thought.

"It was a lottery where whoever pulled a winner would get…

um, a grand prize of five hundred yen. Suzumiya was drawing people in with a megaphone, and…"

No doubt she was trying to raise money for the club.

Asahina continued her explanation, but with difficulty.

"I was in charge of handing out goods. There were a lot of people, so it was kinda scary…"

I wondered if Haruhi was trying to get revenge for the Setsubun event.

"Asahina, what were you wearing? Was it by any chance a shrine maiden's outfit?"

"Wha—? How did you know?"

Because it sounded like the kind of thing Haruhi would do. It was Haruhi's policy, when trying to command attention, to start with costume design. Whatever stood out the most was the best, in her view. Asahina's features by themselves were enough to draw the eye, but when decorated, their power inexplicably grew far greater. In terms of character statistics, I guess you'd call it her charm.

"I handed out prizes to the winners, shook their hands, and took photos with them," Asahina said, embarrassed, her hand grabbing onto the fur of Shamisen's cheek. "Then you suddenly took me by the hand and led me to the clubroom. You said we were in a big hurry, and that I should change into my uniform, and I didn't really understand, but I did what you said. Then you told me to get in the broom closet and jump eight days back in time, to three forty-five PM. You said you'd be waiting for me there, and that I should do whatever your past self told me to do."

Asahina looked down, her index finger tracing the calico patterns on Shamisen's back.

"Permission to use the TPDD was granted immediately—so fast I couldn't believe it. It was like they were just waiting for my request."

They must have been. Asahina the Elder would have known all

of this ahead of time. What I didn't understand was why had my future self played a role in the time traveler's plan? I knew that the other, curvier Asahina was the same individual as the one that was here with me, separated only by time. But reason and emotion are different things. How many times was she going to make the younger Asahina travel through time before she was satisfied? *C'mon, Asahina the Elder—give me something to work with, here!*

If she didn't, I was gonna happily puke my guts out pretty soon.

The Asahina in front of me was looking depressed again. A pained expression played over her features, not unlike the time a month ago when she was feeling shame over her own powerlessness. If that was it, she shouldn't have worried—I was plenty powerless myself. Even now, all I could do was try to figure out who I was going to beg for help.

The two of us sighed simultaneously, as Shamisen yawned, bored. Just then—

"Kyon, open up!"

My little sister's voice sounded from the other side of the door. When I did as the voice instructed, she came wobbling into the room, precariously holding a tray with juice and sponge cake. I guess my mom was being pretty considerate, but when I saw that there were three servings, I could tell my sister was planning to stay. I realized it too late. This was a prime chance to be alone with Asahina in my room, but it sure didn't seem like that was going to happen. I stared daggers at my sister, willing her to get out of my room, but she ignored me completely and plopped herself down next to Asahina.

"Shami, want some cake?"

As she watched my sister hold a little piece of cake in front of the cat's nose, Asahina finally faintly smiled.

I guess little sisters can be good for something. As her brother, I hoped she wouldn't lose that innocence as she got older.

*   *   *

After my sister played with Asahina for a little while, the cat sandwiched between them, Asahina and I finally left my house.

My watch indicated six fifteen, and the sky was already dark. The first day of spring wouldn't be until next month.

"Kyon, what shall we do?" Asahina murmured, breathing clouds of white vapor as she walked beside me. She was walking a bit uncertainly, having borrowed a pair of my shoes. I'd figured they'd be better than her school slippers, but now I wondered if they were a bit too big for this particular Cinderella.

"Yeah, hmm," I said, exhaling.

I was starting to want to have her just stay at my house—that would've made my sister happy, but somehow it just didn't seem like it would work. For one thing, my parents would want to know exactly why she couldn't just go home. And if some rumor happened to reach Haruhi's ears, I could wind up in serious danger. Shamisen's fur would grow back if I wound up having to shave a patch, but I couldn't very well erase Asahina's existence. It looked like I'd have to leave the idea of Asahina staying at my house in the realm of fantasy.

The petite junior's footsteps listed diagonally. Her path finally intersected mine, and our arms touched, causing her to twitch back in surprise, even more adorable than usual. It didn't seem like it was just the fault of the ill-fitting shoes. I found myself pleased that she was unconsciously leaning on me, but I couldn't simply enjoy the sensation. I wasn't confident that I'd be able to support her completely. A falling domino causes another to fall, until they've reached the last piece.

So when I started to think about who could be trusted not to fall, there weren't many candidates.

Haruhi was totally out of the question. If anybody were to ask why, I'd feel no shame in going completely *Eraserhead* on them.

60

The other Asahina currently existing in this time period was also out of consideration. Having a matched set of twins walking around would only complicate things—and I had no intention of having to think about time paradoxes any more than I already was.

Koizumi seemed a bit more trustworthy, but I didn't know how his Agency treated time travelers, and who knew what would happen to Asahina if I handed her over to that mysterious syndicate. Mori, Arakawa, and the Tamaru brothers were all good people, but Koizumi himself had admitted that they were no better than underlings, and I didn't have enough faith in them to also trust whoever was controlling things over their heads.

Thus, a simple process of elimination led me to a single name. The shadowy power behind the scenes of the SOS Brigade, the one who already knew what was going on. Though she was still backed by an unknown, unknowable boss, it had a less corporeal existence than Koizumi's superiors.

Yes, the only one remaining was her.

Thus it came to pass that when I started to think about where to go, there was only one option.

It was time to see Yuki Nagato. Having another problem like this was enough to make you want to say "What, this again?" Maybe it was time to start thinking of the alien and the time traveler as a matched set. It seemed like the route from the future to the past always involved a trip to Nagato's room.

And also— I thought.

Nagato was the one who had pulled Asahina (current) out of the room such that Asahina the Current's gaze wouldn't fall upon Asahina (future). Nagato might even be able to tell me just what was going on here.

"Are we going to Nagato's place?" asked Asahina, her steps slowing.

"You'll be fine with her," I said, trying to cheer her up. "She's got an extra room, and I'm sure she'll let you stay for a week."

Heck, I should've brought my own pajamas. I even had a good excuse.

"But..." Asahina replied, her eyes a bit downcast. "Being alone with Nagato is a little...um...for a whole week?"

There wasn't anything to be afraid of. Nagato would never do anything to hurt Asahina. We'd relied on Nagato plenty of times in the past, and she'd even been our companion in our most recent time-travel episode.

"I-I know, but..." Strangely, Asahina looked at me with accusation in her eyes. "I don't think Nagato will enjoy it very much if I stay with her..."

"Huh? Why's that?"

How would Asahina know what Nagato *did* enjoy? I doubted Nagato would so much as flinch even if someone stripped all their clothes off and started dancing around six inches away from her.

I looked at her, waiting for an answer, but Asahina just puffed her cheeks in irritation and faced ahead.

"...Fine then," she said.

Nagato's specialty was saying things using the fewest words possible, and this time was no different. In the foyer of her apartment building, I punched her apartment number into the now-familiar keypad and hit the buzzer, to be greeted with—

"..."

The same wordless reaction as always.

"It's me. Asahina's with me. There's a problem."

"Come in."

How many times had we had this conversation? I'd brought both the large and small versions of Asahina here, let's see...four times. The first time was during Tanabata four years ago, the second was also that day. The third time was January second, just last month.

Asahina had the same anxious look on her face, and I'd gotten used to it remaining all the way down the seventh floor hallway on the way to Nagato's apartment. She clung to my sleeve looking for all the world like some small, frightened animal, and if that sight wasn't enough to make me want to protect her, then surely nothing else in the world ever could.

"..."

Nagato's apartment door was open, and she leaned partway through it as she waited for us. She was wearing her school uniform, as usual. The first time I'd seen her in street clothes was during our summer trip, and the last time was during our winter trip. She looked at us, and although her gaze didn't seem to carry particular meaning, Asahina still shrank away from it.

"Um...excuse us, Nagato. It seems we've come to trouble you again..." she said.

Which was quite true.

"It's fine." Nagato gave a cool nod. "Come in."

Asahina's total fright indicated that she was about as close to getting used to Nagato's manner as our solar system was to Barnard's Star. I put my hand on her shoulder and gently urged her forward, at which she finally stepped inside. She was so reluctant that it was hard to imagine that she'd ever slept in this very apartment's guest room.

"Excuse us..." she said.

Nagato's apartment had once been completely bare of anything but the basic necessities for living. But now, for the first time since I'd first visited last spring, there hung a set of paisley-patterned winter curtains in the large living room window. That alone would've been enough to make an impression on me. The Twister game mat we'd used at Christmas was rolled up and leaning against the wall, although there was still no television or

Nagaru Tanigawa

carpet. As we passed through the living room, the only other furnishing was a low, bare table. For a moment I really wanted to get a look in the bedroom to see what, if anything, there was in there, but then suddenly I felt like that was a bad idea. If it was fancy wallpaper or lacy ornamentation, or a canopy bed with big pillows and a fuzzy stuffed animal like a lamb or something, I'd have to reset all preexisting data I thought I had on Nagato. On that matter, the comment I can give is that you could go all the way back to the Mesopotamian era and you still wouldn't find any trace of anything like that. And when tomorrow came, I already had good intelligence from Asahina.

What I needed to ask about was something else.

"So, Nagato, you know that Asahina here is from the future…" Well, that was a stupid thing to say—obviously she was from the future. "No, what I mean is, you know that this is another Asahina, who came from eight days in the future. Right?" I asked, sitting at the low living room table.

"I know."

Nagato sat directly across from me, looking up at Asahina, who was still standing. Asahina flinched, then hurriedly sat next to me, her eyes downcast.

"Apparently Asahina herself doesn't know why she came to this time," I explained. "She says that I told her to come. So—do you have any idea what this is all about, Nagato?"

Even if she didn't know, there was a high probability that she'd be able to tell me something about the future.

So when she quickly said, "I don't know," I wasn't worried. So long as she would find out for me. I asked her to just do that synchronization-whatever thing.

But Nagato completely betrayed my expectations.

"I cannot. Currently, I am unable to synchronize with selves from either future or past space-time continuities."

Before I could ask why, she continued.

"Execution prevention code was applied."

I definitely didn't understand that, I told her. Why?

"Because it was determined that it could cause irregularities in my autonomous functioning."

So was it her boss that had sealed that ability? I asked.

"The Data Overmind concurred." Something was strangely cheerful about Nagato's expressionless face. "But it was my decision," she said, sounding like she was reading a telegram aloud. "The release code is encrypted and held by a different humanoid interface. I cannot release the lock of my own volition. Nor do I intend to."

Uh, so, in other words, Nagato couldn't exchange information with her future self, nor did she have any way of knowing future events. So, obviously, she didn't know the reason why Asahina had come from eight days in the future. So what was I supposed to do? I asked.

"You should act according to your own judgment." I saw myself reflected tinily in her black pupils. "Just as I am doing."

All I could do was drop my jaw. Nagato was speaking of her own volition. Had I just gotten a lecture from her?

"By losing the ability to synchronize, I have gained the right to greater autonomy. I am currently able to act according to my own judgment. I am not constrained by the future."

Nagato was being extremely talkative, by her usual standards. What was bringing this on? I asked.

"I have determined that my responsibility of determining my future self is carried by my current self." Nagato continued to stare at me. "Which is true of you, as well."

She spoke very slowly.

"That is your future."

I closed my eyes and thought.

Suppose I had the ability to predict the future and could know exactly what actions I would take in the next eight days. Likewise, suppose I knew that whatever I did, I couldn't change the ultimate result. So no matter what I did, I couldn't change the future, and I would have to arrive at that result—did that then mean that I should give up trying to do anything at all?

Could it be said that the result of all that struggle was that it would all come to naught, that I shouldn't have done anything from the start, and that if the place we arrived at was going to be the same, that everything else would *also* be the same?

Nagato must have struggled too. She knew she was going to commit an error. Trying to avoid that while knowing it would be futile must have been hard. Knowing in advance might have even been the cause, but in any case the outcome had been what it was. It was my fault. I'd noticed Nagato was changing but hadn't done anything about it. Part of me wanted to let Haruhi take some of the blame, but this was a psychological burden only I could bear.

Last month, this Nagato had spoken to the past Nagato.

—*I don't want to.*

She didn't want to be forced to know what to do, and she didn't want to know herself.

Nagato had known that she would do what she had to. She had trusted herself.

I didn't have to remind myself of this—I'd been doing it all along, hadn't I?

I'd heard the words of my future self, then I'd gone back into the past to tell myself those same words. I hadn't asked myself what to do, nor had I told myself what to do.

—Because I already knew that things would work out.

And things *would* work out. Because here I was.

"It will be all right."

The sound of Nagato's voice brought me out of my reverie. Her dark, emotionless eyes were shining.

"My highest priority remains the safety of you and Haruhi Suzumiya."

I wished she'd included Asahina in that statement. And maybe Koizumi too. In the snowy mountain incident, he'd said some very supportive things about her, I reminded her.

Nagato nodded. "Yes, in cases of enemy interference."

What did she mean by "enemy"? I asked.

"Macro-spatial cosmic beings unrelated to the Data Overmind. They once sealed us in a different dimension."

Those were the bastards who were behind the snowy mountain incident.

"They exist in a far-removed"—Nagato closed her mouth as she searched for the right word—"*place* from the Data Overmind. Each knew of the existence of the other, but there was no contact, as it was decided that mutual understanding was impossible. However, they have now come to a realization."

A realization of what? I asked.

"Of Haruhi Suzumiya."

How can I describe the familiar feeling that came over me? Everyone and their uncle took special notice of Haruhi, watched her movements carefully, and occasionally tried to mess with her.

"So the snowy mountain disaster was their doing, eh...?"

"Yes. They put me under heavy load, making it difficult for me to avert the danger with my own abilities."

So what had her boss been doing? I asked. Napping?

"A humanoid interface like me does not have the capability to fully understand the will of the Data Overmind." Nagato then turned her head down two millimeters. "I could recognize it as a form of communication."

What the hell kind of conversation was that? They'd just gone and sealed us off. That kind of approach wasn't going to fly in the modern world, I said.

"They are utterly unlike us. It is impossible to understand their cognitive processes. It is surmised that they are likewise unable to understand our thinking."

So that was it, then? I really wanted to know what they thought of Haruhi, I said.

"Perfect data transfer is impossible."

Well, obviously—if they were so stupid as to say "Hello" by sending the blizzard of the century.

"However, some communication may be possible." Nagato straightened her neck. "If they were to construct a humanoid interface similar to myself, verbal communication, although imperfect, could take place."

Surely there weren't any already around here, were there? I asked.

"There may be."

Although I didn't especially hope they existed, I had a weird feeling like it would be stranger if they *didn't* show up.

"Oh…" Asahina said, exhaling. "It couldn't be…"

She seemed to have realized something and looked to Nagato, surprised. Nagato looked back at her. A bit surprised, I watched the time traveler and the alien regarding each other.

"What is it?"

"Oh, um, it's nothing. Really, nothing…"

As I was sitting there stunned by Asahina's suddenly confused expression, Nagato suddenly stood.

"I will make some tea," she said, looking down at us before she turned and headed for the kitchen. Halfway there, she stopped and looked over her shoulder. "Or—" she started. I opened my mouth and waited for her to finish; she concluded with a simple question: "—Dinner?"

Nagato's menu for the evening was instant canned curry. Preparation consisted of her opening the giant can, which could've fed a family of five, pouring its contents into a hot pot, and heating it up—the whole process was indescribably Nagato-like. If Haruhi'd been here, I imagined that she would've added all kinds of superfluous ingredients, which notion I likewise found indescribable, as far as which would've been more delicious or more fun.

It was definitely dinnertime, though.

Asahina sat at the table and fidgeted, as Nagato had ordered her to stay. When Asahina had offered to help, Nagato had said only, "You are a guest," and gone about the preparations herself—although that merely entailed getting a can of curry out of the cupboard and finely slicing an entire head of cabbage.

Eventually she ladled the curry over big bowls of rice. In the simplicity of the main dish there was also a kind of magnificence, and the curry was served to Asahina and me alongside large cabbage-only salads. Bowing almost apologetically, Asahina looked down to her dish, and a sweat broke out on her face as her expression stiffened, as though she were trying to gulp down the stomachache that eating such a gigantic serving of curry rice would surely bring.

Nagato sat at her own place. "Eat," she said.

"L-let's eat!"

I put my hands together too, since the instant I'd first smelled the curry my stomach had been growling. It was a bit unfortunate that it wasn't homemade, but curry from a can had its own charm. The sight of Nagato wordlessly destroying her serving and Asahina politely eating her own went pretty well with the food, honestly. Although there was no conversation (had Haruhi been there, she would've just talked to herself), the dining milieu left nothing to be desired.

After that, once a dazed Asahina had shoveled the remaining half of her own serving of curry onto Nagato's dish and we were drinking the after-dinner tea Nagato had brewed, I spoke up.

"That was delicious. So I guess I'll be heading home in a second—"

"Huh? You're not staying, Kyon?" Asahina looked at me

goggle-eyed as she daintily held her teacup, and even Nagato froze midsip and looked at me.

"No, I, uh…"

The fantasy of saying, "Sure, that's fine," rocketed through my mind like a Bussard ramjet–powered spacecraft. The scene flickered, then disappeared: Asahina fresh from the bath, wearing pajamas borrowed from Nagato and bashfully toweling dry her hair, Nagato herself drinking a glass of milk, her hair still steaming—my memory went back to the two futons laid out in the spare room, and then for some reason it was all interrupted by Haruhi's face, sticking her tongue out at me in my mind's eye as I snapped back to reality.

"I'm going home tonight. I'll come by after school tomorrow." I turned to the owner of the room. "Is that all right, Nagato?"

Nagato nodded.

I faced the trembling Asahina. "Just stay here until I show up. Things'll work out, you'll see."

I wasn't just trying to make her feel better. If things got really bad, Nagato could always freeze her in time again. The first time we'd done that, it had been to travel three years into the future from that first Tanabata, so a week would be a piece of cake. And I had another matter to think about. Asahina hadn't traveled back in time for no reason, and my future self must have had a purpose in sending her back. It was weird to be saying "had" about future events, but this much was certain. The letter I still had in my pocket told me that much.

Isn't that right, Adult Asahina?

I knew she had to be involved in this somehow.

I said my good-byes to an Asahina whose very face incited the desire to protect her and headed home in the winter night, looking up at the sky as I went.

Nagato's confession that she'd limited her own power occupied my thoughts. It looked like Koizumi had been right on the money. The day when Nagato would become a normal high school student, a being unconnected to the Data Overmind, might not be so very far away. If it came to that, when I had a problem I'd have to get along without Nagato's power, without giving her more responsibility. We'd be normal friends who had to face problems together.

And without Nagato's power, I'd be a lot more confused.

But so what?

I'd never regretted what I'd done last December, when I took the world where Haruhi and Koizumi were gone and Asahina didn't know who I was and returned it to the normal state I knew. But misgivings still remained. On my way home the night Asakura had brought stew over to Nagato's place—

—I wanted to see that shy little smile again.

If it could somehow exist in this world, then I was all for it.

CHAPTER TWO

The next day, the first thing waiting for me when I arrived at school was an envelope in my shoe locker.

"I knew it."

I quickly stuffed it into my pocket before anybody else noticed, then hurried to the bathroom after changing into my school slippers. That's right, I was the walking cliché of the guy who opens a secret letter in a bathroom stall.

I opened the envelope and took out the folded sheets within—there were two.

The first was obviously written by her, and on it was written the following:

"At the intersection of XXXX and YYYY, proceed south until you find an unpaved alley. Please leave the object at that intersection, as directed on the map, between 6:12 and 6:15 PM.
P.S.—do not forget to bring Mikuru Asahina with you."

That was as far as I could read. At the end of the note, there were some symbols I'd never seen before, but I had no idea what they meant. I wondered if they were a signature of some kind, but in any case the letter was completely incomprehensible, and I tilted my head in confusion.

"What kind of orders are these, anyway?"

The moment I looked at the second sheet, things only got worse.

"What the hell?"

The bizarre thing came with a diagram. Even if I flattered it by calling it "simplified," it was well outside the range of "good." The intersection was marked with an *x*, and the diagram beside that *x* had to be a joke.

"I don't get any of this, Asahina."

Did she really want me to put this stuff on the spot indicated within three minutes of 6:12 this evening?

What would be the point?

I reread the letter several times until I'd memorized it, then shoved it down into the depths of my bag. I absolutely could not let Haruhi see it. This was one thing I'd never be able to think up a good excuse for.

I left the bathroom and ascended the stairs, deep in thought.

This much was becoming clear: Asahina had been sent back from eight days in the future because of this. There was something she needed to do in this time period, and it's something that the current Asahina, the one here at school right now, could not do. But why couldn't she do it?

As I arrived at my classroom, still wrestling with the endless questions, there was Haruhi, looking vaguely subdued as usual.

Haruhi glanced up at me. "How's Shamisen?"

"Ah—" That's right, that had been my excuse. "He's okay."

"Huh."

I sat down in my cold chair and discreetly took in Haruhi's profile.

She didn't seem to have noticed anything. She held her chin in her hands, looking bored, her mouth closed. Recently she'd been spending a lot of time like this. I didn't know what she was thinking about, and I didn't have time to give it much thought.

"Hey, Haruhi."

"What?"

"About Shamisen—I have to take him to the vet again today. It looks like I'll have to do that a lot, actually. So I don't think I can make it to the clubroom. Sorry, but…"

I was positive she was going to stare daggers at me, but no.

"Fine, whatever." Haruhi looked at my stunned expression. "I don't want people ditching for no reason, but if you've got a good excuse, I'm an understanding chief, and I won't give you a hard time about it."

I searched my memory for a version of Haruhi that was "understanding" and "wouldn't give you a hard time," and concluded that this was the first time I'd ever seen such a thing.

"I'll come and visit him sometime soon, so tell him I said to get well soon, okay? But I guess Shamisen's got your sister to pamper him to death too."

She didn't seem like she really cared that much; her chin moved around, still cupped between her hands. It was definitely strange to see her so listless, but at the moment I was grateful for it. I still had to figure out the Asahina Problem.

Still, what was this mood? Having the person behind me quietly stare out the window was both nostalgic and strangely novel. If only Haruhi would be like this even half of her waking time…

"Morning, class!"

The morning bell hadn't even finished ringing when Mr. Okabe came striding gallantly into the room.

I understood.

I understood that Haruhi's melancholy would not last long. When I thought about it, this was the first concrete prediction that the time traveler had made. According to Asahina, Haruhi would drag us all into a treasure hunt, and we'd wind up walking all over the place. I'd be fine if Haruhi was like that the *other* half of her waking hours.

For good or ill, that was enough to make me feel at ease.

At lunch, I bolted down my food and hurried to the clubroom.

If she wasn't in her classroom, she'd be here, I reasoned, and sure enough—there was Nagato sitting at her usual spot at the table, absorbed in reading.

"Nagato, how's Asahina?"

I was the one who had made her stay at Nagato's place, so I thought I should make sure everything was okay.

"..."

Nagato turned her lowered gaze up to me, silent as though contemplating the meaning of my question.

"What do you mean by 'how'?"

"She's not causing you any trouble, is she?"

"No."

Thank goodness for that, I thought. I imagined Nagato and Asahina having a pajama party. My heart swelled.

"However," Nagato said in an even voice, "she is uneasy when she is with me."

Her glossy eyes dropped once again to the hardcover in front of her.

I looked at Nagato silently, searching for some kind of expression on her pale face. Regret, or loneliness, say—but no such feelings were evident.

I could understand Asahina's unease. Most people would probably find being shut up in a room with Nagato hard to handle. I could handle it, as could Haruhi and Koizumi, and Tsuruya would probably be fine, but that wasn't the point.

Nagato had understood Asahina's fear and had expressed it to me thus, so there had to be something more.

"It's because Asahina and I both are constantly in your debt. She's being considerate."

"It's mutual," said Nagato, not looking up. "I have also relied on you."

But Nagato was always the one who could do something. She'd saved my life time and time again, I told her. When something happened, she was pretty much the only reliable one. I wouldn't say Koizumi and Asahina were worthless, but if she hadn't been around, there would've been many more times when we'd all have been helpless, I said.

"I was also the cause of many problems."

C'mon, those couldn't be helped, I told her. If she wanted to assign blame, she ought to start with the Data Overmind and me. It wasn't something she could blame herself for. Plus it was thanks to that whole incident that I learned to really appreciate this reality. I got to see Haruhi in a ponytail. When I'd been able to change something, the experience had meant a lot to me.

"I see," murmured Nagato, turning the page. The cold winter wind blew, rattling the glass of the clubroom's windows.

I turned on the electric heater. "What about your boss? They've suppressed the extremist faction, right?"

"The Data Overmind does not have complete consensus. But the main faction still leads."

Interesting. Even pure thought entities had internal disagreements.

"And you're connected to the main faction, right?"

"Yes."

Asakura had been a vanguard of the extremist faction. Wait— were there just two factions? Were there others? I asked.

"So far as I am aware, there is the Moderate, the Revolutionary, the Compromise, and the Contemplative."

And they were all different. Asakura had tried to kill me in order to provoke Haruhi, but Nagato had destroyed her. But the higher-ups were still arguing about it, apparently.

Just as I was visualizing the interactions of all those gods in the sky, Nagato spoke.

"I cannot transmit the thoughts of other factions." She slowly brought her gaze up from the page. "But I am here."

Her voice was perfectly steady, the very sound of trustworthiness.

"I won't let them do as they please."

On the way back from the clubroom, I ran into two familiar faces.

"Heya, Kyon!" Tsuruya waved her hand rapidly.

"Is your kitty okay?" said the person beside her in a worried voice. "I heard he had to go to the vet."

It was Asahina. The normal, native-to-this-time Asahina. She didn't seem to know she'd soon be headed into the past.

"Is he taking medicine?"

Oh, of course—Haruhi had called from the clubroom, and since Asahina had been there, she knew what we'd talked about.

"It's not very serious, but it seems like he'll need some time to recuperate." I shook my head lightly, a bit confused. Obviously, this Asahina looked no different from the other one. If I wasn't careful, I'd fool myself into thinking that Asahina was the one who was supposed to be at Nagato's place right now, and I wouldn't even notice it had happened, unless Asahina herself said something.

"Hard to believe Shamisen could get stressed out about anything!" said Tsuruya with a smile. "But I guess that's better than catching some weird disease. I bet he's not getting enough exercise! No mice at your house, right, Kyon? Sometimes we get mice in our garden—you should totally bring Shamisen over. I bet it'd do him some good!"

"Sure, once he's better, I'll do that."

I wasn't going to take him outside while it was still this cold, but once spring came, Shamisen would probably love that. Once the cherry blossoms bloomed, Haruhi would definitely want to do some kind of flower-viewing garden party, anyway.

"Kyon, will you be coming to the clubroom today?" asked Asahina a bit forlornly.

"I have to take Shamisen to the vet again today," I said, wishing I'd asked the other Asahina what my day was going to contain. "I already told Haruhi."

"Oh, really?" She sounded like she really cared about the cat. "I hope he gets well soon."

It pained me, but I gave a serious nod. "Come by sometime and pet him. It'll help him get better. He's a male too, after all."

The two girls left to get juice for their lunches, and I returned to my classroom. Not having a heater, it was colder than the clubroom I'd just been in. The only source of heat was the breath and warmth of the students in the room, and the most efficient heat source, Haruhi herself, was gone.

I walked toward Taniguchi and Kunikida and joined in their conversation.

Then, after class was over—

I put the school behind me as soon as I could. I had plenty of time until the time given in the letter, but I was worried about Asahina being left by herself, and if I was going to follow Asahina the Elder's instructions, there were some tools I had to assemble.

First I stopped by my house and got a hammer and some nails from the garage, which I threw in my bag, then grabbed my bike and sprinted over to Nagato's apartment building. The winter day was cold enough to make my ears sting, but when I thought about Asahina waiting all by herself, I didn't care. Plus it was practically guaranteed that something fun would be waiting for me. It was the arrival of a scene I'd been hoping for ever since summer vacation.

My strangely high spirits were the lingering results of my talk with Nagato in the clubroom.

Come what may, Nagato would protect Asahina and me, and I wanted to protect them too. Haruhi treated us brigade members like her property, and if anybody messed with us, she'd flip out and turn them right around—plus Koizumi, at least, could probably take care of himself. It was hard to imagine him getting tired, and if he were to falter, I can't say I wouldn't give him a hand. Haruhi would probably order me to, without regard for whether it was convenient for me or not. Not that I cared. I'd been a brigade member for just under a year, and I hadn't been ground down so much that I'd fold now, of all times.

"Whoops."

I skidded the bike to a stop, letting the rear wheel drift out a bit for no real reason, then headed for the console in the apartment foyer. I pushed the button for Nagato's unit.

"...Yes?" I was relieved to hear Asahina's voice.

"It's me. Did anything happen? I hope not."

"Um...no, nothing happened. Ah, I'll be right down, so just wait there, please!"

I'd wanted to come up to Nagato's room and relax for a bit, but Asahina cut off the intercom immediately.

I stood there idly for about five minutes, whereupon Asahina showed up in the foyer, still wearing her school uniform. She held school slippers in one hand.

She looked at me with an expression of relief, but then suddenly turned serious, shivering in the cold as she trotted over to me.

"I borrowed shoes from Nagato. Also, here's the apartment key."

Asahina held a small key in her hand.

"Could you return it to Nagato for me?"

Huh? What was going on? Since she was staying for a while, couldn't she borrow both the shoes and the key?

"About that…" Asahina tucked her chin down, her eyes upturned and looking at me. "I don't think I should stay at Nagato's place."

Why not? I asked.

"How should I put this…" The winter wind tried to disturb her chestnut brown hair; Asahina smoothed it down with her hand. "When I'm alone with Nagato, she just can't calm down."

I'd gotten the same line from Nagato. But no, forget that—I couldn't imagine what Nagato would do that would indicate anxiousness to Asahina, I said.

"Um, well," said Asahina, as though explaining something to a small child. "It's just a feeling, really. When I'm sleeping at night…I mean, we're in separate rooms, I'm sleeping in the spare room, but it's like she's standing right beside my bed, staring down at me…"

C'mon, she's not like a ghost, I said.

"…It's just a feeling, but it's like she's *conscious* of me." Asahina exhaled whitely, staring at my chest. "I don't feel it when we're all in the clubroom, but it's really strong when it's just the two of us at her place. It happened last month too. When we returned from the past, I woke up and you were gone, and I just had the feeling that she'd been staring at me the whole time I was asleep."

What was that supposed to imply? I couldn't imagine Nagato ever doing anything to hurt Asahina, I said.

"I know. That's not what she's thinking. It's just an impression I get…but I know. It's like she's hung up on me somehow."

This was completely incoherent. *I* certainly didn't understand it.

Asahina looked at me accusingly. With a lonely tone to her voice, she said, "It's like…she wants to be like me."

"…?" was my only reply.

"Like doing all kinds of crazy stuff with you, Kyon. I'm always doing stuff like that, right? But Nagato just watches. It was like that on Tanabata and during the endless summer too."

The seal of the SOS Brigade was all over my memories of the previous year. One of them was that Nagato was always the hardest-working member.

"I wonder if that's part of why she changed the past. She's always watching over us, instead of always getting saved, like me."

Asahina breathed into the palm of her hand, then nodded decisively.

"When I think about it like that, it makes sense. What I feel from Nagato, I mean. She might want to become like me, in a way..."

My mind went on a wild flight of fancy. I couldn't help imagining going into the clubroom as usual and encountering a maid-outfit-wearing Nagato there, cheerfully serving me tea. She would smile as she poured out the hot water, then, holding the tray, ask me how it tasted...

If Nagato were to become like that, I couldn't really complain. But what would happen to the Nagato who sat at the corner of the table, reading?

"I think Nagato knows this herself too. That's why I don't think I should be here. It just makes things difficult for her."

Asahina's eyes were serious. It wasn't that she didn't want to be in Nagato's home, it was that she was being considerate of Nagato. We already knew what could happen when too many bugs turned up in Nagato's system, and we knew what caused them to accumulate. As a result, she'd restricted herself. No more synchronization. She was trying to avoid bugs of her own free will. Was Asahina really Nagato's ideal? A person who, unlike herself, takes action without knowledge? A time traveler—her perfect opposite.

It was the ultimate irony. Asahina suffered from her own ignorance, while Nagato knew too much.

I looked up at Nagato's place. "Yeah..."

Asahina might have been right. When I thought about it, the most perceptive people I'd known had all been female—although Haruhi and Tsuruya were a little *too* perceptive.

Nagato had her own virtues, and they were virtues enough. But when she herself didn't realize that, it made things difficult. If pressed about it, she'd just feign ignorance.

It was also possible that Asahina was overthinking this. Nagato might be just fine as she was. She might just occasionally run out of books to read and stare at Asahina without any particular intent. But if Asahina was worried, I would just ignore her concerns.

"I understand. I'll tell Nagato for you. We'll figure out where you're going to stay later."

She could stay at my place as a last resort, but it wasn't like there weren't any alternatives.

"Anyway, there's something else I wanted you to look at. I got another letter in my shoe locker."

Asahina looked at the letter I gave her as though it were a crib sheet for a test she was about to take. "Oh, this is"—she pointed to the very end of the directions—"an order code. The very highest priority."

I hadn't been able to figure out whether the line was a code or a signature of some kind. I asked if it was some kind of future language.

"No, it's not a word…um, it's a code. One that has a special priority for us. It means no matter what the order is, it must be carried out."

"You mean…*this?*" I asked, thinking about the contents of the letter. "What point could there possibly be in a prank like this?"

"That's…" Asahina began, her head cocked, confusion on her face. "I…have no idea."

"What would happen if we ignore this and do nothing?"

"We cannot ignore it," said Asahina flatly. "Having seen that code, I must take action to ensure its execution." She looked at me uncertainly. "And you'll do it too, won't you, Kyon?"

*   *   *

We did as the letter said and proceeded to the location in question. Our method of transportation was a bicycle; it should go without saying that Asahina rode behind me on the luggage rack. In any case, although our target was within the city, it was still some distance on a bicycle.

We killed some time wandering around; by my watch it was now just ten minutes past six. The letter had directed me to set up the materials I now carried between 6:12 and 6:15.

I felt a little lonely, and not just because the sun had already set. The road was a bit removed from the local residences and didn't see much traffic. Then there was a little side path that branched off it, which was unpaved. It didn't seem like a private drive, but neither was it a shortcut to anywhere in particular, which made one wonder why anybody would go to the trouble of using it. The *x* on the hand-drawn map was just at the intersection of that little path and the road, a few centimeters away from the edge of the asphalt.

We were lucky there weren't any pedestrians around. What we were about to do was not exactly upstanding behavior—to put it bluntly, it was a practical joke.

All I needed were three things: a hammer, some nails, and a steel can. You can probably guess what I did.

"All right, I'd better get to it," I said.

"Yes," nodded Asahina.

I'd been hiding behind a telephone pole; I jumped out, ran for the spot, and began pounding nails into the ground. The ground was pretty hard. I had to pound them really hard to get them even halfway in—but I couldn't risk making a lot of noise and possibly catching the eye of a passerby.

I was in a hurry, so I don't think it took me more than thirty seconds, all told.

I covered the nails with the can, then hurried back to the telephone pole, where Asahina awaited. We then found a darker place a bit farther away in which to hide.

So what was going to happen? I was really interested to see what effect this prank was supposed to have.

I didn't have to wait long. It was 6:14.

Opposite the street from where we hid, a male-looking silhouette came walking along at a leisurely pace. I could tell he was wearing a long coat and carrying a shoulder bag. He didn't seem to notice us.

He seemed to be looking down as he walked. He didn't seem particularly cheerful. Suddenly, he stopped. He was looking directly at the empty can.

"Haah…"

I heard a sigh. Just when I was wondering if he were the type to take offense at litter, he lined up a kick (with perfect form) and directed it with all his strength at the can.

Of course, the can did not go sailing between a pair of notional goal posts; in fact, it didn't move from its position at all—

"Gah—?! Aaaaugh!"

The man clutched his foot and fell to the ground.

"What the hell?! Ugh, it hurts!"

He was literally rolling around on the ground, apparently in intense agony.

"Crap, who—who did this? Owwww…"

Asahina and I looked at each other.

Had this been the objective?

Who knew?

We had a silent exchange of glances, then nodded in unison and emerged from the darkness, walking along the path as though just happening to pass by.

"Are you all right?" Asahina asked of the man, who lay face up, holding his foot in his hands. I casually stood next to Asahina, looking down at the man, who continued to groan.

"Huh?"

The face was distorted with pain, and I didn't recognize it; he was a slender man in his twenties. Underneath his long coat, he wore a suit and tie, and he looked like a regular working stiff.

"Do you need a hand?" I said, my conscience torturing itself.

"Uh…yeah, thanks." The man took my hand and stood, wincing as he stood on his other foot. "Crap, who would pull a childish prank like this?"

"Yeah, terrible, huh?" I squatted down and picked up the can. It had a huge dent in it. The nails had been knocked diagonal too. The guy had really taken a serious shot. "Geez, that's dangerous."

I tried to sound plausible as I pulled the nails out of the ground. Thanks to the man's kick, they came out pretty easily. I slipped the nails in my pocket to conceal the evidence.

The man raised a lowered leg several times, each time wincing and clucking his tongue. "What a pain. Doesn't seem like it's broken, though…maybe I twisted my ankle?"

"Um," said Asahina. "Maybe you should go to the hospital?"

"Yeah, you're probably right."

The man hopped toward the edge of the automotive-traffic-bearing road, teetering dangerously as he approached.

"Here, lean on my shoulder," I said, coming alongside him so he wouldn't fall over. "Shall we call an ambulance?"

"Oh, no, that's okay. I'll call a cab. Don't want to make too big a deal out of this. I hate to ask, but could you help me over to the main road?"

"Sure, of course." No matter the reason, this was my fault, after all. I really wanted to apologize.

The man held on to my shoulder as he hopped along. From what I could tell by the light of the streetlights, he seemed pretty good-looking.

"I'm kind of at a dead end at my job," he said apologetically, as we were midway through crossing the street. "It's my own fault for thinking that kicking a can would help me clear my head. I got what I deserve."

"No, I really think it's the fault of whatever jerk set the prank up."

"Yeah, I guess. What kind of nasty little kid still does that kind of thing?"

He looked back and forth between Asahina and me, who was tottering along behind us, and smiled slightly. "Is she your girlfriend?"

After being at a loss for how to answer for a couple of seconds, I replied, "Uh...kinda..." I lied—hey, why not.

"Ah," said the man simply, before his face returned to its pained expression.

We reached the intersection and had the good luck to be able to quickly wave down a passing taxicab, helping the man (who'd broken into a cold sweat, despite the temperature) into the backseat.

"Thanks, you two. And sorry again."

It really was us who should've been apologizing—but this Asahina was completely innocent, so if he ever found out the truth and came to settle the score, I hoped he'd take it up with Asahina the Elder.

As we bowed and backed away from the car, Asahina asked me a question.

"Is that all we have to do?"

"Mmm..."

Asahina hugged herself and sighed, discomfited.

It was half past six.

There was an important restriction on us.

It was this: I could not allow Haruhi and this time's Asahina to see future Asahina and me together. If it were just Haruhi, I could probably figure out some kind of excuse, but it was hard to imagine that present-Asahina would write off seeing an identical copy of herself as a mere look-alike. And if we happened to bump into the entire SOS Brigade on its way home from school, that would be a total disaster.

But according to future-Asahina, she'd never seen her doppelganger during her last eight days, so it stood to reason that we'd be able to walk around without worrying about it—but there was no way to know whether something might go wrong, and if my hard work in the present was being reflected in the future, then I'd still have to make a special effort now to ensure that future, so I couldn't afford not to take the situation seriously... could I?

I had no idea. Why did things always have to be so complicated? If the Asahina that had traveled back from the future had only been Asahina the Elder, instead of the one from eight days in the future, things probably would've gone more smoothly.

I regarded the small upperclassman at my side.

Her North High uniform–clad body looked stiffened by the cold. It probably wasn't much fun braving a windy February night without so much as a jacket. Like her, all I was wearing was my school uniform, and I was freezing.

"Shall we go?" I said, gesturing toward my parked bicycle.

Asahina nodded, replying, "But where? To your house?"

I desperately wanted to do exactly that, but somewhere with fewer tattletales would be better. As her older brother, I knew better than anybody that my sister's mouth could open faster than a grandma's wallet when said grandma was trying to spoil her grandson.

"We'll go to someone else who'll let you stay with her, someone besides Nagato. I doubt she'll ask any questions, if I know her."

I got on the bike and gestured to a confused Asahina to do likewise, whereupon she sat sidesaddle on the luggage rack and off I went, carrying my light schoolmate behind me.

*   *   *

The spot where I stopped my bike would have been familiar to any SOS Brigade member.

Including Asahina.

"This...this isn't—"

She hopped off the bike and looked up at the gate in front of the residence.

I flipped down the bike's kickstand and locked it up. "This person will absolutely help you out. She'd never fail to come to your rescue."

"B-but, we can't let her know—"

"You just leave that to me."

Beside the gigantic traditional-style gate there was a single modern touch—an intercom. But before I pushed the button on it, I had to work something out.

"Asahina, your ear."

"O-okay..."

She obediently tilted her head, brushing her hair back to reveal her perfect ear. I couldn't help but remember when Haruhi bit down on this same ear. I wanted to do the same thing, but I knew full well that this was neither the time nor the place.

"Right, so, this is what I'm thinking of doing..."

Asahina's eyes went wide at my whispered explanation. "Eh, b-but, I don't think I can do that kind of acting!" she protested with a quivering voice. "That's too hard..."

Indeed it would be. If she really had to act, that is.

But I knew there'd be no need for that. All Asahina had to do was be herself. Nobody would ever notice.

"Anyway, just do that. It'll work out fine; trust me."

I smiled optimistically, then hit the intercom button.

" "
...

" "
...

Asahina and I silently waited for a reply. There was only a slim chance that the person I was trying to reach would reply personally, so I rehearsed the exchange over in my head. I was on my third run-through, and had waited close to a minute, when I started to darkly suspect that—surely not!—nobody was home. Just then—

"Hey now, wait there!"

An energetic voice echoed from beyond the gate, followed quickly by a *clunk*. The great wooden door creaked open.

"Hey! Kyon, Mikuru! What're you doing out here at this hour? Is it just the two of you? My, don't you make a couple! I'm practically jealous!" said Tsuruya with a broad smile.

Tsuruya's clothing was rather different from her usual school outfit.

She wore a casual kimono with a traditional short jacket, her long hair tied artlessly back in a bun. It matched the old-fashioned Japanese garden perfectly.

Letting us onto the Tsuruya estate grounds, she then replaced the square timber that kept the great gate locked.

"Still, this is really rare! Kyon and Mikuru out for a hike in the freezing cold? Without Haru-nyan, even?"

"There are some extenuating circumstances…actually, Tsuruya—how did you know it was us at the gate?"

I'd heard only silence from the intercom, after all.

"Oh, yeah, there's a security camera above the gate. It's super easy to tell who's there! When I looked I saw you two, so I figured I'd better come out to see ya. Was that okay?" Tsuruya's wooden sandals clacked against the ground as we walked along the shrine-like path that led to the main wing of the house. She smiled. "Hm? Mikuru? You don't look well—are you all right?"

"Actually, about that," I said, clearing my throat and preparing the lines I'd rehearsed. "We've got a favor to ask you. Could you let Asahina stay at your place for a few days?"

"Wha? I mean, sure, but—" Tsuruya chuckled as though something had occurred to her. She peered at Asahina's face. "You *are* Mikuru…right?"

Asahina looked surprised, at which Tsuruya narrowed her bright eyes. Had we been found out?

"Anyway, it's fine. Is there some kinda problem? Like one that's stopping Mikuru from going to her own house, I mean?"

The conversation was moving right along, thankfully.

"How long does she need to stay, d'you think?"

"Eight days at the most," I said. Eight days from now, Asahina would revert to being the only Asahina in the timeline. "Will that be okay?"

"Sure, I don't mind. Oh, right—she can just use the apartment. It's a separate building, kinda like what we have at the mountain villa. No one's living there right now. It's just a little studio— sometimes I go there to think about stuff, 'cause it's so nice and quiet."

I looked around the grounds that surrounded us, which you could pretty much just call a forest. Who knew what was hidden in the expanse? I'd heard there was even an old-fashioned store-house somewhere in the area.

As I felt a strange combination of admiration and envy, Tsu-ruya's mouth curved into a perfect half circle. "So anyway, Mikuru—what's up? You don't have to be so scaredy-like." Tsu-ruya poked at Mikuru's chin with her finger. "It's not like you."

Before the silent Asahina could say anything, I quickly cut in.

"She's Asahina's younger twin sister, Michiru."

"Twin? Michiru?"

"That's…that's right! They were separated at birth, you see…"

"Wow!"

"And there were some difficult circumstances, and…Asa-

hina...what I mean is, Mikuru doesn't know she has a younger twin."

"Ooh! So why is Michiru here wearing a North High uniform, then?"

Crap. I hadn't thought of that.

"How should I put this...Michiru, here, wanted to sneak into North High to catch a glimpse of her sister. So she got a uniform, but then she wound up not being able to pull off her plan. Then she happened to bump into me, and I got her to tell me the story, and after that..."

Tsuruya patted my shoulder. "Don't worry about it!" she said with a pleased grin. "No need to explain any more. If she's Mikuru's sister, she's practically Mikuru. She only needs a place to stay?"

"Also, you've got to keep her a secret from Asahina."

"But of course!"

"Um..." said Asahina, as though afraid of being left out of the conversation. "Is it really okay?"

"Sure, it's mega-okay! Right, Michiru, come this way! I'll show you the apartment."

Tsuruya took Asahina's hand and dragged her off through the garden. As she went, Tsuruya looked over her shoulder and shot me a broad wink that just about killed me dead.

The apartment was very similar to the mountain villa we'd been invited to earlier. According to Tsuruya's explanation, the villa had been built using this apartment as a model; this was the original. It was a pleasant Japanese-style one-floor building.

Asahina sat politely on the tatami-mat floor, like a pretty French doll placed in a simple house.

The room was warming up, thanks to Tsuruya having turned the heater on, and strangely I didn't really want to leave.

After explaining the hanging scroll that hung in the alcove and telling us where the closet with the futon and sheets was, Tsuruya made herself scarce, saying "I'll bring some nice hot tea."

"Looks like this will work out," I said to Asahina.

"Yes, thank goodness. We'll need to properly thank Tsuruya," agreed Asahina *Michiru*. "Michiru, was it? That's a nice name." She finally smiled.

I stretched my legs out on the tatami mat and looked at the heater, thinking about Asahina's name.

Until Tsuruya returned, carrying a basket filled with a kettle, some teacups, and some clothes.

Tsuruya invited me to stay for dinner, but if I were away from home for two nights running, my mom would probably get irritated, so I instead expressed my sadness at having to go home. Thanks to finally having found a place for Asahina to stay, I was suddenly tired. If I dithered around anymore, I'd wind up deciding to spend the night.

"Hmm, she's like Mikuru and yet not Mikuru. Or, like, she's not Mikuru but she seems Mikuru-ish."

I told Tsuruya I thought I'd already explained she was a twin.

"Ha ha ha! That's true. We'll just leave it at that."

Walking about a step and a half ahead of me, Tsuruya headed for the huge gate.

As I watched her loose bun of hair gently sway, a question occurred to me.

"Tsuruya."

"Yeah?"

"How much do you know? You said before that Asahina and Nagato—that the members of the SOS Brigade weren't normal."

"Yeah, I guess." My long-haired schoolmate bounced slightly as she turned around. Her smiling face was as bright as a star. "I really don't know that much, Kyon. Just that they seem kinda different. At the very least, they're not *normal* normal like you and me."

Even if that was all she knew, that was more than enough. Yet she still hadn't asked any inconvenient questions, and she hadn't tried to figure out what Asahina really was.

"How do you know?"

Tsuruya tucked her hands into her kimono sleeves and laughed broadly. "I just really like watching people have fun. Like when someone gobbles down a delicious meal I made for them, or when I just get to watch someone I've never met having a great time—I really love that. Yeah, so when I watch Haru-nyan, it makes me really happy. It's like, I don't know, she's just having so much fun, y'know?"

Didn't she want to join in herself? I asked. Wasn't it lonely just watching?

"Mm, yeah, y'know—I think movies are super cool, but I don't really want to make movies myself. Just watching is enough. Or like when I watch the World Series or the Super Bowl, it's really fun to cheer and stuff, but I don't start thinking, 'Gosh, I should totally get out there myself and play!' Watching the players out there, giving it their best shot, is the best part. I mean, I wouldn't be any good at it. So I do other stuff, stuff I *can* do."

In a way, she was the exact opposite of Haruhi. When Haruhi saw something she thought was interesting, she just had to butt in and give it a try.

Tsuruya's big eyes cast about. "The SOS Brigade is just like the baseball game! I get a kick out of watching you, Haruhi, Nagato, and Koizumi, whatever it is you're doing!"

Her smile and voice were completely genuine. She was speaking words of truth. I started to feel cheered up just by standing next to her.

"So I really like the position I'm in. I think Haru-nyan understands too. After all, she doesn't try to drag me into things, y'know? Five people is just the right number."

She turned back around with another bounce, facing the gate once again.

"It's totally impossible to figure out everything, y'know? My hands are already full!" She looked over her shoulder at me. "Hang in there, Kyon! The future of humanity's riding on your shoulders!"

The corner of her mouth twitched a couple of times, and she regarded me for a moment, but soon she was unable to keep herself from breaking into giggles. The guileless, childlike laughter made me feel like my merry upperclassman's words were a simple joke.

Tsuruya gasped for air, holding her stomach. "Anyway, make sure you always watch Mikuru's back! But no funny business, you got that? That's the one thing that's not allowed. If you're gonna play tricks, play 'em on Haru-nyan. I'm sure she'll forgive you, totally."

These words, I was sure, were meant sincerely. I don't know why I thought as much—I just did. Not that I'd had any intention of doing anything.

I said goodnight to Tsuruya and pedaled off on my bike, but it wasn't long before I found myself applying the brakes.

"Good evening."

My path was blocked by someone standing alone in the gloom of the street.

"You're certainly working hard. For my part, I can't say I agree with involving Tsuruya, although that's surely the safest place she could possibly be."

I hadn't seen Koizumi's handsome, pleasant smile in two days.

"Hey. What a coincidence, meeting you here."

"You could say that, yes. You could also say that the coincidences started when you and I first met. No, even earlier than that—when you met Haruhi."

Koizumi raised his hand in greeting and began to approach me. How long had he been skulking around in the night streets waiting for me? I asked. He wouldn't have any cause to complain if someone mistook him for a pervert and called the cops on him.

Koizumi chuckled softly. "You seem to be up to something interesting again, but I suppose I haven't won the participation lottery."

I chose to sigh, exhaling whitely. "This is my and Asahina's problem. It's got nothing to do with you. You should just run along and hunt those celestials of yours."

"These days they never call, they never write. Sometimes a man just needs to get out and take a walk."

The only people who were out at this hour without a dog to walk were writers stuck for ideas, I said—and I knew for certain running into him was no coincidence.

"If this were a coincidence, one could hardly be blamed for thinking it was just a little too perfect."

"What do you want?" I asked, but immediately changed subjects. "No, never mind—that much I can guess, more or less. How much do you know?"

"You mean about there being two Asahinas?" Koizumi casually mentioned the crucial point. "How did you manage to explain that to Tsuruya? Twins, I suppose? Surely you didn't tell her the truth."

"Not that it would've mattered."

"Maybe not. It *is* Tsuruya, after all."

He said it like it was the most obvious thing in the world. Just what kind of person was Tsuruya, anyway? Our cheerful school-mate seemed to know everything about us, yet was still keeping her distance.

"My superiors have warned me not to interfere with Tsuruya." Koizumi's face became slightly more serious. "She's actually not related to this. Originally, we weren't supposed to encounter her at all, but there was a mistake somewhere and we wound up coming into contact. That's Suzumiya for you, I suppose."

What mistake, where? Was he talking about Tsuruya being in Asahina's class? I asked. Or her being a substitute player on our sandlot baseball team?

"We do not interfere with her, and in exchange, she is no more involved with us than necessary. Those are the rules by which the Agency and the Tsuruya clan conduct their relationship."

He shouldn't just mention an absurd inside story like that, I told him.

Koizumi chuckled. "To be clearer, the Tsuruya clan is among the many sponsors of the Agency. However, our activities may be irrelevant to them; they are entirely indifferent to everything we do. Which is fine, since it's frankly more convenient for us that way, but Miss Tsuruya is the successor to the entire clan."

Tsuruya, you...I thought. To think we'd been just casually hanging out with a person like that. Now I *really* wanted to know—what was she? I asked.

"She's an ordinary high school student. She's a second-year student at the same public school we attend; she just commutes from a bigger house. Meanwhile, she might be fighting the forces of evil somewhere, or she might have solved some intractable problem, but none of that has anything to do with us."

The words Tsuruya had just recently spoken now were clear in my memory. She'd said she was happy not being too involved with us. Maybe the same was true of us, for her. It would definitely be best to just keep relating to her the way we always had. Whatever she was, whatever she was doing, none of that was important. Just as Haruhi was Haruhi, Tsuruya was Tsuruya. She was Asahina's cheerful, happy, over-perceptive friend. The SOS Brigade's faithful advisor. That was the best way to think about it.

But how much of a coincidence had her meeting Asahina been? Were there parts of the past that were mysterious even to time travelers, in the same way that Haruhi was a mystery to them?

And then I remembered.

"Koizumi, earlier you said things with Asahina would work out just fine. What did you mean by that?"

"I meant that the future can be changed." Then, as though he'd predicted my next question, he continued. "You might be thinking that people from the future regard the past as freely changeable and consider the future to be superior to the past, but the future is actually quite a fuzzy thing."

If you knew past history and could travel back, you could change the future however you wanted to. I'd done it myself—I'd gone back in time with Nagato to fix the world after it had gone all wrong.

Koizumi smiled. "You could also have done the same thing from the past. If you'd known the future in advance, you could've changed it right at that point and time."

"How can you possibly know the future? That's impossible."

"Do you really think so?"

Koizumi's smile turned a bit devilish, surely on purpose. The guy really could be pointlessly nasty sometimes.

"I am an esper—though my abilities and range are a bit limited. But can you be sure that I am the only one? I don't mean anti-Celestials like me. How can we say for certain that there aren't more straightforward superhumans with, for example, the power to see the future, perhaps even attached to the Agency?" His smile returned to its previous pleasant state. "I don't recall ever telling you that such individuals don't exist."

Why you son of a—

"Of course, I never told you they *did* exist either."

Well, which was it? I asked, adding that he'd better not tell me that it could go either way.

"To be completely honest, I don't know. As I said before, I'm an underling. I don't know everything. Asahina's the same way."

That much I could believe. Never had an agent been so deserving of pity as Asahina.

"There's a purpose to her ignorance, of course. If a time traveler from the future knows they are acting with a defined intention, they can simply analyze those actions, and they'll never take actions that would jeopardize their own future. The reason Asahina seems so careless, despite being from the future, is because she doesn't know anything. You could even say she hasn't been *allowed* to know anything. That's the future's countermeasure to stop us in the past from analyzing their intentions. Her presence is required in this time period, but if we were to infer the future from her presence, that puts the future in danger. In a way, you could say she's a perfect time resident. I don't feel any threat from her at the moment, and when push comes to shove I'm sure she'll follow her orders exactly."

Koizumi performed his specialty: the shrug.

"That might very well be the aim of the future group—to make the people in the past think that. Which is why the Agency doesn't get involved. It'd be awfully irritating to just play into their hands, after all. We don't want to be puppets of the future."

So what, did they oppose Asahina? I asked.

"I wouldn't go that far. If I had to sum it up, I'd say we're at a standstill."

A chill ran through my body. Literally.

"Let me make an analogy. Suppose there are two nations, A and B. They oppose each other but have not engaged in direct conflict. Now suppose there appears power C, which opposes A, and power D, which opposes B. From A's perspective, coexistence with C is impossible; they are a direct threat. The same goes for B and D. C and D then join forces and begin cooperating. If one nation was intolerable, the two joined are now all the more so. Now, as the old saying goes, the enemy of my enemy is my friend, so A and B build a grudging and unsteady alliance—which is where we are."

Koizumi regarded me uncertainly.

"Are you listening?"

"Oh, sorry," I said, throwing my leg over my bike seat. "I stopped listening when you started talking about D or whatever. I can remember the first three, but after that it was too much."

"I know it was audible. Your brain chose to listen and process, or not."

He didn't have to answer so seriously. I was just messing with him. Would it kill him to play along with my joke, for once? He'd never be popular with the ladies without a sense of humor, no matter how good-looking he was.

Koizumi grinned. I wondered how many different smiles he had.

"I change my expressions and statements to match the situation and the individual, just like anybody else does. But when I'm talking to you, it always turns into this kind of conversation."

It must be hard to be him, I said.

"I feel the same way, but I think I'll stay like this for a while." Koizumi looked off into the distance for some reason. "I hope the day comes when we'll be friends on a perfectly equal footing, and we'll be able to laugh about the past—just as people, when things like 'mission' and 'duty' no longer matter." He seemed satisfied by that. "Well then, I'll see you in the clubroom."

He raised his hand in a sort of salute, then strolled off into the darkness, as though lazily continuing his evening walk.

Upon returning home, I wolfed down my dinner and immediately shut myself up in my room.

The first thing I did was to phone Nagato. I had to tell her that I'd moved Asahina to Tsuruya's place. Knowing Nagato, she might well already know. Even Koizumi had figured it out, after all.

After three rings, Nagato picked up. She didn't even bother saying hello, proof that she already knew who was calling.

" . . . "

"Nagato, it's me. I'll make this short. It's about Asahina."

I gave her the highlights of what Asahina had told me. Nagato listened to my explanation with her usual silence.

"Understood," she said, without any particular regret, adding, "That is for the best."

"Really? That's a relief."

"Why?"

Why? Even I had misgivings about relying on Nagato too much. And this time we'd unilaterally decided to impose upon her, then unilaterally left—it was really selfish of us.

"Needless worry," said Nagato, her voice calm. "I can understand her position." Then, after a short pause: "I do not wish to become like her. However, sentiment to that effect is valid."

Valid how? I wanted to know.

"If I were in her position, I might have come to the same conclusion."

So, uh, that meant that Nagato could imagine being in Asahina's place, and worrying about Nagato in the way that Asahina currently was? I asked.

There was silence for a while. Then: "I think so."

Her fine voice reached my ears. It was such a pleasant sound that I wished I would've turned on the phone's recording function.

We exchanged a few more words, whereupon I hung up. It seemed that there was no need for me to worry: the alien and the time traveler had come to a mutual understanding. Probably more than either of them realized.

For some reason I grinned and looked to my side. Shamisen was sleeping on my bed. His head was on my pillow as though he were human, his breathing deep and even. Just as I was wondering whether I should shave a patch of his fur off in case Haruhi did happen to turn up, something else occurred to me.

"How long do I have to lie about Shamisen's recuperation?"

I'd forgotten to ask. Asahina should have been able to tell me how many days I skipped club activities for, and when I'd started coming back. If I knew that much, I'd be able to set up a tentative schedule for this week. But the Asahina from a week in the future didn't have a cell phone. If I wanted to call Asahina, I'd have to call Tsuruya, but thanks to that conversation I'd had with Koizumi, I hesitated to contact her. I didn't know how much of what he'd said was true. Since it was Koizumi we were talking about, he might have just made up something plausible-sounding to see the look on my face. Hell, I'd *rather* that were the case.

I aimed the air conditioner's remote control at the cooler, reclining back onto my bed.

Tomorrow, I'd check the contents of my shoe locker and figure out the day's plan.

As I regarded the calico cat, whose eyes were shut as he smacked his lips, I wound up drifting off to sleep myself, only to be awakened by my sister, who'd just gotten out of the bath.

CHAPTER THREE

The next day.

"Go to the mountains. There you will see an oddly shaped rock. Move it approximately three meters west. Your Mikuru Asahina will know the place. It will be very dark after nightfall, so try to finish during the daylight."

A glance at the contents of another envelope torn open in a bathroom stall revealed the preceding message. And just as before, a second sheet contained a crudely drawn gourd-like picture, with a label that went out of its way to say "rock."

That clinched it. Today I'd be a member of the going-home club.

"Which is fine, I guess..."

But what was with these vague instructions? Rocks in the mountains? Which rock, in which mountains? If it was a mountain that Asahina knew about, that meant...

Plop, a pebble tumbled through my mind.

"Oh, right. The treasure hunt."

According to (Michiru) Asahina, we'd be using our next day off school to go on a treasure hunt. That was the day after tomorrow. She'd said it was on a mountain that belonged to the Tsuruya clan. Which meant another Tsuruya appearance. Tsuruya had swallowed the story of the two Asahinas without complaint, and she would probably just smile when confronted by Haruhi and me, but at this rate I was going to become emotionally unstable myself. It would be a problem for Koizumi too—but hold on.

"So this means Haruhi's gonna be back to her usual self soon," I predicted as I headed to the classroom. Tsuruya would bring the treasure map and we'd put it to use the day after tomorrow—so that meant Haruhi would definitely have it in her hands either today or tomorrow. Probably tomorrow. I hadn't gotten a whiff of excitement off of Tsuruya the previous night, after all, which meant she probably hadn't found the map in the storehouse yet. If she had, she would've tried to force it on me to give to Haruhi.

"Hey, Haruhi."

Just as I suspected. She was already in the classroom, taking a page out of Nagato's book and running in low-energy mode as she played the part of the gloomy high school girl.

"How's Shamisen?" she asked without looking at me, the window fogging up with her breath.

"Ah, yeah, he's doing okay, I guess."

"That's good."

She doodled a face in the white condensation on the window.

So strange. Having a regular conversation with Haruhi was rarer than seeing Nagato doing something besides reading in the clubroom. It made me even more worried—no, more like uncertain. I wondered if there were Celestials going crazy somewhere.

"What's wrong? You've been so gloomy lately."

Haruhi sniffed. "What're you talking about? I'm the same as I always am. I've just got stuff on my mind, and tomorr—" She was about to continue, but cut herself off mid-sentence. "What about you? Are you coming to the clubroom today?"

Her expression made it seem like she didn't care one way or the other, which from my perspective was the most convenient expression possible.

"Shamisen's still pretty lonely. I can't just leave him to my little sister, and he has to visit the vet again tomorrow."

"Yeah, that's probably best."

What was strange, though, was Haruhi seemed to think it was convenient too.

"You get lonely when you get sick. Make sure to stay with him until he's fully recovered. I want to play with him when he's well again."

It seemed like Haruhi thought of Shamisen as a brigade member too, in her own way. The part where she told me to take care of him while he was sick, then bring him over to play once he was better was definitely like her, anyway. I ought to just lend him to her for a week, I told her.

"I'll think about it." Haruhi nodded absentmindedly, her breath condensing on the window again.

Nothing makes the passage of time feel slower than sitting there wishing for class to end.

Thus, I gritted my teeth and silently prayed that the teacher wouldn't ask me any questions, aimlessly copying down the contents of the blackboard, passing the time without remembering a single thing from class, which now that I think about it is what I usually do, realizing anew that this sort of thing was why my grades hadn't risen one bit, though I found some consolation in telling myself that it was all the fault of having too much SOS Brigade stuff to think about. Yes, definitely. Please ignore the fact that Taniguchi's grades are just as bad as mine, but he's a member of the go-home-and-do-nothing club.

Thanks to having shoved my good-for-nothing textbooks into my desk, my bag was nice and light as I picked it up and headed out of the classroom—whereupon Taniguchi (whose turn it was to clean the classroom) called out to me, a broom over his shoulder.

"Yo, Kyon."

His eyes seemed kind of flat. I didn't know why, but I didn't have time to find out. Asahina was waiting for me. It was just like in *Run, Melos!*, with Selinuntius waiting for Melos's return to save him from certain death. I had to make haste.

But Taniguchi blocked my way, pointing his broom's handle at me.

"I envy you, Kyon."

There was a note of bitterness in his voice. What could he possibly envy? I could only think of about a dozen things, I told him.

"That many? No, there are three, at best," replied Taniguchi irritably. He sighed.

I half wondered whether Haruhi's melancholy had gone airborne and infected Taniguchi.

"Oh, about Taniguchi—" Kunikida's face popped out, and he began to explain, gesturing with a dustpan he held. "Turns out he and his girlfriend just split up. So that's why he's down. Guess it makes sense."

"That's too bad," I said, half smiling as I patted Taniguchi's back. I guess the girlfriend in question must have been the one he'd gotten just before Christmas. I'll bet he felt good and sorry for me, since my own Christmas Eve had been spent enjoying a Haruhi Hot Pot Special.

"Ha ha. With that face, you must've been the one who got dumped. I see how it is."

"Shut up," he said. The friend I should've had sympathy for pretended to brandish his broom, then held it limply at his side. "Just go home already. I've gotta clean the classroom and you're in the way."

Kunikida gave a pained grin. "I hate to say it, but it was only a matter of time, Taniguchi. I admit I never met or saw your girlfriend, but from what you said, she just didn't sound serious about you."

"Oh, like you'd understand. Well, that's fine. I don't *want* you to understand."

"And c'mon, I mean, her reason for going out with you was way too weird. Like—"

"Whoa, hey! Don't say any more! I'm serious! I just want to forget the whole thing!"

I wanted to stay a little longer to see how this overwhelmingly high school–like conversation between two good friends would play out, but I was in a hurry.

"Well, don't overthink it. A great guy like you will definitely meet a nice girl eventually. Every dog has his day, y'know," I said. I didn't wait for his reply before I headed out into the hallway, walking away without looking back. At least I'd given him some words of encouragement. I'm not such a jerk that I'd turn his heartbreak into a joke—although to be honest, part of me thought he deserved it. I was just happy that the friend who'd gone sprinting ahead of me was now back at the same starting line as the rest of us. We were all in this together.

"But—why was he so jealous of me?"

The thought occurred to me as I was opening my shoe locker, and with it came another, stranger notion: the terrifying possibility that if a romantic entanglement had been the source of Taniguchi's malaise, perhaps the root of Haruhi's gloom was something similar. I shuddered at the very idea, then laughed it off.

"Couldn't be."

The essentially absurd notion of Haruhi being lovesick was about as likely as my being the first-round draft pick in the Major Leagues next year. Which was fine, since I didn't particularly want to get picked, but I had to admit I did want to know what was on Haruhi's mind. I didn't think she was just sitting glumly in an unheated classroom, hand warmers in hand, but...

"Ah, whatever."

I didn't have time to think about any of that right now. And anyway, Haruhi would be back to her usual self in no time. I already knew we'd be going on a treasure hunt the day after tomorrow, and since I knew about it in advance, I couldn't afford to worry about extraneous things. A single misstep could set the entire SOS Brigade on the wrong path, an outcome I definitely wanted to avoid. It would be like exposing a harmless bacterium to radiation, thus creating a deadly disease. Even if it would have served the cause of science, it was too great a risk. I had to keep my priorities straight.

"All right, time to do something about the immediate future."

I wouldn't get anywhere worrying about the future of humanity. For me right now, the most pressing problem was the other Mikuru Asahina.

I first headed home, then picked up my bike and headed immediately for the Tsuruya estate.

On the way over, I'd planned to call ahead for Asahina to come out, but Tsuruya wasn't home from school yet. I thus assumed that it would take some time for me to get a message through to (Michiru) Asahina the freeloader, but the servant who answered the phone seemed to have been informed of the situation by Tsuruya, and all I had to do was give my name, omitting my self-introduction, and I was immediately transferred to Asahina. Tsuruya sure came in handy for times like this. We'd forgotten to arrange it ahead of time, yet she'd perfectly anticipated what I would need. If she were to become a personal assistant or something in the future, she definitely had the talent for it.

And Asahina was every bit as laudable as Tsuruya—"Just wait a moment, I'll be right there," she said over the phone before hanging up. Actions speak louder and more quickly than words. In my pocket was the letter containing the day's instructions, along with a flashlight, just in case.

I'd been to Tsuruya's home several times, so my legs took me smoothly there. I could stand the February cold, and was just happy it wasn't snowing. The wind in my face made my nose and ears tingle as I arrived at Tsuruya's place and rang the bell.

Asahina popped right out the front gate. "Kyon!" she said with a relieved smile, no longer wearing her school uniform but instead pants and a thick, fluffy coat. "I borrowed some clothes from Tsuruya," she said, adjusting her collar as she noticed my gaze. "I can't very well get clothes from home, after all."

"You don't remember any of your clothes going missing?" I asked as I flipped my bike's kickstand up, at which Asahina looked suddenly abashed.

"I don't, um, remember...but I know my usual clothes were all there. But even if they disappeared, I might not have noticed...I mean, not that I have that many clothes, really, it's just—"

She didn't have anything to worry about. If a single pair of underwear went missing from my dresser, I'd never file a police report over it. Even if I managed to notice, I'd just assume I'd misplaced them somewhere.

I gave Asahina a gentle look. Whether they were borrowed or not, I told her, she was definitely clear for launch.

"No, not at all!" Asahina waved her hands, bashful. "The sleeves and hem are too long for me, and also..." She hugged her chest, turning a bit red before stopping. "Um, never mind."

I was feeling calmer and calmer. Clothes that fit the long-limbed, slender Tsuruya would definitely have lacked material in certain places when worn by Asahina. It was easy to guess which part of her outfit was the cause of her stiff demeanor. It was a shame that her upper half was hidden by her coat, but I could worry about that later.

I showed her the message from the future I'd gotten from my shoe locker. "This is what we have to do next. Any ideas?"

Go to a mountain and move a rock—it was like a side-quest from a role-playing game. Worse, the purpose for the quest was far from clear, and since we didn't even know whether we'd get some kind of loot upon completion, it wasn't even a very good game.

"Er—the mountain? The only place I know of is…hmm. A strangely shaped rock…oh, could it be—?" Asahina murmured as she read the letter, the paper fluttering in the breeze, cocking her head curiously like a chipmunk that's lost sight of its nest. "I do have an idea. I think this is where we went for the treasure hunt. Or I mean, that's the only place I know, so…but why?"

Naturally, I had no idea myself. But I could guess.

"Asahina—we didn't find anything, did we? On our treasure hunt?"

"N-no."

My fingertips were already turning numb from the cold as Asahina refolded the letter uncertainly. Something felt strange. "It's strange, though. These directions must have something to do with that treasure hunt."

"Th-that's—" began Asahina, looking down. "I wonder…" She looked deep in thought, as though trying to decide whether to voice the feelings that were welling up inside her. The look in her eyes as she shook her head made me weak at the knees. "No, I can't think of anything. But we should go. Maybe I'll remember something when we get there."

"Yeah, let's."

It was time to have a look. I felt bad for doing location scouting at the treasure hunt site ahead of Haruhi, but she'd forgive me as long as it seemed new to me tomorrow.

I climbed back on my bike and gestured for Asahina to get on behind me. She sat demurely sidesaddle on the luggage rack; I nearly fainted at the arms that wrapped hesitantly around me from behind, but memories of the previous night brought me back to reason.

"What's the matter?" Asahina asked uncertainly as I looked left, then right, before starting off.

"Oh, nothing," was my only answer as I pushed down hard on the pedal.

It was just that I thought I'd spied Koizumi, or somebody Koizumi-like, hiding nearby. Though I had no idea if he was staking out Tsuruya's house or following us around.

The Tsuruya clan's private mountain was east of North High. It was more of a large hill than a mountain, and it didn't have much in the way of altitude. If you really squinted, it did sort of look like a forgotten burial mound, but looking up at the naturally wooded face of the mountain, it didn't matter whether it was a dormant volcano or a forgotten tomb; it would take the same amount of time to climb, and there wasn't a good path. All there was was a steep, narrow animal track, so if the bear wanted to go over the mountain, he wasn't gonna have an easy time of it.

"It's over here. Yes—we climbed up from here."

The sun had started to get low as I rode my bike up hills and along fields at Asahina's direction. At the base of the mountain were drained rice paddies and vegetable plots, and not a single person in sight.

"I wonder if we should just be climbing up somebody's private mountain." I looked wearily up the slope, and Asahina giggled.

"Tsuruya said it was all right. Ah—it was a few days ago that she said…no, wait, relatively speaking, that would be tomorrow, so…right. She'll give you permission tomorrow too, Kyon."

Perhaps having finally become accustomed to her situation, Asahina seemed to feel free to think back on her own past.

"I can't tell you, um, very much. Only that what we did was a treasure hunt and a city patrol…that's all I can say."

What about the Haruhi-sponsored lottery? I asked.

"Oh, yes, that's—"

Asahina looked flustered. I asked if she was forgetting anything else.

"Um, er..."

She was strangely fidgety. Was there something she couldn't tell me? I asked—more classified information?

"Y-yes, that's right. It's classified. Or, well...probably."

So far as I could tell from her expression, her mood wasn't particularly serious. I didn't think that the ever-secretive time traveler would make a joke now of all times, but it seemed likely that this Asahina knew something she wasn't telling me. The only one who was completely in the dark was the other Asahina in this timeline. What a pain. If I were to express it as an inequality, I'd put it this way, more or less: Asahina The Elder > (...) > "Michiru" Asahina > Asahina the Younger.

I must have sighed louder than I meant to, as Asahina's face turned uncertain again.

"Um, Kyon..."

If I turned my back on her I was sure she'd start crying, and I wasn't so much of a sadist that I could ignore those eyes of hers, and in fact a sudden rush of affection made my expression turn as soft as Shamisen's belly.

"No, no, it's fine," I said. "I'm sure I'll figure it out."

According to this Asahina, it had been my eight-days-later self who had directed her to time-jump eight days back. That version of me knew everything and had sent Asahina into the past. Since that was just the future version of me, if I just asked him he'd be able to tell me everything—except I'd *be* him, so there'd be no need to ask. Right?

"Let's get this mission done before it gets dark," I said, laying my hand on Asahina's shoulder.

Asahina looked up at me with her big puppy-dog eyes and nodded. "All right. I'll show you the way. We didn't climb that high, so it'll be close."

We headed into the dense forest. Normally I would've been at the lead, clearing dangerous branches and roots away with a machete, but given that it was winter and all the snakes and bugs were hibernating, there wasn't that much danger. The best thing I could do was stay behind Asahina to make sure she didn't slip and fall.

"Ah—whew...wha—"

Unsurprisingly, helping Asahina safely climb a mountain was tricky—and trickier still, since we barely had a trail. Normally when ascending a slope, you'd follow a switchback pattern, but as far as I could see there was no way to do that. We'd have to step on logs and grab onto craggy rocks to climb our way up.

"Eyaaah!"

I had to smile inwardly at the unexpected side benefits that came with constantly catching the tripping Asahina as we made our way nearly straight up the face of the small mountain. When I looked closely, I saw here and there signs of human passage along the route we were taking. Even so, this was more of a glorified animal track than a proper trail, although if it had been entirely wild, Asahina and I would never have been able to make any progress at all.

After ten-odd minutes of climbing, I caught sight of a more level spot.

"Here—*whew*—it's here. We dug all over the place, but the stone was here." Asahina was short of breath, and she leaned over, bracing her hands against her knees.

I stopped next to her.

"Huh."

While it wasn't very large, there was indeed a flat space on this otherwise sloping mountain. It was completely overgrown with shrubs and vegetation, save for a semicircle of clear space. It wasn't even ten meters across, and it seemed like it had been cleared to make a convenient rest stop while climbing the mountain. I didn't know if it was man-made or not. It might've been the result of a landslide long past. Given the overgrowth, it definitely wasn't a recent addition. Maybe it was natural, after all.

Once she'd caught her breath, Asahina pointed. "I think that's the rock from the message. It looks just like the one in the drawing…"

A gourd-shaped rock. A rock…?

"That's awfully big for a rock," I said.

Asahina had exaggerated a bit when she'd spoken. It did not look "just like" the one in the drawing. If (Michiru) Asahina hadn't been guiding me, I would've been wandering around on this mountain all damn night.

"I suppose it does look a bit like a gourd…" she said.

The rock sat at the nearer side of the clearing. To my eye it looked less like a gourd and more like the arched back of a sea serpent protruding from the surface of the water. Since it was partially sunken into the surrounding earth, it was hard to spot among the fallen leaves and dry grass, despite its whitish surface.

I checked the letter again.

" 'Move this rock three meters west,' huh?"

It was already starting to get dark. It would be dangerous to stay much longer. I didn't want to wind up making a misstep on our way back such that we both went tumbling down the mountain.

I handed my flashlight to Asahina and asked her to illuminate the matter at hand. It was time to try moving the rock.

"Ugh, this is heavy."

Worse, when I actually tried to move it, I discovered a third of it was buried in the ground. This wasn't just a rock. If you were going to label it, you'd have to call it a boulder.

After much effort, I managed to pull it out, whereupon I took a good look at it. I had to admit it did look not unlike a gourd, if I stood the rock on its end.

I heaved the rock up and tottered over in a direction I thought was vaguely westish, figuring four steps would be about three meters.

"It was just a bit past that," Asahina indicated. Of course—this Asahina knew where the stone was after it had been moved. "Right, right there. Right about there."

I dropped the rock onto the ground, where it stuck in the earth with a dull thump. Just as I was about to push it over so it would lay the same way it had previously—

"It was standing," Asahina corrected me. Her eyes then went wide and she drew a sharp breath. "Just like…a marker…"

I looked down at the rock I'd just dropped.

A marker.

When I looked at it like this, the rock was really obvious. I didn't know what kind of mineral it was, but its white color was strangely prominent even in the gloom, and its shape was odd too. If you were to call it the "White Gourdstone" or something and show it off to people as an ancient ruin of some kind, people would definitely believe you.

"Asahina, does Haruhi by any chance make us dig beneath this rock?"

"Yes, that's right. Although the only ones digging were you and Koizumi."

And she'd said we didn't find anything. Was that true? I asked.

"It's true," she said, her eyes downcast. "We didn't find any treasure…"

I heaved a sigh and dusted the filthy palms of my hands off against each other.

So what was I even doing? But this wasn't the time to ask. Not even Asahina had understood the purpose of our prank last night, or the man we'd played it on. The only one who knew for certain was Asahina the Elder. I'd have to ask her. I wasn't gonna allow this kind of unilateral communication again.

I gazed at the rock I'd just erected and realized another unnatural thing. Since it had been partially buried for so long, one side of it was dirty and covered with soil. Anyone could tell at a glance it had recently been moved from somewhere else.

"And the ground there too."

The spot where the stone had lain was now exposed, the crater of black soil obvious.

"What did it look like when you got here?" I asked.

Asahina made a face of concentration as she thought back. "Hmmm, nobody said anything, so I didn't really notice. I guess all Suzumiya cared about was digging holes..."

In which case, we could've just left it be, but I figured we might as well make a bit of an effort.

Asahina and I gathered up dried grass and ivy twigs and scattered them over the crater left behind by the now-moved rock, tamping them down with our feet. We also brushed off the soil that clung to the once-buried side of the rock. It wasn't perfect—the difference between the two sides of the stone, one of which had weathered years' worth of changing seasons while the other was buried in the earth—was too great.

We did our best, but the sky was getting dark, so it was all we could do to finish up at a convenient stopping point. I wasn't sure how hard the work actually was, but it was hard enough.

"Let's go home, Asahina."

I led the way going down. It was a good thing I'd brought a flashlight. The ancients feared and revered the forest's darkness—plus they say the descent takes more of a toll on your body than the ascent does.

Asahina stumbled several times, clinging to my back for support, and by the time we reached the foot of the mountain, it was nighttime proper. Just then—

"Oh!" said Asahina, looking skyward. "Rain!"

Within five minutes, the occasional drops had turned to a gentle rain.

*   *   *

With Asahina on the back, I rode my bike as fast as I could to Tsuruya's house. It was mostly downhill, which made pedaling easier. It took us less than half the time it took to get to the mountain and only a third the effort.

As we arrived through the drizzle, there was someone waiting for us.

"Hey there! Welcome back!" Tsuruya was wearing the same traditional clothing as yesterday, carrying an umbrella in one hand as she smiled cheerfully and opened the gate for us. "Where'd you guys get off to? Nah, never mind! I'm sure you had your reasons! Tsuru-nyan hears no evil and speaks no evil! She does see you, though. Wait—Miku—I mean, Michiru! You're super dirty! Let's get you into the bath, hmm?" Tsuruya said in her usual rapid-fire way. "You must be freezing! C'mon, into the bath with you! We'll take one together! You too, Kyon! I'll wash your back for you. We've even got a traditional cypress bath!"

I would've cried tears of gratitude at the proposal, but I could tell from her face that Tsuruya was only joking. Haruhi would say things she really meant while sounding like she was kidding, but Tsuruya would crack jokes with a straight face.

"I'll just head home. You take care of Asahina—Michiru, I mean."

I turned to leave, but Tsuruya stopped me. "Hang on just a sec."

She held the umbrella over me, then produced from the breast pocket of her traditional jacket a piece of paper that had been rolled up and tied with twine.

"Haru-nyan asked for this. Would you give it to her, Kyon?"

She looked completely serious. The thick, aging parchment was partially bug-eaten in places, looking every inch like the kind of paper that would have a map leading to buried treasure on it.

"What's this?"

"A treasure map!" Tsuruya answered quickly, grinning. "I found it a while ago poking around in the old storehouse. I figured why not give it to Haru-nyan, but then I forgot all about it."

Was it okay to just give it to Haruhi? I asked. I mean, it was a *treasure* map.

"Sure, why not? It'll be a pain to go all the way out there and dig it up. If you find anything, just kick me back ten percent. One of our ancestors was the one who buried it, see, and according to family records, he was a crazy old geezer who loved pranks. I bet he thought he'd get his descendants good! There's either nothing there or something totally pointless."

Surely it would be the former.

I took the rolled-up parchment as respectfully as I could manage, but Tsuruya just flippantly handed it over, so there was only so much graciousness I could show.

"Make sure you give it to Haru-nyan, 'kay?" Tsuruya gave a gleeful smile, one eye closed, while a stiff Asahina looked back and forth between the supposed treasure map and me, hastily looking down when she noticed my gaze. What was going on? I wondered. Was there really classified information regarding the treasure hunt? I knew she was sad about being sent back in time with no idea why, but she seemed to have some hang-up about the treasure hunt as well.

"Here, Kyon, I'll let you borrow the umbrella. Take care on your way home! Bye!"

Tsuruya waved good-bye, and I saw Asahina give a small wave herself before the two disappeared behind the closing gate.

I stood there in the rain, umbrella in one hand, ancient scroll in the other.

A terrible loneliness struck me hard enough that I wanted to break in and help myself to a bath. Was Tsuruya having this effect on me? When you were with someone that cheerful, then left her side, it was like a festival had ended. She was like a one-woman carnival.

"Damn, it's cold out here."

I rested the umbrella over my shoulder and started walking my bike.

Haruhi, Asahina, even Nagato—they could all make me crazy.

"Crap, I'm really hungry."

I didn't see Koizumi on my way back, even though for once I wouldn't have minded talking to him.

The next morning, four days after the other Asahina had appeared in the broom closet, the previous day's rainclouds were quickly moving east, and the clear sky facilitated some serious radiative cooling.

The uphill hike to school helped warm me a bit, but I knew that half an hour in my unheated classroom would make the sweat I'd worked up only chill me further.

I crossed the front grounds and got to the school entryway, then took a deep breath before opening my shoe locker. I knew that the messages from the future wouldn't stop with the last one, and thus I expected there to be another one this morning, and who knew what I'd be ordered to do this time. But my hesitation was pointless, since after all, I had to get my school slippers.

And indeed, there was a letter.

In fact, there were three.

"C'mon, Asahina, you've gotta be kidding me..."

They were even numbered. Each envelope had a number carefully handwritten on it: #3, #4, and #6. Three, four, and...six?

"So were the two earlier ones number one and number two? Guess that makes the first one number zero."

But why did they jump from four to six? What happened to five? Had she written the wrong number?

I shoved them in my pocket and headed directly for the bathroom, which had by this time become routine.

I opened the envelopes in ascending order.

There wasn't much time before the bell would ring, so I scanned them quickly, then headed out of the restroom. On the way out, I caught a glimpse of my own face in the mirror and saw that I looked as confused as I felt.

What was Asahina the Elder trying to get us all to do? And while I'm on the subject, I wouldn't even ask what the point was of sending a completely random man to the hospital, then moving a rock from one place to another. I really wanted to know, though.

I headed to my classroom, filled with half-formed misgivings, where a strangely agitated individual was waiting for me.

"Kyon!"

It was Haruhi who called out my strange nickname and came running over—a girl who, until yesterday, had been strangely melancholy.

"I heard all about it; hurry up and show it to me!"

Just as I was momentarily wondering what the insanely grinning Haruhi was talking about, she interrupted.

"Don't tell me you forgot it. I'm talking about the thing you got from Tsuruya! You know, the super-awesome one."

I knew she was mercurial, but surely even Haruhi's mood swings had a limit. What had happened to the gloomy, almost sick-seeming girl of yesterday? Don't tell me she'd been replaced by an impostor, I told her.

"Don't be stupid. I'm always me, and there's only one me in the whole world!" replied Haruhi with a triumphant smile. "Anyway! C'mon, show it to me! If you forgot it, I'm gonna make you sprint home to get it."

I just bet she would. Our idle classmates were starting to stare at us. I told her that I tried to live as unobtrusively as I could.

"A goal that boring should be written down on a paper airplane and launched off the roof. Living unobtrusively or conspicuously—none of that is relevant. If you want to talk about your life, do it three seconds before you die!"

I didn't want to live a life that could be explained in three seconds, but in any case, I helplessly—well, not quite *helplessly*—got the ancient scroll Tsuruya had given me out of my bag, whereupon it was immediately snatched out of my hand. The owner of the hand that had done the snatching undid the string that held it closed, and then spoke to me in a lowered voice.

"Hey, did you look at this?"

"No, not yet."

"Really?"

"Yeah, I didn't particularly want to."

"Even though it's a treasure map? That doesn't excite you a little bit?"

I already knew there wasn't even one scrap of treasure, so the only phrase that came to mind here was "pointless waste of effort," so tell me, please, how I was supposed to get excited about that? Thus, I'd tossed Tsuruya's terrible souvenir into my bag and hadn't given it a second glance. I'd had other things to worry about, and I still did. To be perfectly honest, I was thinking about trying to talk Haruhi out of this whole treasure-hunting business, but she was already unrolling the scroll.

"Honestly, I don't know what Tsuruya was thinking either—giving this thing to you, when she should've just given it straight to me! I guess it's nice to get it first thing in the morning, but I was gonna make it a surprise after school…"

She seemed pleased despite her muttering, whirling around and returning to her seat. Using her pencil case and textbooks as paperweights, she spread the parchment out on her desk and absorbed herself in studying it.

I gave up and sat back down in my own seat, whereupon a new question occurred to me.

"Hey, Haruhi."

"What?" came her quick reply.

"When did you find out Tsuruya had given me that thing?"

"Last night. I got a phone call from her," Haruhi said without looking up. "You took Shamisen for a walk, right? Tsuruya spotted you going past her house, and that's when she gave it to you, she said. I guess Shamisen's feeling better. Good for him."

I could only purse my lips at Tsuruya's tale. I'd like to see the person who'd take a *cat* for a walk on a freezing, rainy night like that. There was something wrong with Haruhi if she really believed that.

She didn't seem to notice the silence that indicated my exasperation, her eyes shining like they had at Setsubun. "Take a look at this, Kyon! This is *definitely* a treasure map. It says so right here!"

I looked down at Haruhi's desk.

There on the sheet of parchment (which really belonged in a museum) was a picture and a few lines of text, along with the name of the writer. The picture was clear enough. It was done in simple brushstrokes but had skillfully captured the shape of the mountain. The writing was done in squiggly phonetic characters—and since my own classical literature textbook frequently seemed like alien writing to me, I didn't have a prayer of reading this.

Haruhi translated for me.

"'Upon this mountain is buried something rare. Those of my descendants who would seek it, dig ye here.'"

After that came the writer's name.

"'Fusauemon Tsuruya, 1702, Fifteenth Year of the Genroku Era.'"

I didn't know how many generations back *this* Tsuruya was, but he'd sure left quite a thing behind. I mean, why'd he need to bury it? I wondered if it was just as Tsuruya had said, a prank reaching across time. If not, somebody would've dug it up in the centuries between the Genroku period and the modern era.

"So where on the mountain is it buried?" I asked, disinterested.

Haruhi traced her finger over the ink drawing. "It doesn't say. There's no landmark or marker. All it says is that it's somewhere on this mountain. But that's okay." Her energetic gaze assaulted me. "We'll just start digging, and eventually we'll come to it or run out of spots to dig! It'll be Operation Steamroller!"

So who was this "we" she was talking about? Was she just going to get the townsfolk to volunteer? I asked.

"Of course not, stupid." Haruhi rolled the map back up and retied the twine, placing it in her desk. "We'll just do it ourselves, obviously. You don't want your share of the treasure to be any smaller, right?"

If my "share" were actually going to be smaller, I wouldn't have wanted that, but a smaller share of nothing was still nothing. The bell interrupted my internal muttering, and our homeroom teacher, Mr. Okabe, entered the classroom.

"We're meeting after school in the clubroom, got it?" said Haruhi, poking me in the back with her mechanical pencil. "And keep this a secret. I want to surprise everybody. And you better act surprised too. Like you just heard about this for the first time. Seriously, I can't believe Tsuruya spilled the beans like that..."

Haruhi continued to mutter, but it was drowned out by Mr. Okabe's raised voice and the general din of the rest of my classmates.

So here's a reliable technique for burning the contents of a class into your brain cells. You don't actually need any special concentration ability. Just vaguely listen to whatever the teacher's saying and stare at either the chalkboard or the textbook. Of course it's better to take notes, but it's hard to be motivated to take perfect notes every period, which is why you need the technique.

To put it simply, it comes down to this: you don't have to concentrate on class. But you can't think about anything *besides* class. After all, if you're thinking about nothing, you get bored, and your idle brain will just remember whatever's coming in from the ears and eyes.

Just give it a try. But please keep in mind that I got this technique from Haruhi—you could say it's the Haruhi-style Study Technique. You don't have to study, but you can't think about *anything* besides study. But there's no joy in that kind of life, and I found the idea of Haruhi not thinking about anything difficult to believe, so basically this had to be a crock, although there was nothing I could say to the fact that Haruhi's grades were excellent.

All that said, it was a tall order for me at the moment. While Haruhi's vague melancholy had bothered me quite a bit recently, her magic points seemed to have been completely restored by a single sheet of ancient paper—a turn of events I welcomed. It was one less thing for me to worry about.

In exchange, I now had three more letters' worth of orders from Asahina the Elder. With the help of Asahina from eight days hence, I'd have to put them into action somehow. Even if I'd wanted to do so immediately, they were time-dependent, so I couldn't just dash out of the classroom immediately and get to work—but neither could I afford to be lazy...

With all these thoughts in my head, it was no wonder I couldn't absorb any of the class material, but at least I had a unique excuse.

After school, Haruhi herded me off to the clubroom; I felt like a tiny fish being cornered by a cormorant. Thanks to Tsuruya's improvisation, I couldn't use Shamisen's health as an excuse to go home early, and on top of that, I genuinely had no other plans today.

That's right, the letters I'd retrieved from my shoe locker made it clear that today and the next day were free. My duties would fall on the day after tomorrow, and the day after that. The reason three messages had all arrived together today was simple: after today, I wouldn't be back at school for a while. Thanks to the holiday and the entrance exams for middle schoolers, it was a four-day weekend.

Time travelers sure did like using shoe lockers as post office boxes. I wouldn't have minded a bit if she'd just delivered the messages to me in person. I had more than a few things I wanted to ask Asahina the Elder.

Such were the thoughts that occurred to me during class, and even now, being dragged along by Haruhi. Finally, we arrived at the literature club's room.

"Hey! Sorry for the wait!"

I entered the room, pulled after Haruhi as she gave a cheerful yell and opened the door energetically. A strange nostalgia welled up within me, probably because it had been three whole days since I'd last hung out with the entire membership of the brigade. Apparently my attachment to the group was such that I'd have this sort of feeling after only three days.

Still feeling a bit dazed, I closed behind us the door Haruhi'd thrown open, then gave the brigade members inside another look.

My gaze first landed upon a girl sitting in the corner, school-uniformed, hair short-cropped, thick book open in front of her. Nagato regarded both Haruhi and me with her tirelessly blank expression, but soon returned her attention to the text before her. The small-framed organic android wasted neither words nor actions, her stoic, tranquil manner constant as she occupied her corner.

"Hello, there. It's been a while." Koizumi smiled meaningfully, the scattered pieces of a jigsaw puzzle before him. "How's Shamisen the First doing? If necessary, I can recommend an excellent animal hospital. I have a friend whose relative operates it, and I'm told it's very good."

Yeah, I'll bet. All of his connections seemed to be "excellent," I muttered.

"I'm surprisingly well-connected, actually. In many ways," said

Koizumi, snapping a jigsaw puzzle piece into place. "If I follow those connections, I can find nearly anyone. As far as people out-side my network of connections go…" he continued, spreading his arms elegantly wide, as though performing on stage. "They'd have to be people that don't yet exist on this earth."

He already knew aliens and time travelers, so who else could he possibly hope to be acquainted with? I didn't want to meet any extra-dimensional travelers, that was for sure. It'd be nothing but trouble.

Koizumi chuckled and cut off his conversation with me, turn-ing to Haruhi. "I believe you said something about holding a meeting today?"

"That's right! A special emergency meeting." Haruhi tossed her bag onto the brigade chief desk, then plopped down in her chair. "Mikuru! Tea, please."

"Okay!" It was indubitably Mikuru in her maid outfit who answered adorably, then hurried over to the kettle.

Of course it was. There wasn't any problem with Mikuru being here. Still…

"Mmm…" I murmured quietly, my mouth closed. I needed to put my thoughts in order. This wasn't Michiru Asahina, who even now haunted Tsuruya's house. This was the Asahina who hadn't yet traveled a few days back in time.

As she poured hot water from the small, burbling pot, she sud-denly looked up to me.

"Um, Kyon…"

She looked worried—exactly like the other Asahina who had appeared three days ago, from what was then eight days in the future. I guess that was obvious. As I was trying to prepare myself to say something, she continued.

"How is the kitty cat doing? Maybe he's sick because we took him to such a cold place during winter vacation…"

"Uh, n-no…" I stumbled over my words. This Asahina didn't know anything. She had no idea that five days from now, in the evening, she would jump back in time to three days before today. Man, this was getting hard to keep track of.

"Shamisen's been doing better since yesterday. He's probably rolling around in my room right now."

Asahina smiled beautifully, which made me feel even guiltier. (Michiru) Asahina already knew that Shamisen's supposed illness was a total lie, which was why she hadn't said anything about it, but this Asahina was worried about him and was trying to comfort me—all because of that big fat lie. It made me want to bow my head in apology.

"Please do let me play with him again sometime. He's such a cute kitty."

There was nothing cuter than Asahina, though, not within five hundred light-years of this planet, but if she thought a cat was a good excuse to come visit my house, I'd prepare cats aplenty, I told her—although Shamisen was always bringing a black alley cat over; probably his girlfriend.

"Hee hee. That'd be nice. Oh—!" Asahina started. "The tea's spilled."

Hot water had boiled out of the teapot. She'd been distracted by her conversation with me about the cat. This seemed to fit Haruhi's idea of Asahina as the "clumsy maid." Her arms folded in satisfaction, Haruhi watched Asahina wipe the table.

I pulled out a folding chair and sat down next to Koizumi, while Haruhi took out the current object of her obsession and waited to make her announcement.

"Sorry to keep you waiting." Asahina brought a tray with two teacups on it, serving Haruhi and me. I figured Haruhi would only be able to wait until we'd had a single sip of tea, but contrary to my expectations, she didn't seem to have any intention of standing. She sipped her tea, then leaned back in her chair at the brigade chief's desk, a cocky grin on her face as she turned on the computer and idly flipped through a magazine. Our eyes would meet occasionally, whereupon she'd look serious for a moment, then go back to grinning—the woman of a hundred faces, indeed. What did this portend?

Koizumi continued to work on his puzzle, pretending not to notice, while Nagato hadn't reacted at all. Asahina busied herself with the second round of tea, and while things seemed pretty much totally normal, "normal" was totally weird today. What was Haruhi wasting all this time for?

The answer was soon entirely clear.

The room's peace was broken not by a cry from Haruhi or a PA announcement telling students to go home, but rather a rhythmic knock on the door.

"Heya! Here I am! Can I come in?"

I heard a high, familiar voice as Haruhi bolted to her feet.

"We've been waiting! C'mon in, c'mon in!"

In a rare display, the brigade chief opened the door herself to welcome in the guest.

"Hey there, long time no see, everybody-but-Mikuru! Oh, I guess I saw you yesterday, huh, Kyon? Shami's great, you should bring him by again!"

Tsuruya's loud voice rang out. She and Haruhi had their arms around each other's shoulders, and she grinned as though they were about to bust out in a line dance. Here we go again, I thought.

"Yup, that's right! A treasure map! Treasure's about three hundred years old. It'd be great if it's Genroku-era gold coins or something!" Tsuruya sat cross-legged on a folding chair as she munched down on the rice crackers that were served with her tea. "Hadn't been in the storeroom for like five years—we just keep stuff we don't need anymore there, see. Found that scrap of paper in the family storeroom, y'know, in a basket buried under a bunch of junk!"

Tsuruya gulped down tea from the nice guest-use-only teacup, then stood up and pointed at the whiteboard.

The map had been stuck to the whiteboard with magnets at its corners, while Haruhi stood beside it and patted Tsuruya's back with the pointer she held. Haruhi sure seemed happy.

"They've tried to get us to turn that mountain over to the state, but my ancestor said in his will that we can't ever do that. It must be because of the treasure! Is that what you were getting at, Ancestor Guy?" Tsuruya clapped her hands together and made a quick bow toward the sun, as Haruhi smacked the whiteboard with her pointer. "So that's that."

So what was what? All we'd heard was Tsuruya talking about her ancestor's will, I pointed out.

"Obviously we're going to go search for the treasure her ancestor buried. What would be the point of this story, otherwise?" Haruhi's mouth was open wide, her white teeth showing. "That settles it—we're going tomorrow. If we don't hurry, someone might beat us to it. Assemble at the usual station, nine AM. We're heading to the mountains! And don't worry; I'll bring everything we need."

It went without saying that I was completely unsurprised. I was the one who'd gotten the map from Tsuruya yesterday, and I'd heard we were going on a treasure hunt three days earlier from Asahina, and again this morning from Haruhi. I had no confidence in my ability to fake being surprised now. I brought my mostly empty teacup to my lips and pretended to take a drink, but it turned out there was no need.

Only one person in this room was surprised.

"Eh? Wha—? Treasure hunting? Mountain climbing? Ah—I'd better make some lunches!"

Only Asahina.

Nagato, her book still open, followed the tip of Haruhi's pointer in silence.

"Well, now. This could indeed be fascinating, from an anthro-

pological and archaeological perspective. I look forward to it."
Koizumi smiled, ready as ever to support Haruhi's plans.

If Haruhi'd been hoping for everyone to be stunned by her
plan, she'd been sorely mistaken. But she seemed not to take
notice of the lack of surprise. "That's about the size of it. If we
find anything, we'll split it equally—Tsuruya gets a share too, for
her support."

"Sounds good!" said Tsuruya, a little too loudly. "If you find
anything worth money, I'll totally give you guys ninety percent.
And if it's something that great-great-great...actually I forgot
how many greats, but anyway, something that Grandpa Fusauemon left to get a laugh out of his grandchildren, I guess my
family'll hang on to it. Either way, I can't help you out with the
digging! I'm busy tomorrow, see."

Tsuruya gave me a significant look, after which she turned to
Asahina and smiled. Tsuruya's body language made it clear that
she was going to keep her promise not to say anything to *this*
Asahina.

I didn't doubt her. And yet.

For someone who'd claimed she didn't want to be involved
more than necessary, she had given me as much explanation as
anyone short of Koizumi. In spite of that—no, *given* that—her
actions were hard to understand. At least when she helped out
with the baseball tournament, or when we'd borrowed her family's villa, those were requests *we* made of *her*. But this time she'd
gone out of her way to throw Haruhi a bone; it was like she was
trying to be *more* involved with us, rather than less. Maybe she
just liked giving Haruhi things she thought Haruhi would enjoy.

Whatever my suspicions, Tsuruya continued to munch away
on the rice crackers, happy as a clam.

Still stranger was the fact that Koizumi seemed similarly trou-
bled. And when I thought back, I realized that in all the times
Tsuruya had popped into the clubroom, she'd never given him a
significant look. If Koizumi's bosses had told him not to interfere

with Tsuruya, then her showing up all the time might put him in a bad position.

Or maybe...

I looked at Koizumi's excessively mild smile, my mind racing. I didn't know how much of the conversation we'd had that night was true. Maybe there really was some kind of unwritten agreement between Koizumi's Agency and the Tsuruya clan. But even so, that was between the Agency and the family, not Koizumi and Tsuruya specifically. Either one or both of them might not give a crap what their organizations said, and it wasn't as though they had conspired with each other ahead of time.

Tsuruya didn't seem to know anything about Koizumi's, Nagato's, or Asahina's true natures—she only seemed to sense that something about those three (and Haruhi) was different. It wasn't her style to pry further. I generally believed what Tsuruya had told me the night before last, and I even believed most of what Koizumi had said—that if the situation involved weighing the Agency against Nagato, I could choose us instead, for once.

"...Kyon! Hey! Are you even listening?"

A sharp voice reached my ears, and I found myself staring at the business end of a pointer. At the other end stood a very severe-looking Haruhi.

"You got that? Like I said, wear comfortable clothes tomorrow! Stuff you don't mind getting dirty. You and Koizumi don't have to worry about tools. So as for what we're gonna need..."

Haruhi gestured to Asahina to fetch a pen.

Asahina, finding herself in the strange situation of being both maid and secretary, took dictation from Haruhi in her charmingly childish handwriting.

"We'll need two shovels. I'll take care of those. Also—lunches. Mikuru, that's your job. Also blankets to sit on, and in case of emergency, a compass, a lantern, and a map. And not this treasure map either, but the real thing. And we'd probably better have lots of snacks for emergency rations. I wonder what we should do for signal flares..."

Just which mountain did she think we were going to climb? The only ones around here weren't even as tall as the hill the school was on. So long as we didn't encounter any unexpected phenomenon, there weren't going to be any emergencies, and if we *did* encounter something truly dangerous, a compass and a signal flare weren't going to be of any use—the incident at the end of last year came to mind.

I let a soft sigh slip as I watched Nagato's dark eyes, which were fixated on Asahina's clumsy writing.

According to what the Asahina from next week told me, we went safely treasure hunting and came back without incident—completely empty-handed, to boot. If there had been some kind of serious incident on the way, she would've given me some kind of warning.

We climbed up, we ate lunch, and we came back. That was nothing more than a picnic, really—at least it was for everybody besides Koizumi and me, who would be doing all the manual labor.

I finally felt like I understood why Nagato had sealed away her own ability to synchronize with her other selves. It really wasn't any fun at all knowing in advance not just what I was going to do, but what Haruhi was going to say and do as well. I wished I hadn't asked Asahina what would happen.

I supposed it might all balance out in the end. I knew what weekend activity the SOS Brigade had to execute. However, I didn't have the slightest idea what the purpose of the instructions Asahina the Elder was handing down to Michiru Asahina and me was—so perhaps the former canceled out the latter.

Although I couldn't help muttering to myself that it was *all* a loss.

Space on the whiteboard was rapidly disappearing as Haruhi—

now entirely given over to the idea of mountain climbing—rattled off item after item to add to the list, with Asahina being forced to kneel down in order to squeeze "tents" and "Sherpa" onto the bottom of the board in tiny letters.

"C'mon, Haru-nyan, it's not like we're crossing the Tian Shan on foot. It's a pretty tiny mountain, really. It's got cell phone coverage, so if anything happens we can just call for help. They'll send a rescue squad," Tsuruya said, grinning. "I played around on the place all the time as a kid. It's totally bear-free!"

Haruhi smiled back. "Thanks. We'll be counting on you if anything bad happens."

So she hadn't been serious about the preparations? I wondered. Haruhi waved her pointer around.

"All right, everybody! Tsuruya's giving us so much support; we've *got* to bring that treasure out! Let's give it our best shot!"

I realized I was feeling strangely calm, which in turn worried me. Haruhi seemed to have returned to her old self, her eyes shining as she looked at me. That alone was enough to push aside all misgivings, and I suppose I felt reassured, or something like that.

In any case, it was always better when people cheered up. Whatever the reason.

After her unilateral decision to go treasure hunting, Haruhi went to the library and got out every Edo-era reference book, map, and historical novel she could find, in an effort to deduce more about Tsuruya's ancestor (who'd apparently been a headman or merchant), but such deductions were really no more than guesses, and after about an hour of this, our "emergency meeting" was concluded.

Incidentally, Haruhi unreasonably hoped for "something more interesting than boring old coins," but when Nagato closed the paperback she was reading, Haruhi followed suit and shut the encyclopedia of matchlock firearms into which she'd been gazing.

At that point, everybody headed home. I was hoping I'd have the chance to talk with Tsuruya on the way down the hill, but the opportunity never arose. She and Haruhi briskly took up the front; behind them followed Asahina and a silent Nagato, while Koizumi and I brought up the rear. I'd wanted to make sure that (Michiru) Asahina was doing okay over at Tsuruya's place, but I couldn't risk asking while Haruhi might be able to hear.

Oh well. I could call later. I'd have to, in order to discuss upcoming plans with that Asahina. One of the three letters that had come this morning contained instructions that required a bit of preparation. I'd have to set something up beforehand. I was doing more and more unpaid errand-running.

Still, I had to admit I was impressed with Tsuruya. As I watched her rapid exchanges with Haruhi and Asahina, she wasn't letting slip for a moment that she was hosting Asahina's doppelganger at her house—she just seemed like regular old Tsuruya. She was a classmate I could really count on.

"See you tomorrow! Tardiness equals punishment!"

We split into smaller groups within sight of Nagato's apartment, and after I waved in response to Haruhi's voice, all I had to do was pretend to head home.

I ambled along toward my house, pretending to be a high school student returning home. Once I was out of sight of all the other members, I ducked down an alleyway just to be safe, then called Tsuruya's house.

After giving my name to a maid, I was transferred immediately to Asahina.

"Hello? Kyon? It's me."

I thought of Asahina sitting politely in her small room. "I got more letters today."

"Ooh, what are they saying this time?" Her last word trailed off into a sigh.

"That's what I want to talk to you about. We've got free time today and tomorrow, but it looks like things are gonna get busy the day after that."

"Ah, okay. I think I see what you mean..."

Now how would she see that? I asked.

"I told you we did another city patrol on Saturday, didn't I? I did my best to remember how it went, and... well, you were acting a little weird, Kyon."

It was probably better if I didn't ask for details. Tomorrow was going to be tiring enough without having to act purposefully weird the next day.

"We'll talk about that later. Tsuruya's not back yet, is she? I'm heading over, so I'll probably arrive a bit after she does."

The weather made me hurry. I hung up and started off at a brisk walk.

It was again Tsuruya who emerged upon my ringing the doorbell. She must have gotten there just a moment before I did, because she was still wearing her school uniform.

"Hey, I thought you'd show up," said Tsuruya with a smile as she opened the gate and beckoned me inside. "So, what's up? How long's that poor Michiru gonna be cooped up here, anyway?"

I wasn't totally sure, I told her. But it would probably just be for a few more days.

"I like having her over; she can stay as long as she wants. She's so cute, seriously! It's like, just seeing her at school I never knew Mikuru—er, I mean, I never knew she was so cute! I just wanna hug her and go to sleep!"

I sincerely hoped she wasn't actually doing anything so desperately enviable, I told her.

"Oh, no. Only thing we do together is bath time. But Michiru—when she wants to say something, she sorta stops like she's wondering if she should. I mean, that's super cute too, but I feel bad for her. She really doesn't have to worry about it."

Tsuruya led me to the apartment. Asahina was there on the tatami-mat floor, sitting just as politely as I'd imagined. The short rough-spun jacket she wore over her traditional kimono gave her a fresh quality.

"Oh, Kyon—"

The relief she seemed to feel at my arrival made me feel pretty good. It made me want to get down and give her a traditional bow of greeting.

As I ventured to close the door behind me, I ran right into Tsuruya's satisfied smile. She seemed to want to ask me something, and there was indeed something I needed to say.

"Tsuruya, if you'll excuse Michiru and me—we need to speak in private. It will only take a moment."

"Oh reeeally?" Tsuruya peered over my shoulder at Asahina. "Just the two of you? In this little room? I guess..." She watched Asahina's reddening face with amusement. "I guess I'll just go get changed. Hee hee—you two enjoy yourselves!"

Tsuruya strode gracefully back to the main house. I watched her go, then ducked back into the small apartment. Asahina looked tense, and she was staring down as though counting the stitches in the tatami mats. I wanted to tell her not to be so nervous—it made me feel bad.

I swept various carnal desires out of my mind, forcing myself to concentrate on the contents of my school bag.

"I mentioned them on the phone, but here are the letters—the ones that came today."

I presented the envelopes to Asahina—well, #3 and #4, anyway. I'd keep #6 to myself—it was apparently meant for my eyes only. And it was probably the last one too. I assumed there wouldn't be any more. If #5 arrived, that was a separate matter, so I figured we'd just deal with pressing matters within #3 and #4.

First, #3:

> *"Saturday, the day after tomorrow: go south to the pedestrian bridge in [XXXX] county, [XXXX] ward, by dusk. There in front of the bridge, you will see some pansies. Pick up the object that's been dropped there and send it anonymously to the address below. The object is a portable storage device."*

On the second sheet, there was a random address that was some distance away, along with a picture of what seemed to be the storage device. It was reminiscent of a memory stick, but I couldn't be sure. I mean, it wasn't a great picture, to be honest.

Next, #4:

> *"In the row of sakura trees that line the river, there is a bench that you and Asahina should know well. On Sunday, go there by 10:45 AM, and by 10:50 AM, throw a turtle into the river. Any species is fine. A smaller turtle will be more convenient."*

This note also had a second sheet. On it was a cute little illustration of a turtle, with a speech bubble saying, "Take good care of me!"

Both letters had the same postscript: *"P.S. Bring Mikuru Asahina and no one else with you,"* followed by a single line of the symbols only she could read.

Asahina read the letters with a serious face, and after finishing the second one, she sighed. "I just don't understand. A turtle…?"

It would've been stranger if she *had* understood why now, in the middle of freezing winter, we were throwing a turtle into the river. The only part *I* understood was the bench the second letter referred to—it was the same bench on which, last year, Asahina had confessed her true identity as a time traveler to me.

"But we must do it." Asahina traced her finger over the code on the letter, looking up with resolve. "We may not understand the reasons yet, but there is definitely a purpose for all of this. Otherwise..."

Asahina's eyes trembled in sadness for a moment.

I could guess what she was thinking. Otherwise—there wasn't any purpose in her being here. And even *less* purpose for there being *two* of her.

I suddenly wanted to hug her close, but I didn't. I'd been warned off by Tsuruya, for one thing. And I couldn't just ignore my conscience.

"Anyway, Asahina." I attempted an attitude adjustment. "You said we were on city patrol Saturday and Sunday, right? Doesn't that conflict with these directions?"

The Saturday directions were vague, only saying "by dusk," but about Sunday it was very clear: ten forty-five AM. It would be difficult for any SOS Brigade member to pull that off—and I couldn't just sneak off alone either.

"Did you make some kind of excuse for being absent?" I asked.

"No. You were there, Kyon," said Asahina, returning the letters to their envelopes like they were precious things. "But we drew straws to split up into groups, like we always do. I was thinking about it before... on Saturday morning I was with Suzumiya and Nagato, and you were with Koizumi, and then in the afternoon it was Suzumiya, Koizumi, and me, and you were with Nagato..." Asahina nodded slightly as though confirming the contents of her memory. "Yes, I'm sure. Then on Sunday morning it was Suzumiya, Koizumi, and me together, and you and Nagato. Then in the afternoon we were dismissed... wait, what?"

She seemed to realize something mid-sentence—probably the same thing I'd realized myself.

That was an awfully convenient coincidence.

For me to be able to carry out these instructions with *this* Asahina, I would need to be paired up with Nagato. With five people, one of the groups was always going to be a pair, so what were the odds of that pair being the same two people, in two tries out of three? I wasn't going to bother doing the math, but I was sure they were pretty low.

And Nagato already knew the situation. I was sure that rigging the outcome of the straw-drawing would be child's play for her, even now. She'd do it if I asked. And this was the outcome.

"I wonder," said Asahina, uncertain. "But it has to go the way I remember, doesn't it? Did Nagato cooperate with us?"

It was a troubling thought. The pairings in Asahina's memory were fixed. Her memories weren't even a week old, so they had to be correct. So would I naturally be paired up with Nagato, or did we need to rig it?

I didn't agonize over it for very long.

"We'll get Nagato to help," I said. "I know it feels like cheating, but we'll be in real trouble if things don't work out properly. She'll understand."

"I agree," said Asahina readily. "You seemed a little off during the patrol, so that must have been it—I think it was because you asked Nagato to fix the lottery."

So how was I supposed to look? "Off?" What did that mean? I asked.

"That's...um...well, just kinda *off*," Asahina mumbled. It would've been nice if she could've given me a concrete example of the offness, I told her.

"I'm sorry; I don't know how to explain it..."

She didn't have to apologize, I said—it wasn't like it was that important.

"But...oh, right. On Sunday, when Suzumiya, Koizumi, and I were at the bookstore—" Asahina put her finger to her head, as though having remembered something. "Suzumiya got a prank call on her phone."

Who from? I asked.

"From you."

Me? I would go to the trouble of prank-calling Haruhi *now*, of all times?

"Yes, that's what she said. She said she got a weird phone call from you. That your joke wasn't funny at all. Then she hung up right away. I think it might have been right around eleven, maybe?"

So now I had another mysterious prediction I had to fulfill. After I threw the turtle into the river, apparently I had to call up Haruhi and tell her a bad joke.

"Did she say anything about what I said?"

"No, not to me. But then at lunch when we all met back up, you apologized to her."

That went beyond mysterious and right on into absurd. Why the hell would I apologize to her? I asked.

"You said you were sorry for telling a bad joke."

More absurdity. Me, bowing my head in a sincere apology to Haruhi? Let's just say it didn't happen very often.

When I pressed for more information, Asahina just said she didn't know. My exchange with Haruhi had apparently only involved a couple of statements before it was over and we'd moved on to the next subject.

The more I knew about my future actions, the less sense they made. If anybody could interpret them, they were welcome to try. I'd given up, myself.

"Anyway, about that turtle," I said, holding up the #4 envelope. "We're not going to just find a turtle wandering around this time of year, so we're going to have to find one ahead of time."

I didn't have the heart to try to just dig up a hibernating turtle. For one thing, come Sunday I would have done plenty of digging already, thanks to the treasure hunt. Wait—don't tell me the punch line of all this was that we would dig up a turtle while searching for treasure.

"No, we didn't find treasure *or* a turtle."

Right. I'd already heard that our so-called treasure hunt would amount to no more than a hiking trip. Either way, I couldn't imagine that we'd dig up anything lucky. "I guess it can't be helped. We'll have to buy one."

There was a home improvement store in the neighborhood that had a pet corner. I'd go there to buy boxes of canned food for Shamisen, and they also had an aquarium with a bunch of pond turtles moseying around. That was the ticket. I'd pick one up on my way home. I couldn't very well bring it along on Sunday's SOS Brigade activities, so I'd leave it in the care of this Asahina.

The plans were really piling up. So much for enjoying a nice, relaxing weekend.

Asahina and I worked out plans for where we'd meet and what we'd do on Saturday, whereupon I stood up.

She saw me to the apartment's front door; upon opening it, I saw a cold-looking Tsuruya, who'd changed from her school uniform into regular clothes.

"Well, well, well, you two certainly took your time! Are you sure you didn't do anything, Kyon?"

Her grinning face was suspicious. I wondered if she'd sneaked a peek through the door's crack. Good thing I hadn't actually done anything. Getting the crap beaten out of me by a nice upperclassman like Tsuruya wasn't my idea of a good time.

I made some vague excuses and took my leave of the Tsuruya estate, the image of Asahina's reddening cheeks seared into my retinas.

CHAPTER FOUR

I was awakened the next morning by my little sister, who came in to shut off the alarm clock that was ringing next to my pillow.

"That sure is noisy, isn't it, Shami?"

Shamisen was curled into a ball at the foot of my bed; my sister picked the furball up, then shoved him up against my nose.

"Are you gonna have breakfast? Hmm?" Her tone-deaf sing-song voice penetrated my head way more sharply than the alarm.

"Yeah."

My sister was moving Shamisen's paws around like he was a puppet; I brushed them aside and sat up, taking Shamisen out of my sister's arms and putting him on the floor. The cat sniffed in irritation, then climbed back up on my bed.

As I was getting dressed, my sister started pinching Shamisen's furry cheeks, then escalated to grabbing at his angrily twitching tail. Finally he let out a "Nrryaaow" of protest and ran out of the room, my sister chasing closely behind him. I wished they wouldn't start fighting in my room first thing in the morning—although they had gotten me out of bed, I had to admit.

I was on my way to the bathroom when I encountered them again, my sister this time having draped Shamisen around the back of her neck—"Kitty scarf!"—but I ignored them entirely.

I glared at my tense face in the bathroom mirror as I brushed my teeth, wondering just what holiday it was today—not that it mattered. I cursed the cold wind that whistled by outside and wondered when spring would finally get here. I wished I could keep being a freshman whose face nobody knew—without repeating a year, that is—but I was sick of the cold weather. Both treasure-hunting and random city excursions would've been a lot more inviting in a warmer season, but it was February. Freak-in' February!

But no matter the month, once Haruhi said we were doing something, we were doing it, one way or another. We were just lucky she hadn't decided she wanted to salvage an ancient ship-wreck at the bottom of the ocean. Had to stay positive.

Once I finished eating breakfast, I put on a jacket, given that I would be going hiking soon, then headed out for the local train station on foot. I didn't bring my bike, since the only way to get to Tsuruya's mountain from the station was to take a bus. It would've been faster if we'd just met up at the mountain, and the only reason we were meeting up at the station was out of a sense of tradition that wasn't even worth mocking.

I buried my face in my muffler; the north wind was so bad it felt like it had a bet with the sun it was determined not to lose. I wasn't walking particularly quickly, but this wasn't because I'd left myself plenty of time. No, rather it was that no matter how punctual I was, I'd still be the last to arrive. This was another stupid tradition. There'd only been that one time when I'd got-ten to wait for somebody else.

It was about five minutes to nine when I arrived at the station, where I found all the familiar faces of the SOS Brigade already waiting.

Haruhi wore an expression that looked like it had been handed down by Old Man Winter's grouchy boss. "Why are you always the late one, huh? Everybody else was already waiting for me when I got here. Don't you feel bad, making your brigade chief wait?"

Oh, Haruhi was definitely the one who made me feel bad. For one thing, the reason the other three members arrived before she did was to make her treat everybody, and the only reason she didn't have to was because of me. So I wished *she'd* feel a little bad, for once, I told her.

"What're you talking about? *You're* the one who was late," said Haruhi, grinning. "What's your problem? You seem like you're worried about something. Is something up?"

It wasn't just "something." We finally get a holiday, but here we are out in the freezing cold, looking for treasure we're never gonna find, so I was just lamenting my own misfortune, I said.

"Well, cheer up! Or did Shamisen's sickness come back?"

"No," I said, tucking my chin down and looking sideways. "It's just cold."

Haruhi chuckled and held her hands out, as though explaining something she thought was obvious. "You've just gotta adapt to the environment. So today, that means switching to winter mountain-climbing mode. Easy, right?"

I wasn't a plastic model, so I couldn't just swap out parts like that. Humans didn't have mode switches anywhere on them— although I couldn't be sure about the all-weather Haruhi.

While Haruhi and I were exchanging our morning greetings, the other three members stood there in observation mode.

Koizumi, Asahina, and Nagato were dressed in casual, basic, and natural outfits, respectively. Nagato's natural look consisted of a duffle coat over her school uniform, and while there was nothing to say about what part of that was suitable for hiking, I suddenly had the random thought that if I were to take Nagato over to Tsuruya's place and leave her there, Tsuruya would probably dress her up in her hand-me-downs. I'd have to give that a try sometime.

I wanted to ask Koizumi just what catalog he'd jumped out of; his winter jacket looked so sharp on him that you could've swapped him out for a department store mannequin—if you left out the part where he was holding two heavy-duty shovels.

Asahina wore an inoffensive pair of pants along with an inoffensive down jacket. It occurred to me that outside of her school uniform, I'd never seen Asahina wear the same outfit twice.

"I made lunches for everyone." Maybe because she'd totally gotten in the picnicking spirit, Asahina's face was 100 percent charming as she held a large basket. I wanted to pretend I'd come along just to eat her homemade lunch.

And yet it was hard to believe that this Asahina would be half ordered by me to travel into the past. Had the other Asahina really been telling the truth?

"Is something wrong?" Asahina looked up at me, her face uncertain.

"No, no," I answered casually. "I was just thinking I'm looking forward to lunchtime."

"Don't get *too* excited about it, please. I really don't know if it will be tasty or not..."

Her shyness was adorable, but my admiration was interrupted by the usual suspect.

"Lunches are well and good," said Haruhi, breaking into my field of vision, "but don't forget today's objective. We're not here to play around. This is a treasure hunt! We're not taking a lunch break until we've put in enough effort to deserve one!"

As Haruhi spoke, her smile was like the sun outshining the north wind or a child just about to go out and play. I wanted to tell her she needed to keep that smile on ready alert—but I stopped myself.

When I thought about it, I realized that I'd stopped myself because that was Haruhi's usual expression. I'd been deceived by the bad mood she'd been in since the beginning of February. As to why I felt deceived—I had no idea.

*   *   *

For once, the brigade didn't proceed to make a trip to the café at my expense. The trip wasn't canceled, though—just postponed. Haruhi informed me of this as she stood at the bus stop rotary in front of the train station, adding that at the next brigade function, I'd be treating everybody no matter who was the last to arrive.

Perhaps she was worried that if we didn't start looking for treasure immediately, somebody would beat us to it. Whatever the reason, she wanted to get to the mountain as soon as possible. Holding the shovel I'd been handed, I boarded the mountain-bound bus, standing beside Koizumi, who held on to a hanging strap. The two of us definitely stood out, holding shovels like that, but it couldn't be helped. The single saving grace was the fact that there weren't many passengers bound for the mountains that day.

We rattled around the bus for about half an hour. At our stop, Haruhi ordered us off the bus, and we found ourselves so surrounded by nature that the busy train station seemed like a dream. It was hard to believe that we were still in the same city, but thanks to the many field trips I'd taken to this area in elementary and middle school, I was used to the scenery and wasn't actually all that surprised. If we headed north from here, we really *would* be climbing a mountain. Fortunately, Tsuruya's family's mountain was smaller than that, although it was still surprising that such a place was someone's private property. That explained why I'd never climbed this particular mountain, even during a field trip.

"Seems like it'll be easier to climb from this side," said Haruhi, map in hand as she led the way. I exhaled white vapor as I looked up at the peak of Mt. Tsuruya—okay, so I didn't know its real name, but let's stick with Mt. Tsuruya.

We were exactly opposite the face I'd climbed the day before yesterday with Asahina. As to which route was the "back way," it seemed like my earlier path was the likely candidate for that. The way Haruhi was now following was a narrow path that zigzagged from the base of the mountain up to the summit. It would make for an easier hike. Right…?

"Kyon, this is no time to be staring up at the sky! Hurry up and walk!"

Haruhi's voice rang out, and I started to move my feet. Something had been nagging at me, but it now faded away. "I know, I know."

I hefted the shovel and caught back up to the brigade. Aside from Haruhi, who was acting like a rabbit suddenly returning to the forest, there was Asahina, who seemed just like an elementary school student on a hiking field trip; Nagato, who was exactly the same as she always was; and Koizumi, wearing a vaguely chagrined smile. I had major doubts as to how many of these individuals were actually serious about finding treasure. I knew for a fact *I* wasn't serious, which explained my lack of energy. The fact that we'd dig and find nothing was already written in the personalized future schedule I'd gotten from (Michiru) Asahina. Under normal circumstances, since this *was* Haruhi we were talking about, there was every possibility we'd actually dig up treasure, but Asahina would never tell a stupid lie about the past, so it was certain that we weren't going to find the secret treasure of Tsuruya's ancestor.

"Whatever is the matter?" Koizumi walked alongside me, forcing a pleasant smile. "You look as though you believe that everything we're doing is a complete waste of time."

I stayed silent. I had nothing to say to this guy.

Koizumi looked like he believed exactly the same thing—like he knew that this was his job, whether we actually dug something up or not.

He also seemed like he knew there was another Asahina in this time period, in which case I wanted him to come out and say it. Was he waiting for me to come and ask him for advice? If so, he was just gonna have to keep waiting. Now that I had Tsuruya for an accomplice, I didn't need his help. And I didn't feel like giving him any information either. People won't move the way you want them to if you just wait around. If you're not straight with them, they'll just get sick of you.

Whatever he thought of my lack of an answer, Koizumi hefted his shovel and looked ahead. His kept his smile, out of either tolerance or stoicism—either way, he was the same old Koizumi. I found myself relieved for some reason, but in any case I had to focus on mountain climbing now.

Haruhi pushed through a thicket and pointed to the summit. "First we'll head to the peak. If I were going to bury treasure, I'd dig at the easiest spot to find. Tsuruya's ancestor was a human too, after all—he'd obviously bury it somewhere easy to spot."

If he'd wanted it to be easy to spot, why bury it at all? But Haruhi wanted to head to the top. That's why she was the SOS Brigade chief. She was the master and commander of aliens, time travelers, and espers, and she wanted to go to the top.

Asahina was bent over and panting as she climbed; I wanted to give her a push from behind, but with Haruhi in the lead there was no chance for me to do so. After about half an hour of that, we arrived at the peak. That seemed like longer than it should've taken, but the path seemed to have been made to require a minimum of effort on the part of its climbers, and without being conscious of any particularly steep slopes, we'd managed to conquer this small mountain.

I wasn't especially tired, since the mountain itself wasn't more than a glorified hill. My walking endurance had been naturally increased from trudging up the hill to school every day. Unfortunately, what we were about to do would definitely tire me out.

In other words, it was time to dig for treasure. Haruhi was now in her element.

"It should be somewhere around here, right?"

We started digging in the vague area Haruhi'd gestured at. It seemed too obvious a spot to be hiding gold or treasure, even given that I knew there was nothing there. After digging about two meters down, no shovel had impacted wood or stone or anything hard.

And thanks to the discriminatory practice of delegating all excavation duties to males, the only ones digging were Koizumi and me. The three girls simply enjoyed a picnic, with Asahina being the only one who could be relied upon to cheer us on.

Haruhi simply ordered us around—"Next, over there!"—and Nagato had the same Buddha face she always had. It seemed likely that if I prayed to her, she'd tell me where treasure could actually be found, but it would be very strange to strike gold on the first try, so I refrained from Nagato-directed entreaties. And anyway, it wouldn't be good if we actually found something. Plus, no matter how incredible Haruhi's ability to ignore reality was, even she would have to find it a bit strange to dig up hidden treasure without any hard work at all. The problem was that only Koizumi and I were actually doing the hard work, and because Koizumi's pleasant expression seemed permanently carved on his face, I was the only one actually suffering.

It was enough to make me want to try and talk Taniguchi and Kunikida into helping, but Haruhi put the kibosh on that.

"Listen, we're looking for buried treasure. Everybody has to get a share. I'm a fair brigade chief, so I'm going to divide it up evenly. If we brought those jokers in, we'd have to split the treasure seven ways. I am *not* gonna let it go to waste like that, got it?"

If we were actually going to find Genroku-era gold coins, I would've agreed. But this map had come out of the depths of Tsuruya's family's storehouse. The Tsuruya clan had thrived for hundreds of years, so it had definitely weathered some tough times. If an ancestor had buried treasure here, wouldn't their descendants have dug it up and used it at some point? This so-called treasure map had to be the scribbling left behind by one of the clan's heads, or else a grand prank at the expense of his descendants. My guess was that if we dug up anything at all, it'd be a piece of paper containing only the words "Thou hast lost." For some reason, I got the feeling that Tsuruya's ancestor had a lot of free time on his hands. Tsuruya herself had said as much. That's why she'd been happy to give Haruhi the map. I bet Tsuruya would have done the same thing herself, if she were in her ancestor's position, cackling all the while as she imagined people in the future going to all this trouble because of her joke. She was definitely the type to get people all excited at first, then laugh at how exhausted they were.

I wanted to warn them off, but I managed to restrain my own desire, instead silently plunging my shovel into the earth.

Our mountain wasn't a large one, so there wasn't much space at the peak. As we kept digging, the area became full of holes. Koizumi and I labored mightily at Haruhi's urging, and unlike Koizumi (who was happy to play at being a mole man), I began to feel more and more oppressed. It was dangerous to just leave the holes we dug, so we also had the doubly pointless work of shoveling the dug-up earth back into the holes. I started to feel as though I'd been thrown into some kind of inhuman labor camp.

"Stop complaining and focus on the treasure!"

Haruhi sat cross-legged on a rolled-out mat, giving directions with a triumphant smile, like some grand general addressing her army. To her right side knelt Nagato, looking like a faithful page as she read her paperback, while to Haruhi's right sat Asahina, who huddled close to Haruhi as though trying to stay warm.

"Kyon, you're working up enough of a sweat that you might think it's warm, but as you can see it's pretty cold up here. If you don't hurry up and find something, we're gonna freeze. Are you sure you're digging right?"

I was just digging where she told me to. If she wanted to move around, she could do some digging of her own, I told her.

Her arms around Haruhi, Asahina spoke in a tremulous voice. "Um...should I help?"

"No, don't bother," interrupted Haruhi before I could reply. "This is for Kyon's sake too. It's good practice for construction work. If he doesn't get experience now, he's gonna have a hard time later."

I wasn't exactly grateful to receive career counseling from someone my own age, I said.

"The day's gonna come when you'll be glad you did this. That's how the world works. People should do everything they can."

You do it, then.

"Hey, Haruhi," I said, wiping sweat off my forehead. "We're not gonna find anything just digging random holes. I assume you're not planning to try to level the entire mountain. For one thing, we're not even sure if the treasure exists."

"Yeah, and how do you know it *doesn't*? We might just not have found it yet."

"Yeah, we haven't found it yet because it's not here. Let's first prove it exists, then start digging."

Haruhi pursed her lips, though her eyes were smiling. "This *is* that proof." In her hand she held Tsuruya's ancestral treasure map. "It says it's buried somewhere on this mountain, so it's got to be here. I trust Tsuruya's ancestor that much. It's *got* to be here!"

Haruhi's face brimmed with eccentric confidence as she explained her strange reasoning. Her certainty made it sound like she'd seen the spot old Fusauemon Tsuruya had buried his treasure.

"But you've got a point," she said, putting a finger to her chin. "It was hasty to assume it was buried on the peak. It would've been a pain to climb all the way to the top, so maybe it's on a lower spot. Yeah, I definitely want it to be buried in a more interesting spot than this." Haruhi extracted herself from Asahina's arms and stood, putting her shoes back on. "We need to look for a likelier spot. Until then, Kyon—dig over there."

Upon issuing my new orders, Haruhi headed off into the brush, making a rustling sound as she proceeded in roughly the opposite direction from which we'd climbed.

Silently, I watched her go. Assuming my sense of direction wasn't mistaken, if she kept going, she'd come across the flat spot halfway down the mountainside, where she'd find the gourd-shaped stone—a marker that practically shouted, "Dig here!"

It was all well and good to do as I was told and dig, but eventually I got sick of it and tossed the shovel aside, leaving Koizumi to fill the hole back up as I sat down on the mat.

"Here," said Asahina, offering me a paper cup of hot tea. It was the most nutritious thing I could imagine. It was sweet, a sweetness that suited Asahina herself perfectly.

Asahina held her silver thermos carefully and smiled as she watched me tentatively sip at the brown liquid. "It's lovely weather today, isn't it? And such a nice view."

Her eyes looked far off into the distance—to the south, where the world spread out before us. Our far-off city was hazy with distance, and beyond that was the sea.

The mountain wind whistled fiercely, and Asahina shivered. "It would've been nicer to come in the springtime. February's so cold," she said in a lonely voice, even as she kept her soft smile, looking down on the dreary view. "This would be a nicer place if the flowers were blooming."

"We'll come then," I told her. "To see the blossoms. Give it a couple more months, and this cold air mass will have warmed right up."

"Oh, that would be lovely. Blossom watching! I'd love to try that." Asahina held her knees. "That would be in April...I'll be a senior by then."

That was true. In all likelihood, I'd be a junior, and Asahina would be a senior if she advanced—she wasn't going to repeat a year, right? I asked her.

"No, I'll be fine," she said with a sigh. "But...sometimes I think it would be nice to just do my junior year over, because then I'd be the same year as Kyon and everybody else. Right now I'm the only one who's ahead, but I don't feel like an upperclassman at all..."

She had absolutely no reason to worry about that. It had been Haruhi who said we needed a baby-faced, petite, sexy mascot and forced her into the club, and Haruhi who'd brook no complaint on the matter. If she'd wanted Asahina to be in the same year, she would've totally ignored any protest from Asahina and forced her to repeat a year or fail a class or something. For my part, I told her, I was satisfied if she just kept being the SOS Brigade's maid.

Asahina giggled. "Thank you." Possibly taking notice of Nagato reading nearby, she lowered her voice. "I hope I can be a little more worthwhile this year..."

Just as I was experiencing a spastic desire to run my mouth about the other Asahina, the sound of rustling underbrush announced Haruhi's return.

"What, you're taking a break already?"

I didn't want to hear any complaints, I said—I'd already been working for nearly two hours.

"Heh, fine. I'm getting pretty hungry myself." Haruhi seemed happy about something as she trotted over. "C'mon, Mikuru, let's have lunch."

"Uh, okay."

The sight of Asahina opening the picnic basket was a fine one indeed. The handmade sandwiches, rice balls, and side dishes she took out were the *real* treasure, as far as I was concerned. It wasn't an overstatement to say this was the reason I'd come along.

"..."

Nagato silently closed the book she was reading and looked intently at Asahina's handiwork. Koizumi stuck the shovel into the soft earth of the hole he'd just filled and walked over.

"That looks truly delicious," he said by way of his initial impression.

"Of course it looks delicious. You've been exercising," Haruhi butted in, filling her own paper cup from the thermos, then raising the cup into the air. "Well, then, here's to our hopes for successful treasure hunting!"

Now our trip seemed like a real picnic—if you ignored Koizumi's and my dirty clothes, that was.

I looked sideways as I stuffed my face with a seaweed rice ball. From what I could tell, Haruhi was enjoying her lunch with such gusto that it seemed like she'd forgotten all about the treasure hunt. I would've expected her to have gotten frustrated with Koizumi's and my failure to dig up anything interesting, grabbed a shovel, and started digging around herself, but she had been strangely happy all day. Almost as if going on a hike and eating lunch under the blue sky had been her goal all along.

Haruhi's actions lately had been just as incomprehensible as Asahina the Elder's future transmissions. She'd turned suddenly melancholy, then decided it was time for bean-tossing, then just when I thought she'd calmed down again, here we were on a treasure hunt...

It was fine, though. Compared with getting sucked into some stupid dimension filled with Celestials, or having cherry blossoms bloom in autumn, it was like the difference between taking a trip to the moon or the Andromeda nebula. Give me the moon any day of the week. One was a heavenly body on which humans had actually walked, and the other was an undiscovered frontier you'd have to use the galactic railroad to get to—there was a huge difference. Of course, I'd already experienced both closed space *and* unidentified falling blossoms...

Enjoying lunch in the mountains with all five of us was actually very nice. Nagato wasn't hesitating to dig right in, I noticed with relief, and she seemed very much herself. Haruhi seemed brimming with energy, and Koizumi was the usual Koizumi. Asahina was fine too, although when it came to her I knew there was another version holed up at Tsuruya's place, which made it hard for me to feel really at ease.

"Hey, Kyon, if we do find treasure, what're you gonna do with your share?" asked Haruhi, her mouth full of cutlet sandwich. I had fantasies like that all the time, so it was an easy question to answer.

"I'm gonna cash it in and buy a new game system with all the games I've wanted to play, then go to the used bookstore and buy back all the manga my mom made me sell off, then save the rest."

"You make it sound like it's your allowance. You gotta dream bigger than that!" Haruhi gulped down the sandwich in a flash and regarded me with a pitying smile.

So what would *she* do? I demanded.

"I don't really care about money, so even if we find the kind of treasure we'd be able to sell off, I don't think I'd do it. I mean, we went to all that trouble to get it, right? I'd lock it up for a while, then bury it again somewhere. Don't you think leaving a treasure map for your own descendants would be worth more than plain old money?"

Sure, a childish treasure hunt was fun and all, but I wasn't so overflowing with allowance I'd use it that way. If we found something useful, I'd happily keep it for myself, but if I didn't need it,

I'd rather just throw it away than take the trouble to bury it, I said.

"Oh, you're no fun," said Haruhi, her lips pursed in exasperation. But then she smiled. "I guess if you're just going to blow it on pointless stuff like that, I hope we find something you *can't* exchange for money. Right, Mikuru?"

"Eh?" Interrupted midbite, Asahina looked back and forth hesitantly as she simultaneously tried to set down her half-eaten lunch and cover her chewing mouth politely with her hand. "Er...y-yes, I guess—wait, no...um, I mean, maybe that would make everybody happier, or..." She trailed off as her eyes met Haruhi's and mine in turn. She waved her hands frantically. "I mean, I just hope we find some! Treasure, I mean."

"Oh, we'll find some treasure. I know these things."

Haruhi made her usual baseless assertions as she stuffed her face with a sandwich.

Nagato sat on the mat's corner, demolishing her lunch as though wanting to best Haruhi; beside her was Koizumi, down on one knee like a pop idol posing for a teenybopper magazine. He noticed my gaze and tipped his cup slightly, smiling wordlessly as Asahina watched the lunch she'd prepared get taken care of by Haruhi and Nagato.

For just a moment, I wasn't thinking about the letters from the future or the other Asahina hiding out at Tsuruya's house. I was just enjoying having a fun picnic lunch with everybody. Despite the unseasonal hike and the pointless treasure hunt, looking at the high-spirited Haruhi, the thankfully normal Nagato, along with Asahina and Koizumi being their usual selves, for a little while I felt like everything was going to be okay.

No...everything *had* to be okay.

Which made me remember the future that lay before me—there were things I had to do tomorrow and the next day in order to *keep* everything okay.

*   *   *

The pleasant lunch ended, after which Haruhi and I bickered for a bit just to settle our stomachs, though there was no point in relating the details. Finally she clapped and stood. I braced myself; the time had finally come.

"Well, then, time to start the afternoon treasure hunt!" Haruhi picked up the lunch boxes and thermoses and gave Asahina a sidelong glance. "I headed down the mountainside over there. There are so many trees on this mountain that there aren't many places to dig. Which means the treasure must be buried somewhere without trees. You can't dig holes on top of trees, after all."

I picked up my shovel.

"But I found an open space that looks pretty likely," said Haruhi. "Let's head that way. Plus, we can head straight down from there, so it'll be quicker to go home. We shouldn't have bothered to take the bus, really."

I looked and saw that Koizumi had already shouldered his shovel and was heading down the mountain. Nagato rolled up the mat we'd sat on, and Asahina carefully held on to the picnic basket, nodding meekly at Haruhi's pronouncement.

Haruhi bounded down the tree-filled, rock-strewn slope like an antelope. Though we weren't particularly in a hurry, Nagato followed smoothly after.

"Wah—eek!"

Asahina nearly tripped and fell several times, but each time Nagato came to her rescue—Koizumi and I were encumbered with the heavy shovels, and we couldn't help. I wanted to just toss the stupid shovel aside and assist Asahina, but for now I'd leave it to Nagato. Asahina bowed her head every time—*You're reading too much into it, Asahina*, I wanted to say.

Thanks to the nearly straight route we followed down the

mountain, it took almost no time to arrive at our destination, especially compared with how long it'd taken to climb up.

"This is the place. Isn't it strangely flat here? See?"

Haruhi stopped and indicated what she meant. There was no mistaking it. This was the same spot (Michiru) Asahina and I had visited the day before yesterday. This was the place. It was surrounded by tall trees, which kept it gloomy even at midday, and the memory of the crescent-shaped clearing and the fallen leaves that littered the ground was all too familiar to me.

The gourd-shaped rock stood there. It wasn't quite as brilliantly white as it had been before, but that was because of the rain. Having been coated in moisture, it was uniformly faded. The water had also washed off some of the dirt that had clung to it, so that if you didn't look too closely, the difference between the two sides wasn't apparent.

Yet when Haruhi strolled up to the rock, a chill ran through me. She was too damn perceptive, and I hoped she didn't sense anything amiss. Just then, she put her foot on the rock and casually kicked it over. Paying it no further mind, she sat down upon it.

"Kyon, Koizumi—time for phase two. Just start digging somewhere around there, okay?"

She smiled impishly. Koizumi immediately replied with a crisp "Understood" and immediately set to digging, but I had something else I was worried about.

The spot where the rock had originally been—(Michiru) Asahina and I had disguised it a bit, but close inspection would reveal that it had been disturbed. But when I looked—

"..."

Nagato had unrolled the mat on that very spot. I caught a quick glimpse of her expressionless eyes behind her hair. She didn't give me anything that seemed like a signal or a sign. I watched her silently sit on the mat and open her book, Buddha-like.

The corner-loving alien left a large space open on the mat, so Asahina hesitantly sat down as well. The two very different but nonetheless beautiful goddesses sitting in a pair like that made for quite a spectacle. Whoever sat between them would seem like a significant person indeed.

"Hey! Kyon, quit spacing out! Go help Koizumi!"

That "significant person" yelled like a construction foreman making sure nobody was slacking off. She sure did enjoy bossing people around. If some boss somewhere had Haruhi for their subordinate, they'd probably stop coming to work because of the stress. I picked up my shovel, reflecting on the fact that I'd probably never have that problem, and hurried over to Koizumi's side, where he had already started digging into the wet earth.

Let's just skip to the results.

As expected, no matter how much we dug we found not so much as a single fragment of pottery, to say nothing of treasure. That was exactly what (Michiru) Asahina had said would happen, so I wasn't a bit surprised. My shoulders slacked in a complicated feeling of relief, since I'd been constantly worried that by some mistake we would turn something up. This was all fine, but hadn't it been a bit too easy? I wondered.

"We're just not finding any buried treasure, are we?" said Haruhi, her head cocked. She noisily ate a chocolate cookie she'd gotten out as she sat on the gourd-shaped rock.

I took a break from shoveling dirt back into the holes and looked around the area. The once-undisturbed ground had been ravaged. Thanks to the constant excavating and reburying, it looked like a field that had just been plowed. It really would have been better to just leave nature alone.

"Oh well," said Haruhi with uncharacteristic perspective. "I don't really see anywhere else to dig, so we'll wrap things up right here."

She then finished by pointing right at her feet, directly in front of the gourd-rock on which she sat.

Koizumi and I dug as ordered. It was another hole that revealed nothing. We then shoved the soil back into the hole.

All we'd done was make the hard earth a nicer place for earthworms to live.

Just as I was wondering how Haruhi was going to react to not finding any treasure—

"Well, let's go home. The sun's getting low, and if we're up here any longer we're gonna freeze. We'll just go down this way. It comes right out near the road that leads to North High."

Koizumi and I gathered up our supplies, and after taking a moment to rest and have some Asahina Tea, we complied with the order to descend the mountain. It didn't seem like any of the bodies descending the narrow animal trail had any particular attachment to the treasure or the mountain. *C'mon, really?* I thought. *So we just went on a picnic and dug a bunch of holes?*

Koizumi's hand came to rest on my discouraged shoulder. "Come now, it's all right, isn't it?"

I didn't want him to lecture me. He reminded me of the way my mom was when I got angry, I said.

"Apologies. However, I'm quite tired myself, but I do think it would be best to leave the area promptly, before Haruhi spies another spot to excavate."

I agreed with him on that. Asahina and Nagato—who was carrying only the rolled-up mat—were both preparing to leave. I'd just been trying to figure out what was the point of everything I'd just done, I told Koizumi.

"The point?" Koizumi was behind me as I started walking, and I heard a smile creep into his voice. "Why not simply accept that Suzumiya is a capricious girl. Isn't that always so?"

Haruhi strode ahead, her attachment to the idea of treasure totally gone. Behind her walked Asahina, Nagato, and a bit farther, Koizumi and me.

There in the middle of the animal trail, Koizumi lowered his voice and continued. "However, it does seem a bit strange that there really was no treasure."

It was the kind of thing he'd say. For some reason I felt the same way.

"You can be sure of this: if Suzumiya truly believed that something was there, it would not matter whether Tsuruya's long-dead ancestor Fusauemon had actually buried something—we would have found something. Suzumiya has that kind of power."

Apparently so, if the stuff he said was true.

"Nevertheless, we were unable to find anything. This is rather mysterious. Do you know why?"

Because Haruhi herself hadn't really believed it, I guessed. A worthless treasure map like that? It had to be a prank from old man Fusauemon, I said.

Koizumi nodded quietly. "I see you understand the way of it. Suzumiya did not truly want to find Genroku-era treasure. That's the only possibility. We can conclude that all she wanted was to go on a picnic."

She could've just said so, instead of going to all the trouble of this treasure-hunting nonsense. Even I would've been on board for a picnic.

"Who can fathom a maiden's heart? She's been stable ever since winter vacation—*too* stable. Most likely she grew bored."

Well, that just made his job easier, then. It wasn't like the paycheck from his part-time job got lower when those blue giants appeared.

"No, wait." I raised my hand and searched for the words. "You said Haruhi's mental state has been stable? Ever since the beginning of February?"

"Yes. There have been subtle fluctuations, but nothing trending to the negative. If anything, her mood's been elevated."

So what had the vaguely depressed aura I'd felt from Haruhi all this time been? My imagination? I asked.

"Is that what you felt?" Koizumi asked with mild surprise. "She seemed like her usual self to me."

Wasn't he supposed to be the expert on Haruhi's psychology? How come he hadn't picked up on something I'd noticed? Was he planning on quitting his amateur analyst racket? I asked.

"That would be nice," he said, his usual smile returning as he regarded me. "If you're truly better at interpreting Suzumiya's mind than I am, I'll gladly hand over my role—including fighting the Celestials in closed space. You haven't visited that world in a while, after all."

Forget that. I had no desire to go back. All things considered, I preferred it here, I said.

"That's a shame. That said, I haven't been in a while myself."

It must be frustrating to be an esper and never get to use your powers. Why not put together a closed space tour package? I bet all kinds of weirdos would love to see the place, I said.

"I'll take that under advisement. Although it will take a significant amount of courage to deliver such a proposal to my superiors."

As Koizumi and I played verbal catch, we came to the same field-dividing footpath I'd visited the day before yesterday. Having descended ahead of us, Haruhi, along with Nagato and Asahina, was waiting there. The three of them standing there in the golden light of sunset beside the fallow rice field—if an impressionist painter had seen them, he probably would've started painting right away. But before I could take the time to appreciate the view—

"There's no need to head all the way back to the train station. We'll just be dismissed right here." Haruhi collected my shovel and smiled, satisfied. "That was fun. It's good to get out in nature sometimes. We didn't find any treasure, but that's no reason to be depressed. I'm sure we'll find it eventually. And the time will come when we're glad we got this experience. We'll have to tell Tsuruya too. Maybe next time we'll find a Muromachi-era map!"

I didn't care what era the treasure was from; I was finished with maps. You can tell *that* to Tsuruya—that whatever happened, she shouldn't give Haruhi anything else.

But as I watched Haruhi's form recede along the road, bouncing merrily, two shovels in hand, I didn't say the nasty things I was thinking. I didn't know whether or not her strange silence in the classroom had been my imagination or not, but in any case, I was glad she was happy. When she got weirdly quiet like that, it just made me nervous that her internal power gauge was building up to an explosion. Huh? Why did it suddenly seem like I was monologuing to myself?

Once we emerged onto the road that led to North High, we walked as a group for a little while. Eventually we got to the usual spot where we parted ways, whereupon Haruhi turned around, as though having suddenly remembered something.

"Oh, that's right! We're gonna meet up at the station tomorrow too. Same time as today. Got it?"

If I said I couldn't, would she reschedule? I asked.

Haruhi looked at me with a grin. What was up with that grin?

"We're gonna search the city for mysterious phenomena. We haven't done it in a while, after all," said Haruhi, not answering my question at all. She looked at everybody as though checking them out. "You guys got that? And don't be late. Tardiness..."

She drew a deep breath of cold air, then finished her statement the same way she always did.

"...equals punishment!"

The first things I did upon returning to my room were turning on the heater and getting out my cell phone.

By this time it had become part of my normal routine to call—where else?—the Tsuruya house. By now I was well used to the voice of the polite female servant who answered, as well as the smooth transfer to Asahina. By this point, I'd called Tsuruya more often than I'd ever called Koizumi.

"It's me."

"Ah, hello. It's me—Michiru...I mean, Mikuru."

"Is Tsuruya at the house?"

"No...she seems to be out today. She said her family was attending a memorial service."

I got the feeling that it was best not to pry too much into what Tsuruya was doing and where.

"Asahina, we went and did it."

"You mean the treasure hunt...?"

"We didn't find anything, though."

I could hear Asahina let a little sigh slip past her lips. "Thank goodness it turned out the way I remember. If it had been different, I don't know what I would've done."

The phone still pressed to my ear, I furrowed my brow. "Is there any way that could possibly have happened? Isn't the past always the same, no matter where you go?"

"Uh...er, that's, that's true, but..."

I could practically see Asahina holding the receiver as she wavered.

"It's extremely rare, but sometimes things change...er...I don't really understand it myself, but—"

I remembered something as I listened to the hesitant voice. The double loop Koizumi explained, when I told him about the December eighteenth date I'd visited so many times.

When I thought about it, I was the same, insofar as even now I didn't know from when to when the period of fixed events extended. When Nagato had changed an entire year, how had she managed that? According to Koizumi's theory, there were two Decembers the eighteenth. It was too much trouble to have multiple timelines, so this timeline—the one we'd corrected—was the "right" one, I was pretty sure...

So what had that other thing been? Last month, I'd saved a little boy from being killed in a traffic accident. That little glasses-wearing guy living longer must have been a fixed, required event. But what about that car? What if someone had been trying to run that boy down in an effort to manually interfere?

That would mean that there were people trying to destroy the timeline, as well as time travelers from the future like Asahina who were trying to protect it. What if the former were also from the future? Who could oppose them? Only fellow time travelers.

I was starting to see what Asahina the Elder was up to. What she was trying to get me to do.

"I'm sorry, Kyon," said Asahina, dejected. "I'm restricted from telling you the things I want to tell you, and I don't know anything useful... Kyon, I just..."

I could tell she was about to cry. "Anyway, about tomorrow," I said frantically.

Exactly according to the plans Asahina had related to me, Haruhi had said we were doing a city patrol tomorrow. Since Asahina and I had to carry out the instructions of the #3 envelope, we'd need to decide on a place to meet up—someplace where Haruhi and the other Asahina wouldn't spot us.

"Asahina, do you think you could wear a disguise?"

"A disguise?" She sounded confused, and she sniffled. I could picture it very clearly.

"Like sunglasses?... No, I guess that'd be weird. It wouldn't be strange to wear a flu mask this time of year, though, right? Could you do that?"

"Oh, sure. I'll ask Tsuruya for one."

"So about the time. About when did we finish up tomorrow?"

"Umm..." Asahina took only a moment to remember. "It was at five o'clock. We met up at three, then we all went to the café."

I took the #3 envelope out of my desk and opened the contents. The place it indicated was about a ten-minute walk from the train station where the brigade would meet up. Even if it took fifteen minutes, that was still only a half-hour round-trip.

It would be best to have Asahina lay low at Tsuruya's place in the morning, then rendezvous with her a little while after the city patrol started.

Having asked her the details of the day's schedule, I explained where and when we'd meet up.

"Okay then, see you tomorrow. Try to dress as unobtrusively as you can. Oh, also"—I felt a tinge of foreboding in my chest—"if you can, can you get Tsuruya to come along? Tell her I asked her to. Or . . . well, no, I shouldn't get her involved in this. Don't worry about it. It would be good if she could see you off and meet you when we're done, though."

Asahina would have to go from Tsuruya's house to the rendezvous point on her own. Maybe I was overthinking it, but my danger sense was tingling. I didn't want to make her walk alone.

"O-okay. I'll tell her."

Tsuruya was smart—she'd see through my request in an instant. I could count on it.

I hung up, then immediately called Nagato. Here I was, asking another favor of her.

However.

"Huh?"

To my great surprise, her line was busy.

Who could Nagato possibly be talking to? I couldn't think of anybody short of a hard-sell telemarketer. I put down my phone and changed clothes, feeling sympathy for the headset jockey who'd been unlucky enough to wind up talking to Nagato. I threw my muddy pants into the washing machine, then came back to my room and tried again.

This time, she picked up.

"It's me."

" . . . "

Nagato's familiar silence.

"I've got a favor to ask you. It's about tomorrow. You know how we always split up the patrols by drawing straws? Tomorrow and the day after, I want you to rig them."

"I see," answered the cool, clear, high voice.

"Yeah. Tomorrow's afternoon patrol, and the next day's morning one—both of those times, I need to be paired up with you. Can you do it?"

"…" There was a slightly long-seeming silence, then, "I see."

I was pretty sure that was the affirmative, but I thought I'd make sure.

"So you'll do it, then?"

"Understood."

"Thanks, Nagato."

"It's fine."

"By the way, when I called a second ago, the line was busy. Who were you talking to?"

There was another silence, as though time itself had stopped. Just as I was starting to wonder if she was having some kind of side story with somebody I didn't know—

"Haruhi Suzumiya."

Now I *wished* it had been somebody I didn't know. "She called you?"

"Yes."

"What the heck did she want with you?"

"…" A third silence. I strained to hear and was starting to pick up a sense of anxiety over the receiver when Nagato finally replied.

"I cannot say."

Nagato sure had been full of surprises these past few days. To think she'd be using that line on *me*, of all people.

I stayed as silent as a radio that'd been unplugged.

"It is better if you do not know."

That was certainly a terrifying statement—those were just about the least comforting words in the world, I said.

168

"... Do not worry." Her voice had a hesitant tone to it, as though she wasn't sure whether she should say anything but had decided that she wanted me not to worry. And then it came to me.

"Haruhi told you not to say anything, didn't she?"

"Yes."

Which meant Haruhi was up to something weird again, and she was trying to involve Nagato in it.

And whatever it was, it was a secret from me. I didn't know what it was, but based on Nagato's tone, it had to be something big. Like round two of the treasure hunt or something.

This week sure was turning out to be a busy one—like having final exams in math, physics, and world history all on the same day.

"Dammit, Haruhi, what're you gonna make us do *this* time...?"

At this rate, Koizumi was going to wind up being my only true comrade. Haruhi, Nagato, and Asahina were all engaged in activities beyond my influence. Oh, and Tsuruya too. I wondered why it was that no matter the life-form, females always seemed to outmatch the males. The double-X chromosome was a terrifying thing. Explain it to me, please.

I lay down on the floor and spread my arms wide, praying that I'd be able to pass the following week in peace.

CHAPTER FIVE

The next day—Saturday morning.

My upper body ached all over thanks to all the unpaid manual labor I'd done the day before. At least I'd slept well and hadn't had any weird dreams.

I put envelope #3 into my coat pocket as I went out the front door, then got my bike out, whose tire pressure was on the low side as I headed out onto the street through the cold, dry wind.

I didn't want to park illegally and get my bike hauled off by a local merchant, so I paid to park in the new bike parking structure in front of the station, then headed on foot to the meeting place, where as usual I was the last to arrive.

Asahina looked like some new adorable species of pet as she came up to greet me in a warm-looking outfit, while Koizumi was his usual self, handsome enough to get one in five high school girls to turn around and take another look. Nagato wore a hooded duffle coat over her school uniform, standing stock still and looking vaguely like a Jawa.

Wearing a peacoat and a muffler, Haruhi pointed right at me. "We've been waiting, Kyon! Thirty whole seconds!"

It had been a close thing. If I'd just left my bike nearby, I could've been the second-to-last arrival for round one of the Citywide Mysterious Phenomena Search. I would've liked to see Haruhi treat everybody, just once, I said.

"Oh, I'd treat you, all right, if I actually ever arrived last. But let me just say that I hate words like 'last place' and 'runner-up' more than anything. If I think I might oversleep and be late, I'll just arrive the night before and stay all night!"

Haruhi smiled fearlessly. She seriously seemed like she was ready to take on any and all comers. We should've done something like this back when she was depressed. And speaking of the past, I wondered which kind of regret was worse—regretting something you'd done, or something you *hadn't* done?

As I thought it over fruitlessly, Haruhi dragged us all over to the café.

"We didn't find anything yesterday," she said as she drank her hot coffee, "but when I think about it, the purpose of the SOS Brigade isn't to search for lost inheritances, but stuff that's way more mysterious than that. I mean, like…something futuristic, or top secret, or something. There's gotta be at least one thing like that in this city. There's a lot of space in it, after all."

It wasn't a question of land area. The important elements were things like economic prosperity and population density—"Aw, forget it."

I gave up. Prosperity and population don't have anything to do with it, do they, Haruhi? Mysterious phenomena exist right in front of you, and you have no idea. And *because* you have no idea, they can go about their business without anyone being the wiser.

In my case, I hadn't noticed them so much as I'd been *made* to notice them, but I was glad to know. And because you sat right behind me, that was your fault too—or should I say it was thanks to you?

Haruhi marked toothpicks with a ballpoint pen as I silently

monologued to myself, then she held them out such that we could all draw one.

"This is how we'll split up into teams. Two of the toothpicks have marks and three don't."

I reflexively glanced at Nagato. Whoops—too soon. There was no need for me to be forcibly paired up with her this morning. What had Asahina said about that? That's right; it had been Koizumi and me.

"What's wrong? Hurry up and draw." Haruhi thrust the fist containing the five toothpicks at me. "Do you actually care about what the teams are? Oh ho, is there someone in particular you want to pair up with? You're such a baby."

I didn't like the patronizing way she smiled at me. But no matter how much I thought about it, I got nowhere. When she'd delivered her future prediction, Asahina had told me that Koizumi and I would get paired up. I couldn't just pick any toothpick and get the same outcome. The chances of picking a marked one were two in five, so under normal circumstances, there were better odds of getting an unmarked one—but what happened if I did that? Would things still work out even if events diverged from Asahina's memory?

My overthinking went too far. As I silently agonized, Haruhi pulled the toothpicks away from me and had the three other brigade members each draw one. When she got back to me, there were only two left.

I hastily checked Koizumi. The toothpick he elegantly held between his fingertips was indeed marked.

This left just Haruhi and me to draw the remaining two, and since Haruhi's habit was to always save the last lot for herself, the groups would be decided by my draw.

I closed my eyes and took a deep breath, focusing my concentration for ten full seconds on Haruhi's hand.

"What're you doing? Isn't that a bit much?" said Haruhi, irritated, but it was an important step for me. If I couldn't make events match up here, things were only going to get more complicated.

"The hell with it!" I said, moving my right hand quickly. I was going to just randomly grab the first one I touched, but it didn't go the way I'd planned. It was *too* random. I knocked both toothpicks out of Haruhi's hand, and as I realized my mistake one fell to the table while Haruhi grabbed the other one out of midair. The toothpick that had fallen to the table had a spot on one end.

"That's no fun," said Haruhi, her lip twisting. "We're divided into all girls and all boys. How boring."

I'd gotten all worked up for nothing. The morning groupings weren't important to the timeline; if I'd drawn the unmarked toothpick I would've had the double bonus of both Asahina *and* Nagato, which was a lot better than spending my precious day off with Koizumi, and when I thought about it like that, I realized that small changes to the past probably didn't matter. I shouldn't have worried about it.

After idling around for a little while longer, we left the café. I paid, of course. Force of habit can be a terrible thing, and I hated myself for naturally picking up the check without being forced into it.

"Um, I'm sorry, Kyon. Thank you," said Asahina apologetically—she was the only one who made me feel better about having to pay. Koizumi also apologized, but somehow his pleasant smile didn't help my mood.

"If you're concerned about the status of your wallet, I can recommend a good part-time job," said Koizumi quietly, walking alongside me as we exited the café. "It's a very simple job, and once you get used to it, it's very easy. I can guarantee the compensation is good too."

"No thanks."

I had a vision of a demon hiding behind a sweet smile. If I blithely signed the strange contract he gave me, I'd wind up getting whisked away to some terrible laboratory and spread out on an operating table—it didn't bear thinking about. What if they decided to turn me into a part-time esper? I had no desire to go battle against Haruhi's stress level within the confines of that strange, gray dimension, I told him.

"I would handle that. What you would do would be to make sure that I don't *have* to battle her stress level."

He could do that himself, I told him.

"You're the only one who can do it, it seems. At the moment, anyway."

I didn't recall having any supernatural abilities.

"I suppose not." Koizumi pursed the corners of his lips into a smile. "If you ever change your mind, let me know. I'll be happy to explain the job to you. Though for my part I feel I've already told you most of it."

Koizumi sounded uncharacteristically vague, but I didn't pursue the matter. I suspected he'd tell me something I didn't want to hear. If I made some smart remark, he might turn the tables on me, and then I'd wish I hadn't said anything. Sometimes caution was necessary. If you wanted to trap someone, you had to start on the defensive.

Outside the café, Haruhi had waited for me to pay. "We'll meet back up at noon on the dot." Haruhi had her right arm around Nagato's waist and her left around Asahina's, as she grinned as brightly as a tropical flower. "Until then, look for anything mysterious—a manhole that wasn't there yesterday, an extra stripe in the crosswalk, anything! If you keep your eyes peeled you should be able to find something. No—*expect* to find something. If you don't, you'll never find anything!"

There she was, squeezing herself between the ultimate combination of an alien and a time traveler like they were human-size body warmers, and—ah, forget it. If I'd had to find "something mysterious" in a scavenger hunt, I'd grab Haruhi herself and drag her straight to the finish line, but that wasn't the point either. The biggest mystery of all was how I'd wound up being part of this bizarre group, but I couldn't very well lump them all together and show them to Haruhi. Just as she instinctually sought out mysteries, I just wanted to keep living my life. That was the simple truth.

Haruhi proclaimed that they were heading "that way, across the train tracks," so I saw Asahina and Nagato off as they crossed, then retied my muffler.

"Got any idea where we should go?" I asked my companion for the next two hours.

Koizumi managed good cheer despite looking as though the cold was about to freeze him solid. "Even if I did, I very much doubt you'd be willing to follow me. Let's just enjoy a nice walk."

Surprisingly, once we started walking, Koizumi didn't start saying his usual nonsensical things. We watched the silhouettes of the big carp in the canal, impressed at their vigor. We went into a convenience store and browsed the magazines. Basically we acted like two bored high school students.

We talked about the upcoming final exams, what had been on TV the night before—until I suddenly realized that having such a normal conversation with him doubled my suspicion, and I said as much.

"I'm an esper who appears to be a normal high school student. Outward appearances like this are very important," said Koizumi as he crossed the street, appearing to count the stripes on the crosswalk. "It's not as though I want to be an esper forever. If I could pass my powers to someone else, I sometimes feel like I'd happily do so." He smiled at me, as though that were supposed to make me feel better. "Only sometimes. If I had to choose, I'd choose the way I am now. Being able to interact with time travelers and non-terrestrial life-forms is an incredibly rare opportunity. Though I can't compare with you."

From my perspective, he was just as rare as the two people he was talking about, I told him.

"While I don't know when the title of 'esper' might be taken from me, I do know that I'll only be a high school student for a certain amount of time—so long as Suzumiya doesn't repeat a grade. So I've got to make the most of being a high school student, while I still can."

I thought back on the insane events of the past year. "Well, from where I'm standing it looks like you're doing just fine. Especially during the summer and winter trips," I said.

"Those were both because I'm a member of the Agency. Soon it will be four years since I joined, but if I'd never received the strange powers I have, I would never have transferred to North High, and I would've lived a life totally unconcerned with little things like the fate of the entire world."

"So what?" I said as I walked, looking up at the flashing pedestrian signal. "I don't know anything about supernatural powers, but I *do* know that it's thanks to those powers that you're here. Don't blame them. Or are you just frustrated because you wound up in a stupid club like the SOS Brigade? Go ahead and write a resignation letter. Give it a try. I'll even give it to Haruhi for you."

Koizumi's mouth curled into a forced smile. "No thanks," he said after a moment. Then, in an amused tone: "Just as you've now found a certain defiance, I've come to hold Suzumiya, you, and the rest of the brigade in a regard I would've found unimaginable when I first met you. I'm the lieutenant brigade chief and all...but now, there's no need to use that title. Do you remember what I said to you during the snowy mountain incident?"

Of course I did. I'd never forget it. And if he ever went back on the promise he made then, I'd join with Haruhi and come up with a punishment the likes of which he'd never seen, I said.

"That's a relief. If I ever suffer from amnesia, things will be all right—you'll remember for me." Koizumi smiled pleasantly, exhaling white vapor. "While I don't want to think that Nagato will easily find herself in such a predicament very often, I will always do what I can."

I wished he'd express such determination on behalf of the rest of his friends, I said.

"I should think that would go without saying. Asahina's always been the sort of person you want to protect. You just want to take care of her, somehow. That's something of a supernatural ability in and of itself."

Having made it across the crosswalk, Koizumi suddenly stopped and checked his watch, which prompted me to do the same. We'd done quite a bit of wandering around. It would be time to meet back up soon.

Just as I was beginning to head back to the station, I heard Koizumi's quiet voice from about three steps behind me.

"The current Asahina is someone both the Agency and I wish to protect. But please be careful. The same may not be true for the other Asahina, the one with a different outfit from your Asahina."

Asahina the Elder's silhouette flashed across my retinas. I kept walking, not looking back, and Koizumi's voice became more distant.

"There's no guarantee she'll bring us—the SOS Brigade—only good fortune."

Maybe not. But you said this too.

"If so," I said, "we just have to change that future. Starting now."

The three girls were waiting for us when Koizumi and I returned to the station.

"Did you find anything?" Haruhi asked us.

But you can't find what you're not looking for. "No," was my honest answer. "Did you find anything interesting? If you didn't, you can't complain about us."

"Yeah, we didn't really find anything very mysterious," said Haruhi, seeming neither depressed nor irritated. Her smile was actually rather alarming. "But! We went to the department store and ate a bunch of free samples in the supermarket. That was fun, right?"

Haruhi smiled encouragingly at Asahina.

"O-oh, yes, it was," said Asahina, rapidly nodding her head. Her soft chestnut hair fluttered about like butterflies in a garden. "It was nice seeing all the different things. I bought some new tea too."

The happily smiling Asahina seemed to have really gotten in the shopping mood. And when I looked more carefully, I saw that Nagato was holding a bag from the bookstore. Just what "mysterious phenomena" had these three gone in search of, if they'd wound up at the grocery store and the bookstore? I suppose if you wanted mysterious stories, the bookstore was the place to go.

"I don't see what the problem is," said Haruhi nonchalantly. "If you get hasty, you'll just wind up regretting it later. It's when you're in a hurry that you've got to be careful. It's just like driving a car. If you're going too fast, that's gonna be the difference between getting in an accident and avoiding it. It'll happen *because* you were sure it wasn't going to happen."

She was not making a lot of sense, I told her.

"It's very simple, Kyon. Look—" Haruhi said haughtily. "It's like playing Red Light, Green Light. People move when you're not looking, but as soon as you turn around, they freeze. Mysterious phenomena are the same way. But if you never turn around at all, they'll just sneak right by you, so you gotta seize the right moment. It's all about timing, Kyon—*timing.*"

That was even less comprehensible. I suppose it was all consistent in Haruhi's head, but she was talking as though the metaphorical Lady Luck were an *actual lady,* which was not helpful. Only people receiving strange transmissions on unknown wavelengths had any hope of catching an incorporeal concept.

"Anyway, where do you want to go for lunch?"

Apparently my doubts were unimportant.

"There's a new Italian place across from the bank. I heard they've got a good lunch menu, so I made a reservation for the five of us."

Evidently Haruhi was now in full-on city-girl mode. Once she'd made up her mind like this, a monk whispering sutras into the ear of a horse would have a better chance of changing its mind than I would of Haruhi's. At least the monk would be racking up good karma.

"Fine with me," I said. "What about you, Koizumi?"

I wondered what would happen if he said something ridiculous like, "No thanks, I can't stand tomato sauce," but Koizumi would never oppose any plan of Haruhi's. "Sure," he said with a smile.

"It's decided, then." Haruhi reaffirmed the decision she'd obviously already made, then we double-timed it straight over to the Italian place just in time for the lunch rush. By the time we got there my muscles were all aching afresh.

Haruhi was no different from a cat—and there was such a thing as being too mischievous. When she was depressed I'd feel like it was better if she were her usual too-energetic self, but part of me wondered if the day when she was on an even keel would ever come.

I finished the ice water the waiter brought me in about three seconds, and when I looked to see if I'd be able to get a refill—yeah, it looked like it would take about the same amount of time it would take for Asahina the Younger to become Asahina the Elder.

After finishing her reasonably priced lunch—the doria special of the day—Haruhi took out her toothpicks and reshuffled them.

We were approaching the climax of the day. It was a little confusing, since there was Asahina, right in front of me, but the reason I had to worry about what happened here was because of the other Asahina, Michiru Asahina. I hoped she'd be waiting for me.

I looked askance at Nagato, who'd inhaled her lunch and spent the rest of the time silently rereading the menu. Nagato was now watching the five toothpicks dispassionately. I couldn't imagine she'd forgotten my request, so I calmed myself and immediately drew a toothpick.

It had a mark on it.

Nagato was the next to reach out, and she immediately drew the other marked toothpick, then set it carefully on the table.

"Oh, I guess we don't have to keep drawing," said Haruhi.

If she had used some kind of trick, Nagato wasn't so clumsy as to let Haruhi notice. Haruhi flicked the remaining three toothpicks into the ashtray and stood, our meal check in hand. Which is not to say she treated us—no, we split the check evenly, down to the last yen.

We finished paying and reemerged into the cold wind, again to wander aimlessly across the city like migrating fish. But I would leave that to Haruhi, Asahina, and Koizumi. Nagato and I had a different path to walk—along with another Asahina, from three days in the future.

Whenever I walk alone with Nagato, I can't help but remember that first spring day. She'd still been wearing her glasses then, her expression as cold as an ice factory. Come to think of it, that's when Nakagawa had first seen us too.

Nagato followed silently about two steps behind me. She was so quiet that I was constantly checking behind me to make sure she was keeping up. There she was, staring at my muffler, her face as cold and impassive as melting snow.

It was an emotional moment, thanks to our destination. The city library. Nagato went there quite often now, but I was the one who'd first taken her there, back when she'd still had glasses, so it was a memorable place for both of us.

And just like that first time, we'd taken our leave from Haruhi and the others, and I'd brought her here. The only difference was that this time, she already had a library card. And no glasses.

We walked down the street that led to the library, neither of us speaking. It's rare to have someone you can enjoy such silences with. If Haruhi or Koizumi had been that quiet, I would've wondered what they were up to. But with Nagato, it was just the way she was.

Enjoying the companionable silence, I entered the library and surveyed the interior. As though to save me the trouble of looking, a short figure who'd been sitting on one of the couches came trotting over to me.

The figure was wrapped in a long coat and shawl that looked like something Tsuruya would wear, along with a knit cap and white flu mask—her disguise, presumably.

But (Michiru) Asahina couldn't hide her large eyes, which blinked rapidly.

"Kyon...oh, and Nagato..."

It was the library, so we had to keep quiet. Asahina put her hand in front of her mouth in a "shhh" gesture, so I took the cue from her and spoke quietly. "Tsuruya isn't here?"

"No." Asahina hesitantly looked over my shoulder. She really didn't have anything to be afraid of, but still. "She said she had important plans today, so she didn't come along. Oh, but"—Asahina waved her hands—"she had a car take me from her house to here. She told me to take a taxi back and gave me the fare..."

I was a little worried about what Tsuruya's "important plans" were, but Asahina's saucer-wide eyes were my immediate problem. I looked behind me, just to make sure there wasn't a ghost of some kind behind me, in addition to Nagato.

"..."

Nagato regarded Asahina with her unwaveringly expressionless gaze. I suddenly remembered that the night before, I'd only asked her to rig the outcome of the toothpick drawing.

I hadn't told her *why*.

"Oh, uh, Nagato—"

"…"

Asahina's disguise would barely fool a normal person, to say nothing of Nagato.

"This is the other Asahina," I said.

"I know," came Nagato's reply, which was hard to follow up.

"Ah, oh, right. You met her a few days ago."

"…"

"Yeah…that's right."

"…"

"I-I'm sorry."

As I stood there between the inexplicably apologetic Asahina and the inverted icicle of Nagato, the librarian behind the circulation counter stared at me like I was a sleeping panda—I wouldn't forget her glare for days.

However, Nagato was Nagato. After hearing ten seconds of explanation, she intoned, "I see," nodding microscopically even as she stood stock-still.

Incidentally, my explanation consisted of me saying, "I have to go do something with Asahina now, so I'm really sorry, but could you wait here until we get back?" Nagato seemed to have understood everything by the time I got to the "could you wait" part.

She walked off toward a bookshelf filled with gigantic science books, not even glancing as Asahina, who took Nagato's place behind me.

"Shall we go, Asahina?" I said as I watched Nagato's duffle coat disappear behind the bookshelf. The library's wall clock indicated two o'clock in the afternoon.

"…Um, Kyon?" said Asahina in a stiff-sounding tone. "Did you bring Nagato here without explaining anything to her?"

"Uh, yeah, it just slipped my mind."

"That's not—you can't just—" Asahina shook her head. "Even Nagato would be angry at that."

I felt bad. I mean, Asahina seemed like she was angry at me. Not that I thought it was okay if Nagato was angry—

A sigh was directed my way. "I'm…okay. But you should give Nagato a proper apology. Okay?"

Asahina had her older-student vibe at full blast as she turned aside and walked out of the library. For quite some time she stared out at the opposite lane of the street; I didn't know what to do.

After ten minutes of walking in the winter wind, maybe it was because I'd gotten so cold, or maybe it was the fact that without anyone to talk to I'd resorted to reading the number plates on the telephone poles we passed, but in any case the tense mood between Asahina and me faded.

I opened the letter one last time, making sure that we were on the right path, then we stopped in front of a row of flower boxes that were placed alongside the walk.

"Wow, they're really blooming."

The flowers had some serious guts. I wondered if the box that ran along the sidewalk of this north-south prefectural road had been placed by the city government or the prefecture. I was impressed at the blossoms' resistance to the cold of winter and the passing cars' exhaust, but they seemed to be blooming a little too much. Having to search for a lost item among the flower boxes that extended for a good ten meters made it feel like it was my fate to continue the previous day.

I looked over the two sheets, careful not to let them blow away in the wind.

"So we've got to find it somewhere around here…"

It seemed like it would take quite a while to search every corner of the flower box. I hadn't taken that into account.

"I don't think it will take too long," said Asahina, pointing at the box. "Look, the only place pansies are blooming is that corner."

Cursing the fact that I hadn't paid any attention thus far to flower variety, I looked where Asahina was pointing. There grew some small, pale blue flowers, which fluttered in the wind.

"Those over there are pheasant's-eyes, and those other flowers are cyclamen. Next to them are . . . I think they're violas?"

I had no idea she knew so much about flowers, I told her.

Asahina giggled. "I learned all kinds of things after I came here. Including about plants."

Thank goodness. She'd saved me from having to go on another needle-in-a-haystack-type treasure hunt. All I had to do now was look near the pansies.

"Oh, please don't step on the flowers."

I tried to heed the seriousness in Asahina's words as I put my foot on the edge of the flower box and looked down through the pansies; she cared very deeply for the flowers.

The object I was looking for was some kind of data medium. I had no idea why something like that would wind up in a place like this, but I decided to ignore those doubts for the moment. A time traveler had told me it had been dropped here, so it had been dropped here. Otherwise this menial errand wasn't even that.

As Asahina watched over me, I squatted down and gently brushed aside the pansies' stems, and as their leaves parted, I searched the corner of the flower box. I wanted to get this done as soon as I could. This wasn't a spot where there was a lot of passing automotive or pedestrian traffic, but I wouldn't blame anybody for thinking I was vandalizing the flowers. I poked around amid the roots of the pansies, praying a random police car didn't pass by.

*　　*　　*

After about thirty minutes of that, I wiped the dirt off of one hand against my pants while I wiped my forehead with the other.

It was strange.

I couldn't find anything. I'd searched everywhere in the corner with the pansies, with more concentration than I'd ever managed on the sentences for English reading classes. I even gave other groups of flowers the same treatment, searching among the cyclamen and violas as well.

But I didn't find anything more man-made than a rock, to say nothing of a data storage device.

Asahina had joined me midsearch, but even with her carefully double-checking the spots I'd looked at, the two of us toiled in vain.

"What could this mean...?"

If there wasn't anything here, there was no way Asahina the Elder wouldn't know about it. The girl that was kneeling down and hunting around under the flowers, (Michiru) Asahina, was Asahina the Elder's former self. I couldn't imagine her telling us to do something that was doomed from the start.

"What should we do, Kyon?" Asahina asked, on the verge of tears. "If we don't find it, we're gonna be in big trouble. The coded message said I absolutely *had* to. If I don't do what it says, I'll..."

She hadn't noticed that her flu mask had come loose and was dangling from one ear. Asahina's composure had been rattled when we'd met up with Nagato earlier, but now she looked seriously upset. And to be honest, so was I. But just as I'd talked myself into digging up the entire flower bed—

"Is this what you're looking for?"

I heard an unfamiliar voice behind me. It didn't belong to anyone I knew, and something about it made me instinctively rise to my feet. There was no hesitation; my body moved without thought.

I spread my arms out to protect Asahina, and I faced the sidewalk.

About five steps away, there stood a man about my age. I'd never seen him before. This was definitely the first time I'd met him—yet something about him made me instantly loathe him. There was something unmistakably negative about his facial expression.

Between his fingers he held a small stick-like object, which he held up as though it were something filthy. It resembled the black data storage device from the letter.

"What a boring scene this is. Rummaging around in the flowers for half an hour—I'm seriously impressed. I'd never be able to do it." He twisted his cruel lips into a thin sneer—I may be insensitive, but I could tell this guy was mocking me.

"You're quite commendable." He gazed at me as though looking down at something very small. "Doing these filthy chores without even knowing why; you just live your obedient little life. I certainly couldn't do it. Don't you have anything better to do?"

The past year of crazy events had instilled in me an instinctive sense for dangerous situations, and it was getting into the yellow zone. But there was no point in just knowing when you were in danger—it was only by actually avoiding it that you could later tell the story and say, "Man, that was a close one." When the danger you expected actually showed up, it could still wind up being the end of you, so you couldn't take it easy just because you'd expected it. Once you'd perceived the unwelcome arrival of your demise, you had to *do* something about it—and this was that moment.

"Where'd you get that?" I asked, at which the bastard just grinned.

"Right out of that flower bed. I made sure to grab it just before you two showed up. It was easy, really."

"Hand it over." I tried to sound as forceful as I could, but the guy just snickered through his nose.

"It's not yours, is it, so why should I? Lost items should be turned over to the police."

"I'll give it to them. Or better yet, I'll give it to its owner. That's faster than giving it to the police."

"Heh." His laugh was infuriating. "So you think the name and address that's on that letter is the person who dropped this? Who told you that? Was it the alien?"

That bastard! So he knew about Nagato? No, wait—how did he know about the letter? I'd only showed it to Asahina.

Which meant he was a...

Asahina held my arm, trembling. "Do you know this guy?" I asked her, my voice a mix of surprise and confusion.

"No!" she said, shaking her head. "I don't know him. He's not in my...um...he's not one of the people I know."

"It doesn't matter who I am. It's not like I'm going to just eat you guys up right now. I just thought this would be a nice opportunity."

He blew on the object he held as though blowing dust off of it, then grinned a loathsome grin. It was the kind of smile an evil version of Koizumi might use. His fine features made it seem even more threatening.

So, what to do? If I went in to slug him, could I get the data storage device back? But if he were some kind of aberration, our chances of victory were slim, even two-on-one. Damn—I should've brought Nagato with me.

I agonized over whether to clench my fists in a fighting pose or try to reach my pocketed cell phone.

"Hmph." He sniffed as though having lost interest, and he snapped his fingers. The small object arced through the air and toward the earth in front of me. I reached out to catch it before it hit the ground. "You can have it. Those're my orders, anyway.

You just keep doing as you're told—being past puppets for your future masters."

I looked at the object in my hands. It looked like a memory card for a digital camera, but it was a variety I'd never seen before—I wasn't an expert, so it was hard to be sure. It was slightly dirty, probably from having been dropped in the flower bed.

We'd gotten what we came for, which, no matter the method, was a good thing. What wasn't good was the man standing in front of us.

"Who are you? And how did you know we were coming?"

"Hm." The man's thin lips became still thinner. "Isn't there something you should be asking before that? Why did you come here? Why is that? Don't you need to know that first?"

Being lectured sanctimoniously by a guy my age really ticked me off. But I had to take the long view. I wouldn't let my feelings get the best of me.

And I had to think of Asahina, who directed a terrified gaze at the stranger.

"I'm not the one you should be cross-examining," he said, his dangerous eyes slipping from me to her. "Isn't that right, Mikuru Asahina?"

Asahina flinched, her grip suddenly tightening. "Wha—what are you talking about? I don't know you. Have we...?" she said, clinging to my coat.

The guy's lips curled into a sneer. "That's about it. We'll just leave it that this is the first time you've said hello to me. You pass—very good. But I'll be saying a different sort of hello to you. Do you understand what I'm saying, Mikuru Asahina?"

It would've been hard to forgive even a fraction of this, but now he'd definitely crossed the line. There was nothing but malice in his eyes for Asahina. He was her enemy.

It might not have been relevant, but he definitely seemed human to me. It had been a long time since I'd met someone so obviously hostile. He hadn't even pretended to be nice—he hadn't tried to hide anything. Everything he said was just as nasty as he was. At least it saved time. Both Haruhi and I hated that kind of sneakiness.

"If you've got something to say, just say it." I always found myself feeling bolder when shady characters showed up. I had enough vague double-talk with Koizumi around. I put a little bit more power into my voice. "If it's business with me, then I'm listening. Or should I pass a message on to Haruhi? Hell, I'll introduce you to her for free."

"No thanks. Haruhi Suzumiya? I've no need to see her."

Now that was unexpected. I'd been sure he was a member of some mysterious organization obsessed with Haruhi.

"I'm not like Mikuru Asahina." He narrowed his eyes, glaring at the SOS Brigade's token time traveler who peeked out from behind me, then directing the same glare at me. "You shouldn't just blindly follow her directions. There's not just one single reality. Of course, I've been under the same restrictions. That memory device is very important for the future. Whether you pick it up or someone gives it to you, the outcome won't change. You have it. Isn't that right?"

It wasn't even close to right. My instructions never said a single word about a guy like him showing up, I said.

"You fool. Don't you understand that the fact I came here makes no significant difference? Why do you think you're even here?"

"How the hell would I know?" I said without thinking. I had an appointment with a brigade member who did that kind of thinking for me. If he wanted to ponder Zen riddles, he should've been bothering our lieutenant chief, I told him.

"I have no such plans. I'll pass," said the stranger, backing up as though blown by the wind. "Today was simply for introductions. Just a bit of fun. I have my own instructions to follow, you see. Though I don't know if that was part of your little time traveler's plans. And beyond that—heh—it's classified."

He turned on his heel and strolled off. The way he'd just showed up and said his piece without bothering to introduce himself made me want to teach him some manners, and for a moment I thought about following after him, but in the end I just watched him go.

That was because Asahina was standing as still as a bronze statue, still clinging to my arm. Rooted to the ground, the terrified girl watched the disagreeable bastard recede, and it wasn't until he finally turned a corner that she fully relaxed.

"Whew..." said the petite upperclassman, the strength finally going out of her clenched hands as she slumped and leaned against me. I felt the warmth Haruhi was so fond of grabbing onto against my hand, but this was no time to be enjoying such things.

"You didn't even recognize him a little bit, Asahina?"

Asahina somehow managed to straighten, and she spoke in a very small voice. "...I don't know for sure, but...he's probably from the future..."

That much I figured. His wording matched up with Asahina's. My limited deductive capacity could get that far. But what had he come for? Showing up ahead of time and finding the object before we could get to it couldn't be a good thing. He definitely hadn't done it just to watch Asahina and me crawl around in the dirt for half an hour.

Another time traveler. And he was Asahina's enemy.

I felt a chill that had nothing to do with the cold winter wind. So, just like there was a rival faction of cosmic entities, there were also people from the future with different priorities. Come to think of it, even Koizumi had alluded to organizations that were rivals to his Agency. I didn't know what they'd been doing all this time, but it seemed like they were starting to show themselves.

"Looks like there are all kinds of people in the future."

"Yes. Er..." Asahina began to respond to my plaintive-sounding statement, but after opening and closing her mouth she just looked away. "It's classified information—I tried to say it, but I can't."

It was enough. I told her that I wouldn't worry about it, so she shouldn't worry either.

"But this is definitely important. I knew we'd meet someone like him eventually. But . . . this is such an unstable time, so . . ."

"Unstable?"

"Yes. Because the original 'me' is with Suzumiya right now."

That might actually be why this other guy was here.

I put the letter back in the outside pocket of my coat. Assuming that Asahina's and my encounter with that guy was a predetermined event, it would've been impossible, given that Asahina the Younger was now with Koizumi and Haruhi. The only thing that made it possible was the fact that (Michiru) Asahina had come back from eight days in the future to work with me.

I suddenly became aware of the memory device, still clasped in my sweaty hand. It was the object of today's mission, but now I was more worried about another matter entirely. I put it in the same pocket with the letter, feeling a fresh surge of anger at the recently departed stranger. I wouldn't forgive anyone who gave Asahina a hard time, be they from the past, present, or future. Neither would Tsuruya. Come to think of it, neither would Haruhi, and I doubted Nagato or Koizumi would let it slide either.

"I get the feeling we're gonna see him again."

"Probably." Asahina nodded surprisingly readily. Her fearful expression was shifting into confusion, as though she was thinking about something. Happily, she didn't seem to have noticed she was still clinging to my arm as she said, "He also said something about a predetermined event. He's probably not much different from me. And—"

She cut herself off. More classified information? I asked.

"No," said Asahina, finally detaching herself from me. "He didn't seem like that bad of a person to me. What did you think, Kyon?"

What did I think? I thought that anybody who would talk to

Asahina and me like that was the worst. There were only a few people who could get away with that, and a mouthy jerk I'd just met for the first time definitely wasn't one of them.

Of course, I wouldn't have been exactly pleased if he'd used my nickname either.

We'd wasted a lot of time mucking around in the flower box, then being sidetracked by the mysterious stranger. We had to meet back up with Haruhi in front of the station at four o'clock, and it was already past three. There was enough time to go to the library and drag Nagato away from the bookshelves, then go to the station, but I couldn't very well leave Asahina on her own. Even if I called her a cab, there was no guarantee the driver wouldn't be one of our enemies, and the cold smile of the stranger only worsened my worry.

It would destroy my wallet, but there was no other way—I'd ride in the taxi with Asahina to Tsuruya's place, then continue on to the library.

I hailed a passing cab and got in with Asahina, closing the door behind me.

"Do you remember Tsuruya's address?"

"Oh—um, I don't really know," she said. "What ward was it again...?"

"You mean the big Tsuruya mansion? If that's what you're talking about, I know the place," the middle-aged cab driver interjected affably.

The talkative driver wanted to know what school year we were in, how high school was going, and was furthermore happy to tell us about his own son, who was in elementary school, and by the time he'd told us he was thinking of sending said son to a nice private middle school, we had arrived at the front gate of the Tsuruya estate.

Getting out of the car, Asahina thanked both the driver and me profusely before disappearing behind the gate. I could breathe a sigh of relief. No new time traveler would be able to mess with her in there. It was good to have classmates you could count on.

"The library, and step on it," I said, leaning back in the seat and feeling some of the tension finally drain out of me.

When I got back to the library, I saw Nagato there, still standing and reading. I was impressed at her ability to hold a big hardback book for so long.

"Sorry I kept you waiting."

"It's fine."

Nagato closed the book—it looked like a dictionary—with a *thwap*, then replaced it on the shelf in front of her. She kept pace with me as we strode toward the exit.

"Nagato, do you know what this is?"

Outside the exit, Nagato slowly turned her head to face me, still walking as she looked at the object I held up.

"It was like this—" I started to tell her the story as we headed north to the station. I didn't have to keep any secrets from Nagato. I told her everything, from the letters in my shoe locker to the events that had just transpired.

"...I see." Nagato nodded expressionlessly as she answered in her usual flat voice. "There is damaged data recorded on that device," she said, staring at the small chip as though she were performing a CT scan with her eyes. "Over half the data has been destroyed. In its current form, it cannot be interpreted."

What kind of data? I asked.

"Insufficient information. The degree of damage is too high, the omitted portions too numerous."

So it had something on it even Nagato couldn't make sense of. That had to mean that no normal human would be able to interpret it either, but that I was going to have to send it to someone who could.

"If a restoration process were applied, it is possible that entirely different data would result." Nagato looked away from the chip, as though having read the entirety of its contents. "A conjecture is possible."

The hood of the duffle coat shook slightly with each step she took.

"There are two hundred and eighteen sectors of the damaged data where a variant input method was used, and if read on a different device than was intended for that storage medium, it would be possible to extract the fundamental principles underlying a new technology."

Before I could even ask what that meant, Nagato faced me and continued.

"The time travel technology utilized by Mikuru Asahina."

However—Nagato explained to me.

Even if someone were able to obtain that data, human science and technology were at present insufficient to interpret it, and it would not lead to the immediate development of a time machine. But it was still crucial data. Without it, a time machine would never be built, and humanity would never unlock the secrets of time travel. Asahina's method of time travel depended on thousands of accidental discoveries and developments. And at the root of them all was—

"—This? Is that what you're saying?"

"Yes."

Her flat expression seemed disinterested, and Nagato didn't even slacken her pace. I couldn't help but slow down, though. The fate of the future lay in the palm of my hand, and having been entrusted with it I felt an indescribable pressure.

"It could also be a dummy," said Nagato, unwittingly throwing cold water on my emotions. "It is unlikely that is the only copy of the data. It would be natural to have several backups."

That made sense. That's how it always went—when something really valuable was being transported, there would be an original and a dummy, and each would take separate routes. A vision of Asahina the Elder appeared in my mind; she winked and put her finger to her lips, smiling softly. But even she had a weak subject—and it was standing right in front of me.

"Oh, that's right, Nagato—" I said to the back of the rapidly advancing girl. "Sorry about today."

Nagato's progress slowed, and she looked over her shoulder with a blankly questioning expression.

"No, I mean, yesterday I didn't tell you I was going to bring Asahina along today, right? I just asked you for a favor with no explanation, which was kinda...yeah."

"..."

Nagato continued walking while looking at me. After ten seconds under her searching gaze, I finally cracked.

"Asahina told me I should apologize. Anyway, I'm sorry."

"...I see."

She finally looked ahead. Nagato kept walking, speaking again after about five seconds.

"I see."

In front of the station, Haruhi and Asahina leaned on each other like puppies exhausted after a day of playing, while beside them Koizumi stood, a beatific smile on his face.

After meeting up, we found ourselves piling back into the café in order to report our findings. Of course, nothing I could report to Haruhi had happened since the last time we'd done this, and I wasn't going to tell her about the weird guy who'd shown up either. Fortunately, when I reported "We found nothing mysterious or mysterious-seeming," Haruhi's mood didn't take an instant turn for the worse, unlike last year.

"Oh, well—you win some, you lose some."

Had we ever won some?

Haruhi was in surprisingly good spirits as she sipped her cappuccino. "Let's meet up again tomorrow. Those mysterious phenomena won't expect us to be on the lookout two days running! We gotta preserve the element of surprise, then grab 'em by the tail. They'll probably pop out from the strangest places. We might just run right into 'em!"

Yeah, like a voice suddenly calling out to you from behind. Just remembering it made me angry. Just the thought of him smirking as he watched Asahina and me toil away was enough to make my café au lait taste like black coffee. He'd better be ready, the next time I saw him. I'd grab him by the scruff of the neck and make him kneel in front of Haruhi or Nagato—that'd show him.

My irritation must've shown on my face, because Haruhi peered at me curiously. But in the end she let it pass with no comment, then smiled an inexplicable smile.

"Oh, well. We've got tomorrow. A new day brings new possibilities! It wouldn't be any fun to just repeat the same day over and over, would it? My guess is that Sunday is the best target, anyway. It just feels the laziest and most laid-back, right? Like it doesn't get along with Monday, that's what I think."

As I listened to Haruhi anthropomorphize the days of the week, I realized that Monday was a vacation day too, and just as I was suddenly afraid I'd wind up looking for mysterious phenomena three days running, I remembered that (Michiru) Asahina hadn't said anything about that—and anyway, the sight of Asahina the Younger's bashful laugher at Haruhi's affable chatter did my heart good.

"So that'll wrap things up for today," said Haruhi, dismissing us.

Just as I'd been told, it was exactly five o'clock.

*   *   *

Man, oh man. Today had certainly given me a lot to think about.

Riding my bike into the wind, I reflected on the day's events—Koizumi's words before lunch, the two Asahinas, the nameless jerk and his boasting, Nagato's unwavering face, and Haruhi's unexpected good spirits. I didn't even want to think about anything else happening, but things weren't done yet. I wasn't so forgetful that I'd just trudge home empty-handed, I couldn't pretend I hadn't seen the object in my pocket—and there was tomorrow to think about.

So it was that I stopped by the convenience store and bought a stamp and envelope, then headed over to the home center.

Once there, I wandered over to the pet corner. I found myself rather taken with the dogs and cats there, which, unlike Shamisen, were purebred. Pushing the temptation aside, I found the aquarium tank, inside of which was a clump of pond turtles and green turtles; they seemed to be getting along well. I wished I'd had Asahina with me. I would've loved to see her face as she exclaimed at the American shorthairs and shelties in the display. I'd seen my sister do it one too many times.

I looked into the turtle tank.

"All right, then, which one should I get?"

I began my evaluation. The small turtles were mostly unmoving and sat very still upon the rocks, like they were in a diorama. Which was sort of charming, in and of itself. I could understand why one would be a turtle fancier. It seemed a little rude to keep them cooped up like this, but it was winter, so I guessed that couldn't be helped. On the other hand, I was going to toss one of them into a freezing-cold river tomorrow, which wasn't much of an improvement. Which one would a turtle enjoy more? Which had more appeal—a cozy life in an aquarium, or returning to the harsh freedom of nature?

Perhaps sensing my intent gaze, one of the pond turtles craned his neck around to look up at me. Losing his balance, he fell off the rock and plopped into the water, and after drifting about in the bubbles that frothed out of the tank's filter, finally managed to climb back onto the backs of his comrades—perhaps the water was cold. Yup, I'd found my turtle.

I flagged down a shop attendant to pull out the little guy for me, indicating to the young man—maybe a college student working a part-time job—which turtle I wished to purchase. He happily took out a wide variety of turtle-care-type items. For my part I would've been fine with just a paper bag to put the turtle in, but it would've been awkward to explain that no, I didn't plan to keep it as a pet, I was just going to throw it in the river—he'd want to know why, and the fact was, I wanted to know why myself.

In the end, as I was trying to mumble that I didn't have cash on me to cover all this, he'd already covered the bottom of a small plastic tank with gravel and filled it with water, then carefully picked up my turtle and placed it inside, then handed it over to me along with a box of feed. "This comes free with the turtle," he said with a big smile as he led me to the register.

It seemed like this shop attendant really liked turtles.

"If you've ever got any questions about turtles, just ask," he said, ringing it up at the register and paying for the case and feed out of his own wallet. I wanted to apologize, since this turtle was going straight into the river tomorrow.

Feeling a bit guilty, I carried the now-turtle-filled case out of the home center, putting it and the feed in my bicycle's basket and setting off once again.

The sky was now well and truly dark, but I still couldn't head home. There was one more thing I had to take care of—one more thing to do.

*   *   *

"Heya! Kyon! I figured you'd be back! Evenin'!"

My destination was none other than the Tsuruya mansion, where a certain cheerful girl dressed in a perfect traditional Japanese-style outfit let me and my bike through the gate, beneath the starry sky.

"Huh? What's that? A souvenir?" said Tsuruya, peering into the bike basket. "Aw, a pond turtle. Thanks, but our garden's pond is already lousy with the things. They just multiplied like crazy. If you put a little guy like that back there, they'd just beat up on him."

Sorry, Tsuruya—this wasn't a present for her. I'd actually gotten it for Asahina, sort of, I told her.

"Oh, too bad! Also, Kyon, I'm sorry I couldn't take Michiru to the library today. I just couldn't skip out on my thing."

I leaned my bike up in the corner of the absurdly large garden, then walked alongside Tsuruya, carrying the turtle case with me.

"Did you have plans?" I asked.

"It was a memorial service. The whole family gets together to remember our ancestors. It was my dad's grandfather this time— he actually had a really interesting life. With so many crazy episodes, his memorial was really busy!" Tsuruya chattered like she was a hare racing a tortoise and had just decided to take the race seriously. "But are you really that worried about Michiru? Do you want to sleep in the same room with her? I'd sleep next to her too, but if you don't feel like it, that's fine."

Tsuruya smiled at me cheerfully. She sounded just like a fairy godmother bringing Cinderella a fancy ball gown, but I knew that if I naively took her up on her offer, she'd really give me an earful. I wouldn't fall into such an obvious trap. Tsuruya knew that too, which was why she'd laid it in the first place.

"I think I'll pass; thanks."

Tsuruya was smart enough to get my drift. And even if somehow it'd become a reality, if I were to sleep between two older schoolmates like that, I'd be way too nervous to sleep even a little bit. I'd only wind up more exhausted.

Maybe because of the cold, the little pond turtle had retreated into his shell in one corner of the case, and he stayed there, unmoving. I felt like it would've been kinder to leave him in the Tsuruya family's pond, but I couldn't very well go against Asahina the Elder's instructions, though the dilemma still nagged at me.

"Oh, Kyon?"

I was let into the apartment, at which point I was greeted by (Michiru) Asahina's surprised voice. She probably hadn't expected to see me again so soon after we'd parted ways, but she'd forgotten about the turtle. I presented her with the case.

"Could you bring this tomorrow?" I asked.

Consider, if you will, the contents of letter #4: *"On Sunday, by 10:50 AM, throw a turtle into the river."* That was going to be the last action Asahina and I would carry out. Since we'd be doing another city patrol tomorrow, it made the most sense to leave the turtle with this Asahina now, since I'd have to meet up with Haruhi and the rest at nine AM, and we'd lose around an hour to eating at the café and drawing lots. If I showed up with a turtle, there'd be no end of questions to answer from Haruhi.

"Oh, yes. That's right," answered Asahina. "You didn't bring anything to the patrol, I remember."

Ahem. I heard a deliberate-sounding cough. It was Tsuruya, preparing tea on the tea table. She closed one eye in a half wink. "Should I take Michiru somewhere else tomorrow?"

"Would you mind?" I asked.

Tsuruya smiled. "About that—I'm swamped tomorrow too. I've got to show up at this family meeting. But don't you worry! I'll have someone from the house drive her. About what time?"

I asked her to take Asahina to the riverside cherry blossom grove at ten forty-five. Asahina would know the exact place—not even *she* has such a lousy sense of direction that she'd forget that fateful park bench.

"Okay, gotcha. Leave it to me! Just use a taxi for the way back, 'kay?" Tsuruya smacked her chest smartly. "I understand why you're worried, Kyon. I walk around the shopping streets with Mikuru all the time, y'know? She gets hit on every couple hundred meters. Such a pain! I guess it's her superpower."

I figured Tsuruya's superpower might also have something to do with that.

"Mikuru just looks so defenseless, though. That's what worries me. I'd feel a little better if she had a nice boyfriend."

That wouldn't make me feel better at all. I'd spend my days imagining things I didn't want to imagine, I told her.

"Ha ha! So what *would* make you feel better, Kyon m'boy?"

"Kyon m'boy" couldn't think of anything that would make him feel better, but Asahina had turned beet red at Tsuruya's words and was frantically waving her hands. Her strangely ineffable expression must have come from the fact that she was trying to preserve the fiction that she was not *Mikuru* Asahina, but rather *Michiru* Asahina. I didn't really care about that now, and I doubted Tsuruya did either, but Asahina might as well keep her secret. I'd told her to, after all.

The preparations for tomorrow were pretty much settled. I drank some of the bitter tea Tsuruya had brewed, looking at Asahina. I couldn't help but smile as she looked at the little turtle, tapping lightly on his case. I wondered how long I should keep her here. At this rate, this Asahina would come to replace Asahina the Younger in this timeline, but was that really safe? Or did I need to find a way to return her to eight days—no, *three* days now—in the future?

I thought about the numbers on the letters I'd gotten: #3, #4, and #6. Assuming that counting systems hadn't changed in the future such that six came after four, that meant letter #5 was still out there somewhere. It just hadn't reached me yet.

I'd kept the contents of #6 a secret from this Asahina. There was really nothing I could say about it. It was this:

"When everything is over, come to the park bench where you and I met on Tanabata."

The tea at Tsuruya's house was fancier than what we usually drank in the clubroom. I was grateful to Tsuruya for not asking unnecessary questions about the turtle I'd brought with me. I watched my two older schoolmates peer into the case as my mind wandered.

When everything is over— In other words, Asahina traveling eight days into the past was a predetermined event from the perspective of Asahina the Elder. This would all be concluded after not too long.

You and I— "I" had to mean Asahina the Elder, and not the Younger or Michiru. And Tanabata referred to the Tanabata of four years ago. I'd met the same person there, two different times.

I pursed my lips, wondering if I should just tell Asahina everything—tell her that it was the future version of her who was leaving these letters in my shoe locker. How far ahead had Asahina the Elder read? Would this all become a predetermined event?

And how much had this Asahina realized, from the instructions from the future, and from my following them? I'd done nothing but prevaricate. Had that been the right thing to do ...?

I shook my head slightly.

This wasn't good. If all I was going to do was come up with bad ideas, I might as well be asleep. This was all thanks to the stuff that jerk had said to Asahina and me. There was no point trying to figure out who was right. That was one of the things Nagato had taught me.

Nothing could come from agonizing about the future. Your

present self was responsible for your future self. That's why you'd wind up cursing at your past self. At the moment, I was just trying to avoid being cursed by my eventual future self. I didn't have time to think about it.

I just had to move.

Eventually I took my leave of the Tsuruya house and returned home. Shamisen was asleep on my bed, his face the image of serenity. If he was so unconcerned about the world, then the world must be okay. And no matter what happened, I couldn't imagine him getting insomnia over it.

"Guess it all happens tomorrow..."

I'd put an end to all this tomorrow. On day two of Haruhi's citywide investigation, I'd leave the turtle in the river. That was all I had to do. There wasn't anything particularly difficult about it. I wouldn't be digging holes in search of treasure I'd never find, nor taking perfect strangers to the hospital, nor moving random rocks, nor retrieving data storage devices—oh, wait. I still had to deal with that before I forgot about it again.

I wrote the name and address from letter #3 on the envelope I'd bought at the convenience store, then put the memory chip inside it. I stuck enough stamps on the envelope to get it anywhere in the world, then stashed it back in my coat pocket. Naturally, I didn't include a return address.

After I'd dropped it in a post office mailbox, I prayed there wouldn't be an accident. There was a limit to what I could plan for—I hoped Asahina the Elder realized that.

I was sure my hopes would be answered. I'd definitely ask her about that—on that Tanabata bench, when everything was over.

CHAPTER SIX

The fated Sunday arrived.

I rode my bike to the station front at nine AM, just as I had the day previous. And just like the previous day, everyone else was already there, so we visited the café on my dime and drew lots, whereupon Nagato and I were once again grouped together. Nagato would never forget anything I said to her. I knew I could trust her. It was a lesson I needed to learn myself, honestly. For Nagato more than anyone, I wanted to keep every promise I made her, even if it killed me. That's how much she'd done for me.

I was mindful of the time we spent at the café, and though Haruhi was even more carefree than she'd been before, I didn't have time to worry about that. She'd been this way ever since the treasure hunt, so she must have just felt physically unwell during her bad mood early in the month.

It was strange to see Haruhi grinning and whispering something into Asahina's ear; whatever she said, it made Asahina smile brightly. I wanted to know what it was, but in any case, Koizumi and Nagato were their usual selves, so it didn't seem like any cataclysms were imminent.

I slurped the foam that remained in the bottom of my mostly

empty cup of espresso, as Haruhi slid the check over to me and stood up.

It was ten o'clock on the dot.

There was plenty of time to walk over to the river.

We were to meet back up at noon, which gave me more than enough time to go put the turtle in the river and return.

I watched Haruhi, Koizumi, and Asahina recede into the distance. "Sorry," I said to Nagato. "Would you mind going to the library on your own? I should be able to come and get you in an hour."

"I see," Nagato answered, drawing her duffle coat's hood up, which completely hid her head.

"Nagato, do you know what it is that Asahina and I are doing?"

"Something necessary," Nagato murmured as she began to walk down the road that would take her to the library.

"Necessary for whom?"

"For you and for Mikuru Asahina."

Not for her? Not for Haruhi or Koizumi? I asked.

". . ."

Nagato continued to silently walk. Eventually I heard her voice from within her hood. "That possibility exists. It is still unclear."

From where I stood, I could see her shoulders slacken, whereupon she suddenly turned and fixed my face in her crystalline pupils.

"However—" Her hair shifted in the wind. "It will become clear soon. In which case, I will move. As will Itsuki Koizumi."

Nagato's short, declarative speaking style had always been that way, ever since I'd met her.

"Our direction is the same. Mine and yours."

Having seemingly reached a conclusion, Nagato turned and began to walk quietly away. This time, I didn't follow her.

"Thanks, Nagato."

Embarrassment made my voice low. I didn't know whether the receding hooded figure could hear me or not, but I was certain she understood my feelings. Nagato was certainly clever enough to do that much.

Along the way, I'd figured something else out—that Nagato, Koizumi, Asahina, and I were all jointly and mutually responsible. In the center shone the brilliant star known as Haruhi, and we were all planets that orbited around her. I didn't know how long it had been that way, but if Mars or Venus were to suddenly disappear from the night sky, not only would it be rather sad, it would be a big problem for astrologers. And for me. Until we knew with total certainty that Martians and Venusians didn't exist, I didn't want them to just up and disappear. There are a lot of things that you take for granted until they're gone. Like lead for your mechanical pencil, when you're in the middle of a test. Okay, that was a stupid example. But in any case, I didn't want to feel the terrible sense of loss I'd felt last December ever again.

"Nagato's taught me something again."

She'd taught me that the path I should take had been long since decided.

Half an hour later, I arrived at the riverbank. The abnormal autumnally blooming cherry blossoms were nowhere to be seen; there were only bare brown branches, waiting frigidly for spring's arrival. As I made my way to the bench, I looked down the river, which was at low ebb. It was a typical raised-bed river, with a distance of maybe three meters between the bank and the surface of the water. Thanks to the prudent construction of the dikes on either side, the river had a tidy feel to it. With only a few centimeters of water in the bottom, the river was low, but it was still very pleasant. Come summer, there would be children chasing wildly after the small fish it contained, but here in the dead of winter none wanted to approach the frigid flow.

That may or may not have been the reason, but in any case the bench where Asahina had once confessed her true identity as a time traveler was unoccupied. Despite it being Sunday, there weren't many people who wanted to take a nice riverside walk when it was this cold out, so the tree-lined path was nearly deserted. There was one bored-looking dog being silently walked by its shivering owner, but that was it.

Just as I was listening to the babble of the flowing water and really playing the part of the lonely high school lad to the hilt, my clever reverie was interrupted.

"Kyon!"

Having descended the stairs that led from the roadside, Asahina stepped onto the riverbank. She was indeed carrying the turtle's container, but had forgotten to wear her flu mask from yesterday—but with her knit cap and shawl, she still gave off a very different impression from the usual Asahina look, so I supposed it was all right. This would be the last day, anyway.

Asahina faced me and waved, then looked back over her shoulder at the road. When I looked, I saw what must have been the car from the Tsuruya estate driving away—it was a fancy domestic auto, every inch the wealthy family's second car. We'd have to make sure to thank the driver.

It was ten forty-four AM. Once I walked to the river's edge with Asahina, it was ten forty-five. Perfect timing.

"The water looks so cold..." Asahina looked down at the lazily flowing river, then held the case that contained the turtle up to her eye level. "I wonder if the turtle will be able to grow up healthy." My petite older classmate showed kindness to even the smallest animal. "Wait just a moment."

She placed the case on the ground and opened the lid, then produced the box of feed from her coat pocket. The pond turtle craned his neck up toward the suddenly vanished roof, and when Asahina brought the feed closer, it gulped the treat down in a single bite. It had gotten quite fond of her in just a single night. That was Asahina for you.

I felt bad separating the two of them, but soon the time would be upon us. There were only three minutes to go until ten fifty.

"We'll come again in spring," I said soothingly, as I picked up the pond turtle. Unconcerned, the turtle sat quietly in the palm of my hand. "I'm sure we'll be able to see him again once he's gotten bigger."

It was all I could say, though I had no reason to believe it was true. I shook off Asahina's worried gaze, wound up for the throw. Just as I leaned back in preparation for my underhand toss—

"Excuse me!"

I heard a sudden voice from behind me and nearly wound up tumbling into the river, still holding the turtle. I tottered and stumbled, but managed to steady myself on dry ground, whereupon I immediately turned around.

"Thank you very much for helping me!"

It was a young boy wearing glasses, his voice youthful and his head politely bowed. It was the same boy I'd saved from being killed in a traffic accident a month earlier, and nearby whom Haruhi lived and occasionally served as his tutor.

"Ah…"

Asahina seemed surprised; I certainly was. I never thought we'd meet again.

"What are you doing?" The boy's features were very different from my sister's—sharp and intelligent. He looked at Asahina and me, and at the turtle I held. Just as I was about to tell him that that was a question *we* should be asking *him*—

"I'm on my way to cram school," he said clearly, before I even had the chance to ask. He indicated the book bag over his shoulder. "I always come this way. That's what I was doing that day too."

He bowed again, then looked confusedly down at the case on the ground, then at the now struggling shelled reptile in my hand.

"Are you going to let that turtle go?"

"Uh, yeah…" I answered, feeling freshly guilty. Both Asahina and the boy seemed to overflow with sympathy for the turtle as they looked at it. I felt their wordless appeal—*Why do you have to throw this poor little turtle into a freezing river?* But there wasn't anything I could do. I had to do this.

My watch indicated one minute to go. I couldn't just stand here doing nothing. I racked my slow-witted brain for some kind of solution.

"Hey, kid, are pets allowed in your house? I mean—would your parents be okay if you came home with this little guy?"

The boy pushed his glasses up. "I think so. If I took care of him, I mean."

"I see. Hang on a sec."

Still holding the turtle by his back, I crouched down beside the river. With three meters separating the riverbank where we were from the water's surface, the distance wasn't too far. The current was weak, so I wouldn't lose sight of the turtle.

I gave the turtle a gentle toss—like tossing a feather, trying to keep the impact from being too forceful.

The turtle fell into the river with a *plop*, leaving behind a series of concentric ripples that moved lazily downriver.

The boy watched the scene as though holding his breath.

Having sunk, the turtle seemed to kick off the river bottom, then stuck his head out. He almost looked bewildered at the ripples he was causing as he floated along. After a short time, he started swimming, and finally he climbed atop a rock and stuck his neck out. He didn't really seem like he was saying good-bye to us—more likely he was marveling in his turtle-ish way at his suddenly expanded world.

The ripples he made were washed away, but the turtle remained.

I didn't know what Asahina the Elder had anticipated, but her instructions only went as far as throwing the turtle in the river. Which meant that once I'd done that, I could do whatever I wanted with the turtle after that. That's what I kept telling myself as I removed my shoes and socks. Once I'd rolled up the legs of my pants, I was ready to go, and as Asahina and the boy watched wide-eyed, I climbed down from the bank. The water was just as cold as it looked, and the bottom was coated in some kind of slimy, mossy substance that did not feel good, but I'd played in many a stream with my cousins in the countryside when I was little, so this was nothing.

"Sorry, turtle."

The pond turtle lifted his head up. He didn't try to escape when I brought my hand near, and I was able to easily retrieve him. For the turtle's part, he probably wanted to ask me why the hell I threw him in the river, if I was just going to go in and fetch him back. Fortunately I had no facility in turtle-ese. Holding him in one hand, I climbed back up onto the bank. By the time I put the turtle back in his case, the chill had crept from my feet all the way up to my neck. Ugh, I was going to have stomach trouble later, I could tell.

I sat down and lifted my feet into the air to shake off the excess water.

"All right, kid, the turtle's all yours."

"Can I really have it?" the boy asked hesitantly. He'd seen everything I'd done. "I mean, didn't you have a reason for throwing this turtle into the river?"

I was no better equipped than the turtle himself to satisfy his childish curiosity—after all, even I didn't understand the purpose of what I was doing.

"Don't worry about that," I said. "I don't think the turtle really wanted to get tossed into a freezing river in the middle of winter. If you'll take care of him, I think he'd like that a lot better."

I wondered about Asahina. She'd said the directions in the

letter absolutely had to be followed, but nothing I'd done went against them. I was a little worried about it, but then I saw Asahina gently handing the box of food to the boy.

"Take this too. It's turtle food." Then, sounding big-sisterish: "Make sure you take good care of him. Promise?"

"I promise."

He was a little bit of a brat, but he didn't seem like a bad kid. He hugged the turtle case and feed box tightly. "I'll always take good care of him," he said sincerely—more sincerely than he needed to show, honestly.

"Oh, hey, kid, promise me one more thing." I had to make sure of one thing. I'd been careless last time, and it had almost been a disaster. The memory still echoed in my mind. "There's a Haruhi Suzumiya who lives close to you, right?"

"Yes. Haruhi's always taking care of me; she's like my big sister."

The words "big sister" sounded very strange in the context of Haruhi.

"You've gotta keep this a secret from Haruhi, got that? You can't tell her that you saw me or Asahina... I mean, the bunny lady, and you can't tell her we gave you the turtle. Can you promise me that?"

"I promise." The boy nodded, his face serious. Well, that was one thing I didn't have to worry about anymore.

"Are you sure you'll be able to take him home?" Asahina piped up. "Your parents won't tell you not to take things from strangers?"

"It'll be okay. I'll just tell them something else." The boy straightened. "I'll tell them that some people were doing experiments on the turtle, and they didn't need him anymore so they were gonna throw him away, but I happened to pass by and felt sorry for him, so they let me have him. That's what I'll say. My folks'll definitely let me keep him."

The kid had his business together. My little sister could have stood to learn a thing or two from him. They were the same age, but there was a huge difference—I guessed it came down to environment.

"I have to get to cram school now, so I'll be going."

The boy bowed dutifully. Asahina laid the palm of her hand on his head.

"Don't forget the promise you made before. Be careful of cars. Make sure you don't get in any accidents—and make sure to study hard. If you do, I'm sure you'll grow up to be an important person. One whom everyone will remember for a very long time."

Asahina extended her little finger, at which the boy showed a bashfulness appropriate to his age. He hesitantly hooked his little finger around hers, thus completing the pinky promise. Seeing the two of them with their linked pinkies like that was ridiculously adorable.

The boy ticklishly pulled his pinky away, then, holding the turtle case as though it were the most precious treasure, walked off, occasionally looking over his shoulder and dipping his head in a bow. Asahina waved to him until he had vanished from sight, and I'd completely dried my feet and gotten my shoes back on before she finally dropped her hand.

"Whew…" She sighed. Apparently for her—or for her future—that boy was an important figure. It was like if I'd traveled back in time and met a towering historical figure from the Edo period. That much I knew without having to ask. And that whoever he was, it would be classified information.

"Whew." I let a sigh escape myself, the sigh of having accomplished my mission. This was the last thing I had to do with Asahina. The empty can prank, the gourd-shaped stone, the mysterious data storage device, and the turtle.

The problem was I didn't really know what to do next, and it hadn't been written on letter #6. I could rest easy so long as Asahina stayed at Tsuruya's apartment and didn't go wandering around. If she just did that for two more days, she'd be able to catch up to her own original timeline. Then in exchange, I would have to instruct the current Asahina to travel back in time, but that would happen the day after tomorrow. For now, I felt like a load had been taken off my back.

"Asahina, I know you just got here, but let's head back to Tsuruya's place. We'll catch a cab, and I'll escort you back. After that, I've gotta get back to the library—Nagato's waiting for me."

"Okay…"

Asahina started walking a bit absentmindedly. I led us down to the road that ran alongside the row of cherry trees. As we stood there on the road's shoulder waiting for a taxi, Asahina said little, and she seemed rather depressed.

As I waited for a cab to pass by, I took a look around, wondering if the stranger from yesterday was going to show up again. He was obviously malicious, but that was the problem—he was too over-the-top; he needed to improve his game. To be completely honest, I wasn't the least bit scared of him. If someone like Koizumi had approached us yesterday instead, that would've been much more frightening—it was a mistake in either direction or casting.

Aha! I found myself impressed with my own reliable disposition. And it was true, wasn't it? Throughout the past year I'd been involved in unthinkable, astounding events, and every time I learned something new. I'm sure I'd been shaken before. But now things were different. I wasn't at Nagato's level yet, but I'd had enough time to develop an unshakable core. I'd no longer worry about my own place in the world.

No taxi had come yet; indeed, there were few cars of any kind on the road. I was happy to stand there and loiter for a while beside Asahina, but having sent Nagato off to the library alone, I needed to get to her as soon as I could.

Maybe it was my fault for letting my mind wander so idly.

The next moment, I witnessed something unbelievable.

*   *   *

I hadn't checked my watch. There hadn't been an opportunity. I didn't know the exact time, but it was definitely before eleven o'clock.

The incident played out like this:

As Asahina and I stood there on the left side of the road, dazedly watching for a taxi, a minivan approached us slowly. This wasn't a highway, so the vehicle's slow speed itself didn't strike me as strange, and I paid it no mind.

But soon the van decelerated even more, and although there was no traffic signal in sight, it came to a complete stop—directly in front of us.

I'm not sure if I even had time to think, "What?"

Because it was barely a split second later that the sliding door of the minivan suddenly opened, and arms reached out from within the car and grabbed Asahina's body, pulling her into the vehicle.

"Ah—?!"

By the time I'd realized that the cry had come from Asahina, the moss-green minivan had accelerated away, its exhaust blasting into me as though mocking me, sliding door still open, and disappeared into the distance.

"Wha—"

It took a couple of seconds before I recovered from my stupor. The van was already gone.

Wait. Wait just a second.

What the hell was this? Asahina had disappeared right before my eyes. She'd been pulled into the van, and the van was already out of sight, and here I was, standing alone at the edge of the road. What was going on?

"A kidnapping…"

And right before my eyes. I had been standing right next to her. She had been close enough that I could've reached out my hand or simply grabbed onto her. She had been next to me just a few seconds ago. And now she was gone. How could something so ridiculous actually happen?

"God dammit! What the hell!"

I hadn't been so freaked out since last December, when I'd realized that Haruhi wasn't in my class anymore, and sitting behind me instead of her was Asakura.

"Crap!"

Had it been that bastard from yesterday? Was this his doing? If it was, I'd underestimated him. Had his appearance and attitude been a setup to get me to let my guard down? If it had all been a ruse to distract me—

"Asahina!" A loud noise assaulted my eardrums. It wasn't the sound of the wind through the cherry blossoms. It was the sound of the blood rushing through my head.

I whipped my cell phone out. I had to get somebody, anybody, to help me. If they'd help me get Asahina back, I didn't care who they were—the police, the fire department, the self-defense forces, or the chamber of commerce. My fingers moved automatically, and the phone was ringing before I even knew who I'd dialed. They picked up immediately.

"What's up, Kyon?"

It was Haruhi's voice. In the moment I'd been so flustered that I'd called Haruhi. By this time, I was far past rationality.

"Haruhi, we're in trouble! Asahina's been kidnapped!" I shouted.

"Huh? What're you talking about?"

Haruhi's voice was entirely calm. My stomach churned and I yelled into the phone again.

"I told you, Asahina's been kidnapped! We've got to help her—"

"Listen, Kyon," Haruhi began, almost kindly. "I don't know what you're getting at, but if you're going to start making prank calls, you're going to have to do better than that. I mean, really.

Are you kidding me? Mikuru's been here with me the whole time. If you'd said it was Yuki, that would've made more sense."

"No, it's not Nagato—it's Asahina, she's—" I started, but then I realized it was futile. That's right—Asahina was with Haruhi. That Asahina was the original one, not the one who'd appeared in the broom closet, who'd now been taken away in a car—

"That's one point off for you, Kyon, which is less than you deserve for such a lame prank. And by the way, jokes are supposed to be funny. Bye, stupid Kyon!"

"Wait—!"

She hung up.

My hand shook as it held my cell phone. A situation where every second counts was no time to be calling Haruhi. I was such an idiot. If I had an urgent message to deliver, I should've called—

My phone started to ring.

I hit the talk button without bothering to check who it was.

"Hello?"

It was Koizumi's voice. Before I could say anything, he started talking.

"Don't worry. I got away from Haruhi and the others before I called. I told them I was going to the bathroom."

Who cared about that? That didn't matter, what was important was—

"Koizumi! It's Asahina, she's—"

"I understand the situation. Leave it to me. They'll be with you shortly."

"Who'll be with me?!"

Almost giddy, I looked up to see a car stopping right in front of me. It was a black taxi. I couldn't tell what cab company it was from, but it seemed familiar. I'd ridden in a similar cab once—when I was taken to see the Celestials.

The back door of the car opened. "Please get in. Hurry."

The passenger sitting in the back seat beckoned me into the cab. I leaped in. There was a familiar passenger in the backseat of this familiar car. The door closed behind me before I had time to take in the situation and sudden g-forces pressed me into the seat's back.

"We'll catch them soon," said a crisp, clear voice beside me—a voice I'd heard before. I'd never forget her voice, not after the many times she'd bailed us out in the past year.

"Mori...Sono Mori?!"

"My apologies for being so long out of contact."

It had only been a month—that wasn't "long out of contact." And anyway, what was Mori doing here? And not wearing her maid outfit, but instead in a totally ordinary set of office clothes?

Mori gave her usual calm smile. "Didn't Koizumi explain? I am also a member of the Agency. The maid disguise is only for when I'm working with you and your friends."

My eyes went to the driver, at which Mori spoke as though to put me at ease.

"Not just me—him, as well."

The driver brought his left hand up to adjust the rearview mirror, through which his eyes met mine.

"Arakawa..."

"Indeed," said the middle-aged butler who excelled at cooking and—apparently—high-speed cab driving. "To kidnap such a lovely young lady—it's a disgrace. We won't let them get away."

He stomped down on the accelerator, pushing me still harder into the seat. Riding in a car traveling at such a tremendous speed was terrifying, but it was also helping to thaw my shock-frozen brain.

Mori and Arakawa. I knew the two of them were Koizumi's cohorts, and that the maid and butler roles were just part-time jobs for them. But I'd never expected to meet them like this, their car arriving immediately after Asahina had been kidnapped, as though they had expected it— Oh. Now I understood.

"You knew this was going to happen," I managed to say. "You and Koizumi knew that Asahina was going to be kidnapped. That's why you were standing by so close."

"No," said Mori, smiling like a female version of Koizumi. "It wasn't you that we'd marked. It was them. When we saw their car approach you, we were unsure what they would do. Their actions surprised us as much as they did you."

"What do you mean by 'them'?"

"Koizumi didn't explain that either? Asahina's kidnappers are from an organization that opposes the Agency."

It didn't really matter who they were. I wouldn't let them get away with this, whether they were time travelers or espers.

"Why did they take her, of all people...?"

"They acted rashly. No doubt they want to secure a privileged position in the future while they still can."

Privileged? I asked.

"Yes. I expect they plan to use her to bargain with the future. However, they've made a mistake. They should have kidnapped the Mikuru Asahina who is now with Koizumi." Mori explained the absurdity like it was nothing special. "It was a sloppy plan. They must be desperate. We need to know what has made them need to move so quickly."

That weirdo from before appeared suddenly too. Another time traveler. Was this because of his appearance?

Mori seemed to agree, as though having read my mind. "They seem to have joined forces in earnest. We cannot allow this."

"So is the Agency..." I wanted to say "my," but somehow restrained myself. "...Is it our ally?"

"Our goal is to maintain the status quo. Is that not enough?"

It was precisely enough. But what were the bastards who had kidnapped Asahina thinking? I asked. And what *were* they? If they weren't our allies, were they enemies? What kind of people were they?

"They consist of an organization that works against the Agency, a group of time travelers who oppose Mikuru Asahina, and a cosmic entity other than the one that created Yuki Nagato," said Mori plainly. "We knew they would interfere soon, having heard

Koizumi's report regarding the snow mountain late last year. It was conceivable that they would join forces—rather, it was inevitable. There is significant potential payoff in gambling on Haruhi Suzumiya. They might lose everything, but they stand to gain much."

Bouncing and swaying, the black cab flew through a railroad crossing without stopping, then threaded through an S-curve, barely so much as slowing down, tires squealing.

"As does Koizumi, and you and your friends."

I was starting to feel carsick. "So you knew about the other Asahina? You knew that she'd come back from one week in the future, and that she was holed up at Tsuruya's place?"

"It is likely that without her, the original Mikuru Asahina would have been kidnapped. Before Haruhi Suzumiya's very eyes."

That was the worst possible scenario. There was no telling what Haruhi would do.

"Which means…"

It meant that the Asahina who'd come from the future had been kidnapped instead of the current Asahina. In other words, her future self had saved her past self. Was that why (Michiru) Asahina had to come? I could have carried out all of the instructions in Asahina the Elder's letters on my own. So what had been the meaning of the things I'd done with Asahina? The other group of time travelers. The turtle and the boy. And the kidnapping. Only Asahina the Elder knew everything.

A strange emotion settled over me.

"Don't lose them, Arakawa," said Mori.

"Understood."

Their exchange brought my attention front and center. The moss-green car was in view. Both vehicles were still traveling at high speed. Given the way we were going, it wouldn't have been surprising if we'd gotten into three or four accidents by now, but Arakawa's driving technique was as good as any rally racer's. He was no ordinary butler.

The kidnappers' car seemed to be heading for the mountains. If we kept going, we'd soon reach the forest park where we'd shot our movie, then keep heading north. Past that there was little but mountain roads, and few people or buildings. Damn, what were they planning to do to Asahina there? I wouldn't let them get away with it.

I glared at the rear end of the van ahead of us—the moss-green minivan. It looked just like the one from before—the vehicle that had nearly run over the boy in glasses. There was no mistaking it; whoever was in that van, they weren't our allies.

Still driving at an insane speed, the kidnappers' van swerved off the paved roadway and onto a true mountain road. Arakawa pulled on the steering wheel and followed. The road seemed to have been forcibly carved out of the cliff; it was barely wide enough for two cars to pass each other, and there was no guard-rail. If the driver slipped up, we'd wind up tumbling to the foot of the mountain.

I never thought I'd be in a high-speed car chase before, but I wasn't levelheaded enough to appreciate that fact. All I could focus on was how badly I wanted to beat the crap out of the kidnappers.

A cell phone started ringing, as if to throw cold water on the flames of my fighting spirit. It wasn't my phone, though; Mori took her own phone out and put it to her ear.

I couldn't make out the words, but it sounded like a man's voice. Mori was silent for a while, listening.

"Understood. According to the plan, then," she replied simply, then raised her elegant voice and directed it at the driver's seat. "Arakawa, just a bit farther."

"Very well," said Arakawa in a reliable-sounding tone, nodding. He downshifted, revving the engine. There was no chance for me to ask what they were planning to do.

"Whoa—!"

We were approaching a bowlike curve in the unpaved road. A

police car appeared ahead, coming toward us around the bend. It slammed on its parking brake and executed a perfect drift turn, coming to a stop in the middle of the road, totally blocking the way.

With nowhere to go, the minivan braked hard, kicking up a cloud of dust as it skidded. My blood ran cold when one of its wheels seemed about to go over the edge of the cliff, but the kidnappers' driver was pretty good, managing to force the car back on course, where it completed a full spin and an additional half revolution. The van's nose faced the mountainside as it came to a stop alongside the police car.

Arakawa executed a similar, if slower, maneuver, bringing the black cab to a sideways-facing stop. The minivan was trapped. The only place it could go was off the edge of the cliff.

"Arakawa, stand by here," said Mori, then opened her door and stepped out onto the mountain road. I followed, but just as I was about to dash over to the minivan, Mori grabbed my arm.

She stopped me with a sharp glance, then called out to the van in a clear voice. "Turn off your engine and step out of the vehicle! You still have time!"

Her tone was polite as ever, but it had a different timbre to it than the one I remembered from the island mansion and Tsuruya's mountain villa.

An officer got out of the police car. When I looked at the smartly uniformed figure, I was stunned. Underneath the policeman's cap was the youthful face of the younger Tamaru brother, Yutaka; he gave me a thumbs-up. Still in the driver's seat of the patrol car was his older brother, Keiichi, who met my eye and nodded.

Had these been the people Mori was on the phone with?

"Release Asahina Mikuru. You have failed. There is no need to continue this!"

Mori's clear voice brought my attention back to the van. Its windows were tinted, so I couldn't make out the interior. Unable to contain my impatience, I was just about to run over and give it a kick or something when the idling engine fell silent, and the moss-green sliding door began to move. It was opening so slowly, though, that I wondered if they intended to resist.

But when the kidnappers revealed themselves, my eyes went wide at their appearance. The group that emerged from the van was not comprised of tough-looking criminals or soldiers, but normal-looking young men and women like you'd see just walking around town. The fact that there wasn't a vicious-looking one among them made me even more worried.

All those thoughts were blasted away as soon as I saw Asahina slumped inside the van. The last kidnappar to emerge carried her out—her body was slack, evidently unconscious.

I'd never forgive them.

Before I could run at them, Mori stopped me again.

"You must know this already, but I'll say it again. If you so much as leave a single scratch on her..."

My body went slack at the sight of her cold expression. I'd never dreamed a beautiful woman's smile could be so terrifying. Haruhi had an angry grin that she sometimes used, but this was on an entirely different level.

Perhaps sensing my fear, Mori turned to me and gave me her normal maid-like smile, then focused her attention on the idiotic kidnappers once again. "Leave peacefully. We will allow you to go free. Return to your organization and go where you like. Otherwise—" Mori's smile turned still more threatening, making me dizzy. If I'd been one of the kidnappers, I would've been petrified.

But the kidnappers just stood there and snorted, then released Asahina. The unconscious girl slumped back and down, leaning against the van's tire. The kidnappers saved themselves by handling her very carefully. If they'd just shoved my lovely Asahina off, I probably would've charged toward them, raising a cry, fists at the ready.

"We will have your vehicle sent back to you later. Leave the area on foot."

Mori pointed at the cliff's edge, indicating that they should climb down from there. It wouldn't be impossible, but descending without any climbing equipment would certainly be difficult. It served them right.

"Oh well," said one of the kidnappers, sounding cheerful enough that I wondered if she really understood her own position. "I guess I expected this. Too bad, though. Maybe it was fate, after all."

She was the only woman in the group, and the one who'd set Asahina down. When I looked more closely at her, she seemed to be in her mid-teens. Age-wise, she wasn't far from me.

The woman pierced me with a brilliant smile. "Hello, there. I'm sorry these are the circumstances, but I'm honored to finally meet you. I'd hoped to properly introduce myself someday."

She gave a signal to her cohorts with her body language. Leaving their female companion behind, the cohorts seemed not at all reluctant to go. The last of them looked about college-age, and he conscientiously closed the van door before he went, then headed to the near-perpendicular edge of the cliff. One by one, they disappeared down into the forest; neither Mori nor Yutaka Tamaru seemed to want to catch any of them.

I wanted to run immediately over to Asahina, but Mori again took my arm and wouldn't let go. I heard a giggle—it was the kidnapper woman.

"You don't have to worry. We did not harm your little time traveler in the slightest. She's only sleeping because of the tranquilizer we gave her, and I doubt she'll even remember what happened. She fell asleep so quickly it surprised even us. Has she gotten used to being knocked out?"

The woman—no, girl—was still composed, even with her cohorts gone. How long was Mori going to let her get away with that? These guys were kidnappers! What about the Tamaru brothers—if they were gonna dress like cops, they should at least have a set or two of handcuffs.

I was just about to voice my protest, when the sliding door of the supposedly empty minivan was opened again—from the inside.

"What a pain." A man's face popped out, with a smile five times more malicious than anything I'd seen from Koizumi. "You got us way too easily. It was so easy to steal Sleeping Beauty here that I wish we could've held on to her a little longer. This is just going to backfire on us now."

He made no move to leave the van, simply leaning back in his seat. It was him—the guy from yesterday. The other time traveler, whose appearance seemed so strangely significant.

"This, too, was predetermined—for us, as well. So I don't really care."

"You should leave too," said Mori in a kind, big-sisterly voice, smiling with lips like the petals of a poisonous flower. "Or do you plan to stay for a while? We'll be happy to prepare you a bed."

"I won't waste your time." The bastard looked down at Asahina, snorting, then turned his malicious eyes to me. "This wasn't a failure. It's historical fact. You all did very well—you and Asahina too. Tell me, is it fun, being made to dance like that? Count me out. I'm sick of just playing a part."

"Oh? Are you really?" It was the kidnapper girl. "So how much of the future is decided, then? It takes some skill to follow the path that leads to the correct outcome, doesn't it? Anyone can dance, but dancing correctly is quite difficult."

"Hmph. You go right ahead and dance, then. I wasn't counting on help from you people anyway."

"Is that so?" said the girl, amused. "That may be fine for you, but are we not assembling at the same place? Let's join forces."

The bastard's face twisted in annoyance, and he glared at me again. I wanted to tell him that he was going to have to do better than that—Haruhi had gotten me used to being glared at. If he wanted a staring contest, I'd take him on any day.

Maybe he sensed my anger; his face was full of loathing. "Fools, all of you. You don't understand anything. Your ignorance is terrifying." He put his hand on the door's handle and gave me one last parting line. "I'll come again. You'll see me many times—it's ridiculous, but it's my duty."

He closed the van door; evidently that was all he had to say.

Nobody moved. Mori was still, continuing to stare right through the kidnapper girl, and I took my cue from her. The unnamed kidnapper girl stood there smiling, then went over to the van, as though having suddenly remembering something, and opened the door.

I already knew there would be no one inside. The interior of the car was empty. That malicious jerk was nowhere to be seen. I didn't know if he'd used teleportation or time travel, but either way I was happy he was gone.

"I'll be going as well." The girl dusted off her hands, as though having finished her work, and looked down the mountain road. "I suppose I'll walk back. Oh, feel free to take care of the car. You needn't return it. It's yours."

"Thank you," replied Mori, finally letting go of my arm. I dashed toward Asahina like a mother bird returning to the nest where she's left her babies.

"Asahina!" I lifted her up. The soft sound of her breath and periodic rising of her chest were proof that she was still alive. I gave one last angry glare in the direction of the kidnappers, but the girl had already started making her way down the cliff.

Mori leaned over beside me, drawing close to Asahina's sleeping face. She put a finger to Asahina's neck and brought her lips close to the unconscious girl's mouth.

"She is unhurt. I expect she'll awaken in a couple of hours. Please, take her to the car."

I carried her, of course. I was well used to carrying Asahina around. It was one job I didn't want anyone else doing for me.

We returned to the black taxi. Arakawa gave Asahina a fond

look as though she were his own grandchild, then regarded me similarly. I relaxed my arms and let Asahina gently come to rest in the car's backseat. I had no idea what was going to happen, but I was elated at having gotten her back. When I thought about what it would've been like if they'd gotten away...no, I didn't want to think about it, and it couldn't have happened anyway.

It must have been nice to be Asahina the Elder and believe in predetermined events. For her to do something like this, it must have been absolutely necessary in order for this Asahina to eventually become her. *Right, Asahina?*

I continued to gaze at my younger-seeming older schoolmate, not noticing when Mori got back into the car, nor saying anything to the Tamaru brothers. I only came out of my reverie when the car began to move.

"Where shall we go?" Mori asked me, and only then did I realize that the taxi was heading back down the highway we'd come up before.

"...The library."

At the moment, I just wanted to see Nagato's face and calm down. I sat back in the seat, feeling about as exhausted as Asahina looked.

I'd thought my work was done once I'd put the turtle in the water, then retrieved it, but the fact that Asahina's kidnapping awaited soon after was more than just unexpected. Despite my psychological exhaustion, I managed to move my mouth and speak.

"Mori...have those guys always targeted Asahina? Have there been failed kidnapping attempts all along? Are there going to be more...?"

"She will not be kidnapped in this time period."

"Well, then, what was it that just happened?"

"I believe that what I am saying is correct. Her current self is completely unharmed. After all, someone else was kidnapped in her stead." Mori's face was filled with affection. "Mikuru Asahina

227

enjoys the protection of many. Yours, Yuki Nagato's, and even ours. We are all alike in that we don't wish to hand her over to anyone."

Just as I trusted Koizumi, I supposed I could trust Mori.

"As for the rest, I suggest you ask your lovely maid—the older one, from further in the future."

That much was obvious. I exhaled, then voiced the sudden question that came to mind. "Mori, are you Koizumi's superior? Something about the way you talk makes me think so."

Mori giggled and smiled a strangely ageless smile. "You needn't concern yourself with that. We're like a company; all the employees are quite close and don't stick to formalities, not even with the company president."

I could tell she was dodging the question, but the truth was I wasn't very interested in the internal hierarchy of the Agency. If I really wanted to know, I could just lean on Koizumi to tell me. He probably wouldn't tell me the truth, but then again, neither would Mori. If he wanted to tell me, Koizumi wouldn't wait for me to ask before delivering his whole spiel. Maybe that was the Agency style of doing things. He'd give me an earful eventually; that much was certain.

All I had to do was wait.

I got out of the taxi in front of the library, and with Mori's help got the still-sleeping Asahina safely situated on my back.

"Take care. Until we meet again," she said with a smile that came right out of her maid era. Arakawa gave me a silent bow, and the black taxi sped away, heading north up the highway.

I wondered if it had been Arakawa in the driver's seat when Koizumi took me to see the Celestials. I'd have to ask about that. And thank him too—Arakawa and the Tamaru brothers both.

Heading to the library's entrance with Asahina on my back, I saw Nagato waiting for me there. She stood stock-still, apparently unaffected by the cold.

"I am glad she is unhurt," said Nagato, before I could say anything. Her crystalline eyes regarded Asahina, whose cheek rested on my shoulder. "I heard what happened."

From whom? I asked. Koizumi?

Nagato shook her head slowly, then even more slowly held a hand out to me.

She was holding an envelope. Beside the fancy design on it, there was a single handwritten numeral.

Number 5.

The missing message had been delivered to Nagato. I hardly had to ask who the sender was, but Nagato told me.

"Mikuru Asahina's temporal variant. We met roughly one hour ago."

So Asahina the Elder *had* been here. But to think she'd go to Nagato!

"What did she say?"

"She said to take care of herself," said Nagato simply, then reached out with her index finger and touched Asahina on the forehead.

"...Mm...ah...Whaa...?"

It was a magic touch. Asahina's eyes blinked open.

"Waah...Kyon...huh? Why are you carrying...oh, N-Nagato..."

Shamisen struggled the same way when someone picked him up. Asahina had started squirming immediately upon awakening, and although I would've been happy to carry her a bit longer, she seemed unlikely to calm down—and Nagato was watching. I let Asahina down. According to what Mori had said, the tranquilizer was supposed to keep Asahina asleep for two hours, but perhaps because of something Nagato did, Asahina seemed perfectly steady once her feet were on the ground.

Her eyes a bit red at the corners, Asahina looked up at me.

"Um…what happened to me? We gave the turtle to the boy, and then…then all of a sudden there was a car, and it stopped, and…"

Apparently she'd been given the tranquilizer immediately thereafter. She didn't remember anything, so I explained the rest. As the story progressed, her face went from pale to flushed, and when I finished the tale of the car chase, she smiled, much to my surprise.

"So that's what happened. I guess even I can be useful sometimes. I managed to protect my other self in this time line."

Asahina's straightforward smile blasted all the psychological fatigue out of me. She was right. If it hadn't been for (Michiru) Asahina, the kidnappers would've resorted to more extreme methods to capture Asahina the Younger. They might've done it right in front of Haruhi. Koizumi and his comrades could have tried to stop them without worrying about the consequences, but that would've been a terrifying turn of events. Haruhi would be shocked, and Koizumi's Agency could hardly stand by and do nothing. But even our enemies would realize that, now—that they couldn't get away with kidnapping even the comparatively harmless (Michiru) Asahina.

We'd managed to get Asahina back without relying on Nagato. I'll bet our antagonists were well aware of what might have happened if she *had* been involved. If they wanted to be our enemies, I looked forward to seeing them get the treatment they deserved.

"Oh, that letter…" Asahina's eyes fell upon envelope #5. "When did it…?"

Just a while ago. It was for Nagato, I said.

"For Nagato…" Her long eyelashes fluttering, Asahina addressed her petite fellow brigade member. "N-Nagato. Who was it that gave you this letter—was it…?"

"I cannot say," came Nagato's flat refusal. The expressionless alien continued, as though to remind Asahina. "You will understand eventually."

Asahina's mouth opened, and she froze.

"You of all people should understand that," added Nagato, in a voice that sounded like a snow sculpture given life. She then pulled the hood of her duffle coat over her head.

I guess I wasn't the only one who wanted to remind Asahina that it wasn't that we didn't want to tell her—it was that she should've known without asking.

I suddenly felt strangely uncomfortable sandwiched between the two silent girls, so I opened the letter and read it.

The contents of letter #5 were as follows: *"This is the end. Please tell your Mikuru Asahina to return to her original temporal posting. You are free to choose the time designation. And location as well, if you like. Do as you will."*

"Do as you will," huh? I wouldn't mind hearing that phrase under different circumstances, just once. From the original Asahina, of course.

Of course, since this is me we're talking about, even if that wish were granted, I'd probably just stand there and faint dead away, sleeping soundly until Haruhi came along to pound wakefulness into me. I wasn't like Haruhi—I wouldn't wish for the Earth's rotation to reverse. It was better to just seal away wishes you didn't actually want to come true. The world was best left as it was.

Which was why we had to send Asahina back. I placed my hand on the shoulder of the dazed-looking Asahina, and showed her letter #5. She seemed to be more concerned about the sender's identity than the content, but she read it through to the end, her face showing her acceptance.

"I understand. I've finished what I needed to do." She then continued, sounding a bit lonely. "But it was an indirect order. If it hadn't come through you, I wouldn't be able to return to my own time." Her sad expression soon disappeared, though, and she smiled. "Someday I'll be able to do all of this on my own. You'll see. That's when I'll come and save you, Kyon, and everybody else. I don't know when it will happen, but surely…"

Her wish would come true, so long as she didn't lose sight of her resolve at that moment.

I glanced down at my watch. "So, about the time we'll return you to…"

This Asahina had appeared in the broom closet six days earlier, at three forty-five PM, and at the time she'd explained she'd come from eight days in the future, at four fifteen PM—thus her correct temporal posting was two days from now, after four fifteen. Anytime before that, and her situation wouldn't be any different than it was at this moment. We wanted to avoid another instance of two Asahinas existing simultaneously. A sixty-two-second time lag would do nicely.

"Two days from now will be Tuesday. Shall we say four sixteen in the afternoon? That way only one minute will pass without your existence. The same place should work—we'll send you right back into the clubroom's broom closet."

"That sounds fine, since you were the only person in the room then, Kyon," said Asahina.

"Uniform and school slippers," said Nagato, reminding me.

This Asahina was wearing things she'd borrowed from Nagato. Her school uniform was back at Tsuruya's house. But if I went with her to get them now, I'd miss the scheduled rendezvous time with the rest of the brigade. I didn't like the idea of sending Asahina back to fetch them alone either.

"Let's do this. You go back to your correct time in those clothes, and I'll get your uniform and shoes from Tsuruya later today and figure something out."

"I will leave that to you, then. Oh, um…" Asahina bowed, then looked up at me seriously, opening her mouth, then shutting it as though having forgotten what she wanted to say. I wondered if it was my imagination that she seemed to be worried about Nagato.

"It's...it's nothing. We'll talk about it after I get back."

It bothered me, but it probably wasn't too important. If it was something I didn't need to know about for two days, I wouldn't worry about it.

I would not have minded Asahina activating her time-travel mechanism right there on the spot, but she didn't want to be seen doing it. She wanted a place where she could be alone. We went into the library and escorted Asahina to the girls' bathroom.

"Kyon, thank you for everything. I really should thank Koizumi and Tsuruya too."

She could tell Koizumi anytime, but Mori would have to be thanked whenever we met her next. As for Tsuruya, I said, she probably already understood, but I'd make sure to thank her too.

"Well then...Kyon, Nagato—I'll see you soon."

Reluctant to say good-bye right up to the end, Asahina sighed and entered the bathroom. I heard the sound of a stall door closing, but no further Foley reached my ears after that. Nagato looked up quietly.

"She has disappeared from current space-time," she explained.

It was over, then. All I had to do now was wait two days. I left the library with Nagato and heaved a deep sigh.

"Hey, Nagato. Just since yesterday, Asahina and I have met a time traveler from a different faction and a group that opposes Koizumi's organization."

"I see."

"Yeah. So I was thinking maybe the other aliens are also around."

"Are you afraid?" Nagato asked, her gaze perfectly still.

I offered her her own answer. "I am not afraid."

You've got that right, Nagato. I had the same opinion. I bet Asahina and Koizumi would agree with me too. Us birds of a feather had to get along, I said.

Nagato faced silently ahead, and I closed my mouth and continued to walk.

I knew full well that I didn't have to come right out and say something so obvious. The SOS Brigade wasn't a group of five people. It was a single unit. There was no need to explain that to the person who'd long since understood that far better than I ever had.

CHAPTER SEVEN

At the station front, Haruhi spotted Nagato and me and waved her hands hugely, like a cheerleader with a great flag. Asahina was there, right next to her, with Koizumi a bit removed. Haruhi was in fine form, Asahina had a happier-than-usual smile, and Koizumi made eye contact with me but said nothing, only brushing aside his bangs with a finger.

"Kyon, Yuki, you guys sure took your time. Where did you end up?" asked Haruhi, entwining her arm around Nagato's. "Don't tell me you spent the whole time at the library keeping warm. I guess that'd be okay if there were any mysterious spots around there, though. So were there?"

"Hell no," I said.

There were no books that would suck you into their world upon opening them, nor were there books whose characters would leap from their pages into the real world. Maybe in the stacks of a bigger or older library—but not there, I told her.

"Good point; we'll have to try to find a place like that next time, an antique bookstore or something. I'd love to rummage through Tsuruya's family-only storehouse, but there's probably nothing but her ancestors' last testaments."

Haruhi started walking without explaining where she was going. Maybe Asahina and Koizumi already knew; they happily followed her. As did Nagato and I.

I was well aware that putting to Haruhi the question of where she was headed would be pointless. She'd keep walking even if the destination were totally unknown, eventually stopping and pointing at her feet, proudly declaring, "We're here!" The *SS SOS Brigade* had Captain Suzumiya at the tiller, and if it were really a seagoing vessel, we'd probably end up in Bermuda. As it was, Haruhi took us to the same Italian restaurant we'd visited the previous day.

I gazed at Asahina as I ate lunch, full of complicated emotions. She was placidly eating her seafood carbonara with a knife and spoon. It was a calming scene, but soon she'd be heading back in time to flail around for me for days. I wanted to tell her—at the very least, about the kidnapping part.

As I agonized over it, an irritated Haruhi prodded my plate with her fork.

"Kyon, what're you so spaced out about? Got something on your mind? Tell me all about it, and I'll give you some good advice, as your brigade chief." Her eyes shone with energy, the eyes of someone happily taken in by even the most childish April Fool's prank. "Also, about that phone call. Did you forget? The prank call. What *was* that?"

"Oh, that was—" I took a drink of water to buy myself some time. "It was just a stupid joke. I just felt like making a prank call, I guess. I really shouldn't have. I'm sorry."

I glanced briefly at Asahina; Haruhi did likewise. Asahina made a confused expression, her utensils freezing in place halfway to bringing a bite of pasta to her mouth. The next moment, Haruhi's and my eyes met again.

"I guess it's okay," said Haruhi generously. "Just make it a better prank next time, okay? You'll get bonus points if it makes me laugh. If you get enough, you can trade 'em in for a special prize from me. But if the joke's stupid, I'll dock points without mercy! Remember that!"

It felt like Haruhi's roundabout way of asking me to prank-call her. As I was agonizing over having to think of jokes every time I called her, Haruhi and Asahina giggled conspiratorially.

Once lunchtime was over, Haruhi was happy to call it a day. I'd known this would happen, thanks to (Michiru) Asahina, but it was still impressive to see how after two consecutive days of patrolling, even Haruhi would get tired, though her face remained as energetic as always.

Asahina hid her smiling mouth with her hand as she nodded to me in parting. Nagato wore her standard lack of expression, and Koizumi had the same pleasant smile I was sick of, as we all went our separate ways.

After a short while, I caught up with Koizumi.

"I should thank you."

Koizumi smiled as though it were nothing. "You're quite welcome. The idea is to avoid such things before they happen, so I can't say this was a total success. The car chase was a bit much."

The Tamaru brothers had driven the police car—had they been the real thing? I asked. I doubted if they were even really brothers.

"Let's leave it that they're my colleagues, who sometimes assume the identity of the master of a mansion and his younger brother, sometimes a venture capitalist and his younger brother, and sometimes a pair of police officers."

And what about Mori and Arakawa? I'd become particularly suspicious of Mori's true identity.

"Is your organization working with Asahina's and Nagato's bosses?"

"Not directly, no. However, we seem to have come to a tacit

understanding, and there are even times when we unwittingly work toward the same goal. I myself no longer fully understand this world, and the Agency itself is far from united." Koizumi shrugged as we walked down the alleyway. "One extreme viewpoint is that there are no aliens or time travelers. That Nagato and Asahina are just pitiful, deluded girls."

That obviously wasn't true, I said. I'd sign a testament if they wanted me to.

"Ah, but what if Nagato's magic and Asahina's time travel are all the actions of Suzumiya, and the girls are mistaken in believing they are the source of such things?"

If that was the reasoning, you could explain anything that way, I said.

"Or it might be that it's not Suzumiya who possesses this godlike power, but someone else."

Koizumi was probably trying to add some sarcasm to his smile, but all I saw was his usual handsome face.

"The eye of the hurricane is calm, but all around it rages a terrible storm. There may be someone who looks in on the center from outside. Are you not the one who's kept so busy by all these events? If you were the screenwriter, would you cast yourself in such a tiring role?"

This kind of vague explanation was Koizumi's specialty. But I owed him one, so I decided to listen, for once, although it was doubtful that I'd be able to remember everything he said. If I had that kind of memory, my grades would've been a little better than they were.

"If I may speak frankly, my current problem is that I seem to be in the minority. If asked which side I belong to, the SOS Brigade comes to mind, first and foremost. My feelings tend toward it, rather than toward the Agency. So this is what I think. If the Agency gave me an order that ran counter to the interests of the SOS Brigade, I might well find myself upon the horns of a dilemma."

I had prepared myself to listen to another lengthy speech from Koizumi, but just this once, his digression was a brief one. He gave me an easy way and walked away.

I returned home and sat down on the floor of my room, which contained Shamisen and Shamisen's scattered fur.

My activities with (Michiru) Asahina were finished. Asahina the Younger was next. Which meant that I still had work to do.

In my hand was future letter #6.

"When everything is over, go to the park."

Since #5 had instructed me to return (Michiru) Asahina to her previous time plane, all that remained was to follow the instructions in #6. But still...

Would everything really be over then? I couldn't help but feel like there was still something else, though I had no idea why. It was like a tiny sardine bone stuck in my mind.

But no matter how I turned it over in my head, without any new input there would be no new answers, so I reread all the letters I'd gotten from Asahina the Elder. Even now they were still completely incomprehensible, the presumed merits of our actions utterly baffling. Or so they had been.

I was looking at the instructions on the third letter.

"Go to the mountains. There you will see an oddly shaped rock. Move it approximately three meters west. Your Mikuru Asahina will know the place."

This was the only one that was linked with Haruhi's activities. This was the only place where the entire SOS Brigade had been involved. The fruitless treasure hunt. We'd found nothing, as I had known we would...

I felt like I was on the verge of figuring something out when my sister came barging in to inform me that dinner was ready, and I wound up leaving my room with a nagging feeling. I took a bath after dinner, and midway through washing my hair I'd pretty much forgotten whatever I'd nearly hit upon. By the time I got into the bath proper and submerged myself up to my chin in hot water, the only thought in my mind was that of an early bedtime.

But then, right at the end of the day, one last order came in. It wasn't from a time traveler; it was from Haruhi, and it didn't come via a note in my shoe locker, but instead through my sister, carrying the phone.

"Kyon, phone! It's Haru-nyan!" she said, barging right into the bathroom and giving me the handset. I waved my hands and shooed her out of the room, then put the receiver to my ear.

"Hello?"

"Hey. Are you in the bath?"

Haruhi's voice echoed off the walls of the bathroom. I was in the bathroom, but she'd better not get any weird ideas, I told her.

"Like I'd ever do that, stupid. Anyway, we're meeting up at the station tomorrow."

Why was she calling me at this hour? She should've just told me about this before we split up this afternoon, I said.

"Aw, c'mon. I've got my own circumstances, you know."

Did she ever think about anybody's circumstances but her own? I asked.

"Oh, whatever! Anyway, we should meet up in the afternoon. Let's say two o'clock. You don't need to bring anything."

And what about her?

"That's my business. Tomorrow at two. Got it? If you don't come, rest assured you will regret it. Punctuality above all!"

Haruhi-style phone etiquette involved delivering rapid-fire

instructions, then hanging up immediately. I emerged from the bathtub, handset in hand, and thought it over as I toweled myself dry.

So there was something left, after all. What was it this time? So far this February, Haruhi had started out in ennui mode, then done Setsubun, a treasure hunt, and a two-day search for mysterious phenomena. Would this be the last?

Hold on—why hadn't (Michiru) Asahina told me about this? She had never said anything about a station-front rendezvous on Monday. Perhaps she wasn't involved. Perhaps she hadn't told me because she'd never known herself—or perhaps she *did* know and had said nothing.

I just didn't want to hear that this part of history never existed.

Showing up at a specified time, in a specified place was fast becoming a conditioned response for me, and arriving five minutes before two and seeing the rest of the club assembled and waiting for me was more normal than spring following winter.

For once Haruhi didn't berate me for tardiness, nor did she head for the café. Instead we went to the bus terminal, where Haruhi herded me onto a northbound bus.

Asahina, I noticed, was constantly yawning, then hurrying to hide her mouth. When I looked more closely, I saw that Haruhi was rubbing her eyes as though shortchanged on sleep herself. When she noticed me watching her, she gave me a glare and looked out the window as the green of the scenery turned deeper.

Our bus was bound for the mountains, along the same route we'd taken the other day to reach Mt. Tsuruya.

The bus stop we got out at was the same too. And just when it looked like we were going to climb to the summit using the same route—

"If we go this way, it's the long way around. It was the back way originally. We're going to go around to the south side and climb from there."

Haruhi started striding along, followed by Asahina and Nagato, who evidently had no problem with another hiking session. Koizumi scratched his chin for a moment.

"Well, shall we go? We've gotten this far, so neither of us can back out now—we're alike in that way," he said inexplicably, chuckling like a pigeon.

Haruhi circled the base of the mountain, making for the south side. I started to get an idea of where she wanted to go. I'd been there a couple of times myself recently. Two days in a row, in fact.

The only things around us other than mountains were dry fields. The first time I'd been here, I'd been climbing up with (Michiru) Asahina. The second time, I'd been descending the mountain with the SOS Brigade.

Haruhi took the lead up the animal path that led to the spot with the gourd-shaped rock.

"Of course, no wonder…"

The day we'd moved the rock, I'd noticed that Asahina seemed to know the way very well. I now saw that it was because she'd been there twice before.

Asahina ascended rather perilously, being forcibly dragged behind Haruhi, Nagato guarding her from tumbling back down.

We soon reached the spot. As soon as Haruhi emerged into the flat clearing on the mountainside, she sat down on the gourd-shaped rock as though it were a favorite chair.

"Kyon, Koizumi, this is treasure hunt round two! When you think about it, giving up after just one day of digging doesn't show much dedication. Treasure hunting is about keeping at it until you find something!"

Haruhi smiled brilliantly and produced two garden spades from within her coat, offering them to Koizumi and me.

"To be honest, I wanted to use big shovels and dig up every corner like last time, but I'll let you off the hook this time. You can use those spades and just dig right here."

Haruhi indicated the spot right in front of her—in other words, directly beside the gourd rock. It was the same spot Koizumi and I had dug fully two meters down. But before I could complain that we'd already dug there—

"It's pretty common to find lost items in places you think you've already looked, right? Well, treasure's the same way. You've got to look over and over again in the same place for it. And if I say there's treasure, there's treasure."

Haruhi sounded more confident than the dog in "Hanasaka Jiisan," like she was sure we were bound to meet wealth and good fortune. For whatever reason, Asahina just nodded happily in agreement, with Nagato being the only one whose expression was unchanged. There with the spade in my hand for no particular reason, I finally began to understand the meaning of Koizumi's smile.

The digging didn't take much time or effort. The soil had already been dug up and replaced once, so it was soft enough that our spades were more than adequate for the task. We hadn't dug very deeply when our spades' tips bumped into the edge of something hard.

As Haruhi grinned down from above, I dug the object loose and pulled it out of the ground. The rectangular box did not, it must be said, look like something from the Genroku era. It was more like a tin that cookies or rice crackers would come in. It hadn't been here three days earlier, when Koizumi and I had been searching. Someone had to have come up here since then and bury it, I was sure of it—no points for guessing who.

"Open it," said Haruhi, looking like the "Tongue-Cut Sparrow" watching the old man pick the smaller basket. The folktale was about greed and how the smaller basket was filled with treasure instead of monsters, so in this case, she was definitely thinking this was treasure.

I took the tin in hand and popped off the lid.

"…"

I saw neither jewels nor gold coins—but I doubted anyone would dispute me were I to call it "treasure," nonetheless.

There were six small boxes delicately wrapped in beautiful wrapping paper—and tied up with ribbon, obviously.

Finally—finally, was all I could say.

I remembered what day it was. Or maybe it would be more accurate to say I realized. It was a day even more important than July seventh, Tanabata—at least it was for high school guys.

Today was February fourteenth.

In other words: Valentine's Day.

"They're handmade," explained Haruhi, looking askance. "We worked from noon to nightfall to make them. Mikuru, Yuki, and I pulled a late shift for you guys! A late shift! Originally I wanted to make them from pure cacao, but then it was like, 'Let's not get too crazy.' So we went with chocolate cake."

Each of the three girls had written our names on the labels that adorned the wrapped packages—both of us got a cake from each of them.

Koizumi put down his spade, and after carefully brushing off his hands, he picked up one of the packages. "To Koizumi, from Mikuru," it said. Asahina had made treasures just for us.

"You bet she did!" Haruhi fired off like a machine gun. "We all did! It was pretty fun, and we really gave it our all! But whatever, I was just worried that everything was going to get out of hand, and it was making me space out all the time, and to be honest I was sort of worried I was just falling into society's trap, but so what? It's such a broadly accepted tradition; I feel bad for the people who think it's just a conspiracy by candy companies! It's fine! Yuki and Mikuru and I had fun; that's what's important.

We were thinking of putting hot peppers into them, but— Hey, Kyon, what's that look?"

It was nothing. I was just—grateful. It was true. I'd forgotten entirely that today was that day that made men the world over nervous. If I'd remembered, maybe I would've prepared an appropriate reaction, but having weathered this surprise attack, I had nothing to say to the three brigade girls. It was hard to ad-lib clever words to hide your embarrassment. I doubted I had enough life experience to pull it off.

The strength drained from my body. All the riddles had been solved. Haruhi's strange mood and behavior starting in February. Asahina traveling back in time but finding it difficult to talk about the treasure hunt. Taniguchi's sulking and insistence that he envied me.

Haruhi had been thinking about this all along—how to give us chocolates on Valentine's Day. She seriously couldn't get over herself, not even a little. How twisted did someone have to be to make us go on this treasure hunt, dig all these holes, then fill them back up again, instead of just giving chocolate to us in the clubroom? Wait, that meant—ah ha. Tsuruya was in on it too. The treasure map had been a pack of lies. The reason Haruhi had given up on the treasure hunt was because she already knew there was no treasure. The treasure Haruhi had in mind had yet to be buried at that point—the chocolate cake of which Koizumi and I now each had three pieces. That had been the cause of the weeks of uncertainty on Haruhi's part. Nagato and Asahina had gotten dragged into it as well.

What fools we were—both Haruhi, for coming up with such a plan, and me, for not seeing through it.

"These are just friendly chocolates, though! Just friendly. I don't actually want to have to say stuff like 'just friendly,' though. And chocolate cake counts as chocolate, right?"

Haruhi's voice echoing in my head like insects chirping in a thicket, I summoned my strength and looked up.

Haruhi glared at me with an angry face. Asahina wore a gently teasing smile, and Nagato regarded me expressionlessly.

"Thank you very much. I will savor every bite."

Koizumi beat me to the punch.

Haruhi's lips twisted into a smirk. "I recommend eating them as soon as you get home. Just gobble 'em down in one go—don't leave them on the family shrine for your ancestors to eat, got that?" She turned her head away hurriedly, then stood. "Okay then, let's go home. The event's over, and if we don't leave right away, we'll get stuck in traffic. I'm sleepy. We worked on those until sunrise, I'll have you know! And then we came up here in the morning and buried them, and I only caught a couple of hours of sleep at Yuki's place. The same goes for Mikuru and Yuki!"

We were on our way home. As we stood waiting at the bus stop, Haruhi stood as far away from me as possible, gazing off in the distance, avoiding my eyes. *Oh, brother.*

I whispered to Asahina, who stood next to me.

"You didn't give chocolate to someone you have a crush on? Just friends?"

"No," she replied, sounding a bit desolate. "Even if I did have a crush on someone here, I'll eventually have to return to the future. Our separation would be inevitable. It would be so sad..."

It was an extremely honest view to hold. I couldn't think of a single rebuttal. And yet it was the position's obvious correctness that made me hesitate to agree with it.

"You could just stay here," I said. "This time period's not so bad. You could visit the future from time to time, but just keep your home here."

Asahina giggled. "Thanks." Her lips formed a soft smile that made me want to steal a kiss. "But I wasn't born in this time. My

home is there, in the future. No—to me, this is the past. I'm just a visitor. The future is my present, my home. I must return someday."

Just like the princess from "The Bamboo-Cutter's Tale." No matter what measures were taken to stop her, when the time came she had to leave Earth. It wasn't where she belonged. I guess I agreed with Asahina. If I jumped a hundred years into the past, I might find it interesting at first, but I'm sure I would miss the culture and technology of home. I'd want to play video games with ridiculous graphics, heat convenience-store chicken bowls in the microwave, and send stupid text messages with my cell phone. More than anything else, I'd want to nap in my own room and enjoy my own time at my own pace.

Even if she could do all of the same things, Asahina would always be aware that this wasn't her time. She was in the past. It was an unnatural place for her to be in, and I could imagine that she might never really feel comfortable.

"Oh, but—!" she began hastily, waving her hands. "It's not that I don't like being here! It's very important, and I really have to do my best. I'm just really glad you're here with me, Kyon."

It certainly made me happy to hear her say so. I thought I'd try something out.

"So when you go back to the future, how about you take me along?" Not that Haruhi would keep quiet if something like that happened. "We could take everyone on a trip to the future. Haruhi and Nagato and Koizumi too. I wouldn't complain. Heck, I'm starting to think that moving to the future wouldn't be a bad idea."

"Wha—?" Her fairy-like eyes widened; she was totally taken aback. "N-no, definitely not! That is completely forbidden. It's just…"

Asahina's face looked surprised for a while, but eventually she noticed my own expression. She closed her mouth, and the tension drained from her tensed shoulders.

She giggled. "Gosh, Kyon. If you're going to tell a joke, make sure it's jokier next time. You really surprised me!"

"Sorry."

Yes, of course it was a joke. This was my time, my era. I'd encountered terrible challenges, especially the repeated time travel to three and four years ago, but I always came back to this time and place, in the SOS Brigade's clubroom. I hadn't even been a high school student for a year yet, and I was sure Haruhi had a lot of things she still wanted to do here and now. I wondered if the day would ever come when she would finish it all. It was a bit too early to be planning an escape to the future.

The day would come when Asahina had to return to her own time. But for the moment, she was here. That was enough. So long as we kept having fun here, the future would surely become a fun place too. She had once compared different time planes to pages in a flip-book, and if I thought about it that way, if all the pages were full of gags, the last page couldn't possibly be horror. I'd never accept that. I mean, who would?

I'd once lost my friends in the SOS Brigade and gotten them back. I'd never forget the determination I had then. Whatever happened from here on out, whether I stumbled or was defeated, I'd always face ahead. I wasn't such a lightweight that I'd easily go back on a decision I'd made only two months before. But leave me my "Oh, brother." That's special.

In other words, no matter how cheap my pride was, it would have to be a little cheaper before I'd sell it off completely. As long as I faced forward, I could say, "Oh, brother," if I wanted to. They were just words, after all. The same went for, "Haruhi, you idiot," "Take me with you," or even saying nothing, Nagato-style. In a three-legged race, you had to tie your leg to your partner's leg. It was easier for five people to run a six-legged race than it was for one person to do three.

If there was one thing I'd learned this week, that was it.

*　　*　　*

I'd spent the last several days going back and forth between my house and the train station. I would probably enjoy a respite from that for a while. Haruhi continued to ignore me, her back turned, not so much as giving me a proper goodnight. Our honorable brigade chief took large, resolute steps, but I wondered what sort of expression she would wear tomorrow at school.

I gave my thanks to Asahina and Nagato as I reassured myself of the weight of their packages in my pocket. "I'm really sorry I couldn't tell you. Suzumiya made us promise not to say anything," said Asahina, looking particularly regretful, her head bowed. I was impressed that Haruhi had the ability to silence even Nagato. Although I suppose it wasn't that difficult, since it was me who'd forgotten such an important day in the first place. Although things had been complicated for a while, it was as though I'd simply dropped the concept of Valentine's Day entirely.

When I got back to my room, I immediately opened the three packages, though I did not intend to eat them in lieu of dinner as Haruhi had suggested. Inside were plastic cases containing chocolate-coated pieces of cake.

Haruhi's was round, Asahina's was heart-shaped, and Nagato's was in the shape of a star. Each one sported white chocolate lettering on it.

Smack-dab in the middle of Haruhi's was a simple, blunt, "chocolate," while Nagato's sported "Gift" in a neat serif font. Asahina's said "Just Friends" on it, which seemed a bit uncharacteristically blunt to me until I noted another message hidden in the bottom of the cake's plastic case, hurriedly scrawled out on the corner of a paper towel. "Suzumiya made me write that," it said. I imagined the scene of the three of them having a lively time making the cakes in Nagato's kitchen. I put the three cakes in the refrigerator. I couldn't forget to tell my sister not to go and eat them.

*　　*　　*

Once the sun was down, I got on my bike and started to pedal.

The last checkpoint was a certain bench in a certain park near Nagato's apartment.

The park was dark and deserted, and there sat the bench, unoccupied, beneath the streetlight. I stopped my bike, and as I pushed it into the park, I still did not see a soul.

I sat on the chilly bench and raised my voice to the empty space.

"I know you're there, Asahina."

The evergreen shrubs behind the bench rustled, and slowly around the bench came the person I was waiting for.

"May I sit?"

But of course. I expected this to be a long talk, I told her.

She giggled. "I'm afraid I won't be able to tell you much."

I confirmed that it was Asahina the Elder's elegant form on the bench beside me. The winter-wardrobe version of adult Asahina didn't look any different from a random person on the street—assuming you didn't count her heart-melting beauty.

I breathed in the winter air, then spoke. "But you'll explain things, won't you?"

"Where shall I start?"

"The first errand Asahina and I ran—the prank."

We'd pounded nails into the ground, then covered them with a can, and thereby sent a man to the hospital. It seemed like ages ago.

"There was a reason you had to do that." Asahina's face had a faintly visible smile that I could see from an oblique angle. "Kyon, I want you to imagine something. If you could go back into the past, years or even decades"—she sounded serious—"imagine that you could go back and witness history. But what if that history wasn't the history you knew? What if it were different?"

"What do you mean, different?" I didn't understand.

"For example, suppose you traveled exactly one year into the past. What were you doing then?"

Probably playing video games in my room, I told her. I certainly didn't have any memories of getting chocolate from anyone.

Asahina nodded slightly. "Think about if that were different. If you went to your house of a year ago, but you weren't living there. What would you do? Neither you, nor your sister, nor your parents are there. Strangers you've never met live in your house. And your family doesn't live in the house you know, but instead live a totally different life, somewhere far away."

That was absurd.

"When we come to the past and find that the history we're expecting is subtly different, can you see what we in the future would think? Assuming that the past is constantly subject to intervention from the future. Assuming that if left alone, our future will never come to be, and instead a different future will happen."

Asahina's voice sounded distant. As though she were lost in thought.

"A past where a person dies when they were meant to keep on living. A past where two people who were supposed to meet never do. If we knew that, left alone, that past would never lead to our future."

A shadow fell over her already lonely-sounding voice.

"I'll get to the point. The man who injured himself kicking the can you placed will meet a certain woman at the hospital. They will get married, have children, and those children will have children. That is all because he went to the hospital. There is no other point in history where they can meet."

My mind flashed back to the image of the man smiling pleasantly as he looked up at Asahina and me.

"That memory device was the same. The data on it needed to be sent in that form. The person you sent it to ends up accidentally discovering the same data. But in this past, that coincidence wasn't going to happen. Perhaps it was deleted. So we had to send it to him. In as coincidental a form as possible."

Someone picks up the device after it's been dropped in a flower bed and happens to send it to a random address—*his* address, Asahina explained.

I didn't know what to say. There was no way something like that could be a coincidence. Plus that jerk had shown up and *handed* us the data. What had been the point of his interference? I wanted to know.

"He wasn't interfering. That data was necessary for his future too. That's how he was able to come back to this time." Asahina spoke very clearly. "For us in the future, that was a predetermined event. But for you, and the person who will receive the data, it was a mere coincidence. That's just how time works."

"..."

I felt dizzy, possibly because the limits of my imagination had been so easily shattered.

"The turtle and that boy—that was also a coincidence. The boy always remembered getting the turtle from the man and woman at the river. He remembered the ripples in the river when the man threw the turtle into the water, and how he flowed lazily along with the current. Turtles live long lives, and every time he looks at his turtle, he remembers that scene. That gives rise to... a kind of fundamental theory. Though it was the result of many other elements as well."

Could it be—the possibility made me dizzy even as my imagination leaped forward. Was that boy going to be the inventor of the time machine? The near-miss traffic accident, the turtle. Had I changed the future—the future of that boy, and the future of the world? All because of a few insignificant things I had done...

Suddenly a different memory came back to me. A few days before the school festival, when I was in agony trying to finish our film's climax, Nagato had said something to me.

"In order to stabilize the future, the correct values must be input. Asahina Mikuru's job is inputting those values."

My memory was pretty good, but this was not the time to relish it. No, what I was concerned about now was the phrase "in order to stabilize the future." I could no longer assume that there was but one future.

Probably. I wasn't sure, so I couldn't speak with confidence. What understanding I had had gotten me as far as the following, though my mind was wild with question marks.

Was the future not a stable thing?

Were there other futures besides the one from which Asahina came?

I could admit the possibility. But just barely. If the future diverged into separate branches—that could mean there was a future in which that glasses-wearing boy lived and one where he died. Except that I'd erased the possibility of the latter.

Which meant I had single-handedly obliterated an entire future.

I didn't know if that were really true. The basis for the conjecture was so shaky that I would be an idiot to suggest that the proof was "left as an exercise for the reader," yet I could not easily dismiss the wild notion. I was mute, struck dumb. How else could I react?

"The divergence points were concentrated in this time period. While most paths would lead to the same future, everything you did in the past few days was connected to a divergence point—a path that would lead to a different future..."

Her lovely voice got quieter.

"There will soon come an even larger divergence point. There is a very powerful future... if you should choose it, it... it would not be good for our future."

My body felt heavy and sluggish somehow. I tried to look over at Asahina, but my head was strangely stiff.

"But it will be okay. I trust you, after all. Right?"

My consciousness began to blur. A familiar diagram emerged from within the mist. The writing from the whiteboard danced through my mind. I saw two *X*s in the whirl. Koizumi's explanation. There were two *X*s.

It was impossible to completely erase the past. Once modified, history would simply be rewritten over the original time line.

And I had another memory. The loop during summer vacation. We'd repeated the same two weeks tens of thousands of times over.

But no one save Nagato could remember. It was as though those tens of thousands of repetitions had never happened. So the answer was clear.

The past could be negated. In fact, it wasn't a question of whether a certain past had or had not existed. Even if something had happened, if nobody remembered it, it didn't matter. Which was why—

You just had to erase the *memories* of the past.

If my memories of the period from December seventeenth to December twenty-first were erased—my memories of all that running around, of jumping back three years into the past and being stabbed by Asakura—and I'd simply woken on that hospital bed, what then? I would have simply believed Koizumi's explanation, that I'd fallen down the stairs, hit my head, and lost three days of memory.

Nagato the literature club girl, Asahina from the calligraphy club, Haruhi the girl from another school who looked alarmingly good in a ponytail, and Koizumi the normal guy—if my memories of them were erased, I wouldn't have to worry about jumping back to preserve the integrity of the time loop.

But no, that wasn't right.

On the morning of the eighteenth, on the verge of death after being attacked by Asakura, I saw future-us, and so I knew that I would go to that time again. The only one who could repair Nagato was her three-years-previous self, and it was Nagato from this last January second who'd put that repair into action. That much was necessary.

And time was rewritten—

I felt a chill. Haruhi had no idea. Neither did Taniguchi or Kunikida. The only ones who knew were Nagato, Asahina, and me, plus—after hearing my report—Koizumi.

Which meant there was no guarantee I wasn't in the same position as Haruhi. If history had been changed somewhere, even if I had once known of it, without any memory of it, it would be as though it had never happened.

Not just that—there was even the possibility that the version of myself who was thinking these things could be overwritten by another version from another timeline. A timeline in which my present self would cease to exist, and a different me would continue into the future.

I thought of what Nagato had said in the hospital room.

—*Erasure of all your relevant memories.*

—*No guarantee such erasure has not taken place.*

The Asahina who had come from one week in the future told me she had not met her other self. Which was why I'd gone to such lengths to make sure they never *did* meet. But even if they had, it might not have been such a problem.

The current Asahina's memories of such an encounter could simply be erased. If she were then sent back in time after such erasure, it wouldn't much matter whether or not she encountered herself.

A dark feeling rumbled in the pit of my stomach—the same feeling I'd had toward the Data Overmind as I lay in the hospital bed last month. Only this time the emotion was directed at Asahina the Elder.

She was simply using her former self, Asahina the Younger, forcing her to constantly play the confused, unreliable-but-cute classmate. Oh, sure, I knew she had no choice but to do so. I understood that she had to retrace the history that she herself remembered experiencing. "The future's countermeasures against the past," Koizumi had said. But wasn't there some other way?

My neck's curse on my head was finally broken. It felt like it had taken an hour just to look sideways. But when I went to speak the words that came to mind, I realized no one was sitting there.

Asahina had disappeared. I was the only one sitting on the bench in the faint glow of the streetlight. In her place, there had been placed a small box.

A small, square, ribbon-wrapped box.

There was a message card attached to it. I held it up to the light. It carried a single greeting: "Happy Valentine's Day."

The chocolates inside were completely normal. There was nothing futuristic about their flavors or shapes. Either the chocolatiers of Asahina's world had not changed their recipes much, or they'd matched chocolate to its destination era.

"But still, Asahina..."

I didn't want to think that I would concede so easily. Yes, today she'd deviated and provided me with information, but it still wasn't enough. I'd even accept her reasons for not telling me about her kidnapping. But she'd deliberately refrained from saying anything about Haruhi's Valentine's Day plans or the truth of the treasure hunt and gourd stone. That was totally meaningless, even now. Haruhi could have buried those chocolates anywhere. There was no reason it had to be next to that particular rock. And there was no reason for me to move said rock.

Or was this part of your plan too, Asahina the Elder? Were the things I was thinking and doing right now among your predetermined events?

"When everything is over..."

It seemed like that was not today. I'd eventually come here again. And maybe I'd bring the rest of the SOS Brigade along. I'd love to see her try to explain all this to Haruhi and Koizumi. All I was good for was playing the observer.

*   *   *

I placed a phone call from the park.

"Hello? Ah, Tsuruya? It's me. Yeah, about Michiru. She's gone home. I really appreciate everything you did for her, and I'll definitely get your clothes back to you—huh? Oh, really? Oh, also, listen—when you see the Asahina you know tomorrow, she might randomly start apologizing to you, but just let it slide. And there should be a North High uniform she left in your apartment, so could you bring that to school tomorrow? Yeah, to me. Before the end of class."

So far, so good. I listened to Tsuruya's cheerful *"Okay!"* and took a deep breath.

"There's one more thing, and this is the important one. It's about your family's mountain—the one from the treasure map. Yeah, that one. Haruhi used it in this crazy roundabout scheme of hers to...yes. Yes, I got them. Four—I mean, three. It was a lot of fun."

I continued talking over the sound of Tsuruya's laughter. "It's about that treasure map. Did you know there's a trail that leads from the fields at the base straight up the south side? Oh, good, that will make this faster. If you follow it, you'll come to a flat, open area. Oh, you know that too? There's a rock there—if you go about three meters east and dig, you might find something interesting."

Tsuruya's response sounded doubtful.

"I don't have any proof myself, so it's not a one-hundred percent guarantee. But I get the feeling there might be something."

If I hadn't moved the rock, Haruhi would have taken it for a marker the moment she laid eyes on it, and we would've wound up digging right next to it. And we might well have found something. Something we should never have found.

Three meters west. That was how far I'd traveled after picking up the rock. Just that far.

I gave Tsuruya some vague responses, then hung up.

There's your piece of defiance from me, Asahina. I'm not trying to outwit you or your future, but sometimes a guy just wants to give something a try.

After all, I wasn't nearly as audacious as Haruhi.

EPILOGUE

The next morning, I barely arrived at the classroom in time for the first bell. Ignoring the irritated-looking Taniguchi as well as Kunikida, who was already teasing him, I took my seat and spoke to the person behind me.

"Hey, how's it going?"

"Great, obviously." Haruhi flashed a Cheshire cat grin full of intrigue at me. Goodness, but she hadn't even glared at me first—could she, too, flip moods over the course of a single night?

As the bell rang, she leaned forward over her desk and whispered into my ear from behind me.

"And Kyon, let's get something straight. Don't go talking about what happened yesterday. Especially to, say, Taniguchi. You gotta keep it a secret, got that? It would be embarr—well, not *embarrassing*, but still. Don't go spreading rumors. It'll ruin the value of the gift."

What the hell was she mumbling about? I wasn't giving the gift back, I told her. Especially since it was edible.

"I didn't tell you to give it back. If that were the case, I wouldn't have given it to you in the first place. Also, changing the subject. We're gonna be busy after school today, so prepare yourself."

I knew all too well. I'd be busy myself, as it happened. I had to send Asahina eight days back in time, then be there to greet the returning version of herself. And then—finally—this long, long week would be over.

During the lunch period, Tsuruya came by my classroom. Fortunately, Haruhi rarely brought her own lunch from home, and she had gone to the cafeteria to eat. As soon as I heard Tsuruya's "Hey, Kyon!" I set aside my half-eaten lunch and headed out to the hallway, where she waited.

"Not here," she said, dragging me by the necktie to the stairway, then leading me all the way up past the top floor to the roof level, stopping just before the door. Haruhi had dragged me up to the dim little landing here once before, and then, as now, it was scattered with art supplies.

"So I'll just get right to the point," said Tsuruya, smiling cautiously as she produced a stack of photos from her breast pocket. "Kyon, how did you know there was something buried in that spot? I was blown away, seriously."

So there *had* been something there. I asked what it was.

"Something amazing!" Tsuruya fanned out the photos. "The first thing that surprised me when I started digging was this pot just popping up to say hello, and it was…*three hundred years old*!"

She showed me a photo of an earthen pot, covered in cracks, photographed against a plain white background.

"Are you sure it's that old?"

"I'm *super* sure. I even had it carbon-dated. But what was inside was even more of a surprise!"

The second photograph showed an old piece of parchment. It seemed like a name was written on it, but I couldn't make it out. One thing was for sure—at the edge of the paper was a drawing of a very familiar mountain with an X on it. I don't need to tell you what spot the X indicated.

"This was definitely written by Fusauemon Tsuruya, my ancestor. It was the fifteenth year of the Genroku era—1702! A quick translation of it reads, 'I found a strange object, but it made me feel uneasy, so I buried it on the mountain.'"

Haruhi's treasure map. She had said that something similar was written on it. And that one was a fake, but this was for real.

"But what was Old Man Fusauemon thinking? How're we supposed to find the treasure if he buried the map in the same spot?" said Tsuruya, smiling as she indicated a third photograph.

"What's this?"

The photograph gave no sense of the scale, but it looked like a metal rod about ten centimeters long. It was so shiny you'd never think it had been buried for centuries, and close inspection revealed that its surface was covered in spiderweb-fine lines, like a circuit board. Although the pattern looked disorderly at first, I realized that it actually had a beautiful symmetry. Was it really made during the Edo period?

"This and the letter were all that was inside the pot. But here's the real question. Nobody will believe that something like this came out of my ancestor's time capsule!"

"Why not?"

Tsuruya grinned, waving the photos. "Because this thing is made of a titanium-cesium alloy!"

Okay, that was a surprise. I'd have to find Kunikida later so I could tell him and freak myself out all over again.

"Metallurgy from three hundred years ago could never create something like this, y'know? The person I had do the testing had no idea—they said that if this had really come from three hundred years ago, it was either the product of some ancient advanced civilization, or a time traveler from the future had traveled back to 1702 and left it there, or it was a fragment of some alien spaceship."

...I really didn't want it to be from some ancient civilization.

"But doesn't it look like a component for something else?" said Tsuruya, staring at the third photograph, then aiming her smile at me. "What do you think it is, Kyon? Which do you like better, aliens or time travelers?"

The innocent girl's question left me totally speechless.

"You better decide soon, boy!"

The mysterious artifact that had come out of the clay pot, which in turn bore the Tsuruya crest, would be stored securely at the Tsuruya estate. Tsuruya herself promised, so that was one thing I didn't have to worry about. She would definitely do what she said she'd do. The most important thing was to make sure Haruhi didn't find out about it, but I must confess to a certain misgiving. I didn't want things to turn out this way—to be honest, I didn't even want to think about it, but...

...I couldn't escape the feeling that we'd need that artifact eventually.

I wondered if I'd given Tsuruya the location of the treasure too soon. I could also have kept it to myself, neither digging it up nor telling anyone else about it.

But was that really possible? Could I have resisted digging it up once I'd realized there was probably something interesting there? I was a curious guy—when I saw a word I didn't know, I always had to immediately go look it up on the Internet.

Plus there was the other possibility, that for some reason Haruhi would want to go back and dig some more. It was better for the mysterious part to be taken in by Tsuruya's family. If a member of an ancient race, or an alien, or a time traveler showed up and demand it be returned, I doubted very much that Haruhi would simply agree. Plus, I didn't want anyone like that showing up in front of her in the first place. There was no guarantee they'd hide their true forms the way Nagato and Asahina did. Rather than traveling back in time to change the present before it happened, it was better to do what I could in the present to avoid bad outcomes in the future. We did live in the present, after all.

Tsuruya and I parted ways, and I returned to my classroom, where I came upon Haruhi happily eating my lunch.

"Hey, what the—? That's mine."

"I know. Even I wouldn't eat the lunch of someone I don't know, y'know."

Well, if they're someone you *do* know, you should also know you can't just eat their lunch, I said. Give it back. Spit it out.

"Anyway," said Haruhi, putting the chopsticks back in my lunch box and pushing it toward me, then looking up at me with a strange expression. "What're you making that weird face for? Stop grinning."

Grinning? Was there a reason I should grin? But when I put my hand to my face, I found that Haruhi was right—the muscles in my face had somehow relaxed into a smile.

"You look weird," said Haruhi rudely, then turned away. Her hair rustled with the movement, her small ears peeking through.

In that instant, I realized it.

I realized why I was unconsciously grinning. What reason would I have to smile? What had happened to me this past week? Besides wandering all over the place with Asahina, I encountered a new time traveler and a new mysterious organization, which had kidnapped Asahina among other dastardly deeds. Not only did they seem likely to appear again, but likewise the rival alien faction would probably show its face again as well, and now a mysterious artifact had been found on Tsuruya's mountain—it was surely no time to be grinning like an idiot.

Yet anyone who genuinely believes that is a fool, and I had no intention of being a fool. If I was smiling, I had a reason for it. Yes, indeed—and I realized what it was.

I'd already dealt with a series of incredible events, and more seemed likely to come my way—yet I was not even slightly disturbed. Whoever or whatever might come, I didn't care.

I wasn't the least bit afraid of them. If they were going to come, bring it on. I'd face anything. But I wouldn't be alone. When the time came, I'd have Nagato beside me, and Koizumi, and Asahina. In front of me might be Haruhi herself, standing tall; perhaps Tsuruya would be behind me, giggling away. If the mysterious forces of the universe wanted to face all that—then let them come! Be they foe, ally, neutral party, or sharer of some common goal—I didn't care.

I put the lid back on the lunch box that Haruhi returned to me, then wrapped it in a napkin before putting it in my bag.

I might have looked weird, but Haruhi's expression as she regarded me was still weirder. Did I really look that strong?

"Hey, Haruhi."

"What?" Haruhi furrowed her brow.

"You better take care of the SOS Brigade."

Haruhi's mouth hung open for a moment. "Of course I will." The corners of her eyes and mouth curled up in her characteristic smile as she shouted, "I mean, it's *my* brigade, after all!"

After school, I had to arrange for the two Asahinas to switch places, but that wasn't all I had to do—there was still Haruhi's plan. It wasn't that I'd forgotten; Haruhi just hadn't told me she'd planned to raise such a commotion.

I'd been informed that Haruhi would be holding a lottery, with Asahina presenting the prize while wearing a shrine maiden outfit. What I hadn't realized was that the lottery prize would be this:

"The SOS Brigade presents: Mikuru Asahina's Handmade Belated Valentine's Day Chocolate Amidakuji! Five hundred yen to enter!"

...proclaimed Haruhi, wielding a megaphone as I cursed my naiveté at not anticipating this eventuality.

For the Mikuru Asahina's Handmade Belated Valentine's Day Chocolate Amidakuji, we wound up needing a huge amount of paper for the entries, and even with an entry cost of five hundred yen, people were fighting with one another to pay up. It looked like we'd reach five digits of earnings. If it had been the chocolate cake she'd given me, I never would've let it near this accursed market, but Asahina seemed to have made one extra piece in addition to what she'd made for Koizumi and me.

"Actually, it was mostly Nagato who made it..." said Asahina apologetically. The shrine maiden costume she'd been forced to wear was so perfect that if she were teleported to a shrine, she would fit right in. Haruhi had gotten the costume somewhere, and the instant homeroom was over she dragged Asahina off to the clubroom and forced her to change into it. It looked like she took what I said at Setsubun quite seriously.

At Haruhi's behest, Koizumi and I brought the table down from the clubroom into the courtyard while Haruhi ran around with the megaphone. Nagato handled cashier duties.

Male students started to swarm the courtyard like zombies in search of fresh meat, fomenting a terrible atmosphere that made you wonder where this country was headed. I saw Kunikida and Taniguchi in the crowd, and I began to worry for the future of my classmates.

Haruhi gave instructions to the many male and few female students in the crowd. "The cashier is this way! Line up in front of Yuki! Once you've paid your five hundred yen, you'll receive a numbered ticket. Take it to Koizumi, and he'll write it in whatever slot you want. You can draw one horizontal line, wherever you like!"

Nagato was handling the line quite efficiently, and beside her Koizumi was frantically drawing vertical lines on B4 copier paper. It looked like entries would reach three digits, which meant two or three sheets of paper weren't going to be close to enough.

As the number of sheets Koizumi taped together increased, so, too, did the number of times I checked my watch. This was very, very bad. I wasn't going to make it in time.

(Michiru) Asahina would be getting back at four sixteen. I had to send this Asahina back in time by four fifteen, and I'd need time to get her changed out of her shrine maiden outfit before.

It had just passed four o'clock, and Nagato and Koizumi still hadn't finished taking the entries and setting up the grid.

Asahina stood and held the decoratively wrapped prize, her smile looking a bit forced for a mascot. It was too chilly to be dressed as a shrine maiden, but this really wasn't the time to be thinking about details like that. As I was mentally calculating how long it would take her to get out of this outfit and into her school uniform, the amidakuji setup was finally completed. As I expected, if you'd rolled up the series of papers, you'd have a decent-size scroll.

Haruhi casually picked up a pen and chose one of the dozens of vertical lines, at the bottom of which she drew a heart. Then as an afterthought, she added several more horizontal bars, just to mix things up.

"Now, then! Whoever reaches this heart will receive Asahina's chocolate! The winner will surely rejoice! We'll start from...the right side!"

If she'd only start from the heart mark and work backward, this could all be done in one go. Why did she have to waste so much time? I understood her desire to rile up the audience by gradually building tension, but it was incredibly inconvenient for me.

Haruhi had no inkling of my impatience; she set a CD player

down on the table and hit the play button. An energetic classical theme began to fill the space. It was the "Infernal Galop" from *Orpheus in the Underworld*. What was this supposed to be, sports day?

I'd have to resort to my trump card. Fortunately, I was sitting next to the goddess of lotteries.

"Sorry, Nagato." Pretending to look at the pile of bills and coins collecting in the rice cracker tin, I whispered into the ear of the cashier sitting motionless in a folding chair. "I need this to be over after a single draw. There's no time."

"..."

Nagato was gazing at the shrine maiden, who shivered from a combination of cold and nervousness. Her eyes moved to regard me, and then without so much as a word, she stood. Just before Haruhi began tracing lines down with a red pen, Nagato reached her hand out and added a single horizontal segment.

Ten minutes later, I had Asahina's hand in mine and was running with her to the clubroom.

"W-wah—Kyon, wait...! It hurts! Wh-what's the matter?" she cried as I dragged her to keep up with me, but I didn't have time to be considerate. There were barely five minutes left.

"I'll explain later. Right now, we have to hurry."

I carried my petite schoolmate up the stairs three steps at a time.

As far as the amidakuji went, Nagato made my wish come true. The very first student won, which left both Haruhi and the rest of the onlookers feeling let down—but hey, somebody had to win. Haruhi was determined to keep the energy level high, so she switched the background music to "See the Conquering Hero Comes," dragging the student with the winning ticket (number 56) up to stand in front of Asahina. Incidentally, the winner was a curly-haired freshman girl, whose embarrassed fidgeting left an impression on me. Amid the strangely warm atmosphere, Asahina awkwardly handed the prize to the girl, then shook hands with her at Haruhi's behest, at which point everybody inexplicably applauded. I endured it, watching Haruhi produce a Polaroid camera from somewhere and take a snapshot of the two girls, but that was my limit.

I took Asahina's hand without waiting for discussion, and I dragged her off before I'd even had time to think of an excuse. We reached the clubroom.

"Eeek, um…what is…uh, Kyon…?"

Asahina's suspicion was understandable. I quickly pulled her into the room.

"Hurry, change!" Her uniform was hanging on the clothes rack; I thrust it at her. "You've got three minutes! Hurry!"

I don't know if I was intense or simply scary, but either way Asahina nodded but made no move to actually change her clothes. I was just about ready to start removing them myself, when she pointed at the door with a pale fingertip.

"Er…"

"What?!"

"Please wait outside!"

I was out in a single second. I stood in front of the door, glaring at my watch. Twelve minutes, thirty-three seconds.

"Asahina, are you done?"

"…Wait, please!"

There was no time to allow my imagination to run wild with the sounds of rustling fabric. I was anxious enough just worrying about Haruhi following me back to the clubroom.

"Asahina!"

"Just a bit more…"

It was four fourteen. I couldn't wait any longer. I barged back into the room.

"Wah, Kyon! I'm not—Kyon, wha—?"

Asahina froze, her hands at the fastener of her school uniform's blouse. The red trousers and white jacket of her shrine maiden costume were scattered on the floor—proof that she really had been hurrying. I'd pick them up later.

I grabbed both of her shoulders and pushed her against the door of the broom closet.

"Eek, K-Kyo—"

I heard her cries as I pushed her recklessly back, which wasn't a great idea. Her foot slipped, and the force of my pushing made me push her right over, and I fell onto her.

"Wha—! No, don't—"

What the hell was I doing? There was no time to gaze at her weakly shaking head as she was laid out on the floor. I picked up the school-uniformed girl, slammed the steel door of the broom closet open, and shoved her inside.

"Asahina, listen to me. Listen very carefully. Right now, you must travel eight days back in time. Do you understand? Just do it."

Asahina was stunned, tears still in the corners of her eyes. "...B-but, without authorization—"

"Just do it! Right now!"

"Eight days back? Um, what time?"

Crap, I had to remember. What time had it been? What had Asahina said? *Kyon, you told me to go eight days back, to—*

"Three forty-five PM. And hurry!"

"O-okay...huh?" Asahina looked up at me like a small, frightened animal, then placed one hand to her head. "I haven't even made the request yet, and authorization's already come. Space-time coordinates...eight days ago, February seventh, three forty-five PM...to right here? Wha—top priority code...?"

"You'll understand when you get there. I'll be waiting for you. I'll take care of you somehow. And tell him I said hi."

Ten seconds until four fifteen.

I gave the shocked Asahina a nod as I closed the broom closet's door. I heard no breathing from within the steel enclosure.

There's an old saying: what goes around, comes around. If you do something for somebody else, eventually it will come back around to you—and for better or for worse, I'd never felt the truth of that statement more than I did at that moment. The person responsible for my panicked state at this moment was none other than myself, who two days earlier had given Asahina the return time of four sixteen PM. When I'd chosen that time, I never imagined that I'd be cutting things so close. Either way, it was my own fault.

"Asahina?"

I spoke to the closet. There was no answer. I knew it was pointless. I couldn't give any warnings to my past self. I knew, because I hadn't myself heard any such warnings, and Asahina hadn't said anything about them to me. I wanted to say something, but I was out of time.

My watch's display now indicated three seconds past four fifteen.

It was extremely quiet. All I could hear was the sound of the breeze and the noise that rode in on it, that of the chattering in the courtyard. Were they still at it out there?

I stood in front of the broom closet and continued to wait.

Clunk—

That wasn't the sound, exactly, but there was a sound from within the closet. Something that was not a broom.

I couldn't hear breathing, but I sensed someone. At exactly four sixteen, the plain old steel closet felt somehow more like a piece of antique furniture.

I opened the door and said the line I'd prepared especially for the occasion.

"Welcome home, Asahina."

She was wearing the long coat and shawl I hadn't seen in two days—the clothes she'd borrowed from Tsuruya.

"Oh...um..."

Asahina looked down, bashful, then slowly lifted her face back up. Her crystal eyes hesitantly rose to meet mine, then stopped. Finally her faintly smiling lips bloomed into a voice.

"I'm back."

It would have been nice to savor the moment for a while, but the circumstances Asahina and I found ourselves in would not allow that. I had to have her change out of the street clothes she was wearing, but I hadn't gotten her school uniform back from Tsuruya yet.

With no other option, I wound up having Asahina change back into her shrine maiden clothing, as I stood in the hall, slumped against the clubroom door.

Haruhi and the others were sure taking their sweet time. It was convenient for me, sure, but I worried that it was a little too convenient. Meanwhile, along came a person carrying a paper bag in her hand, a person whose arrival would have saved me some trouble if it had been a bit sooner.

"Yoo-hoo! Kyon, apologies! Here, I got Mikuru's uniform and her school shoes. I was gonna give 'em to you during lunch, but I forgot." Tsuruya closed the distance between us with a few steps. "So! Haru-nyan and the others are up to something in the courtyard, but where's Mikuru?"

She grinned as I pointed wordlessly at the clubroom door, then turned the doorknob as though she were casually opening her own refrigerator.

"Heya, Mikuru! Getting changed? Hey, perfect timing. I'll just take those clothes home with me!" Tsuruya winked at me, then went into the room. Staring discreetly at the opposite wall in the hallway, I couldn't see into the room, but it was still easy for me to imagine Asahina's surprised face. I'd seen it many times before, after all.

"Here, lemme help. Time to change, time to change! Was today free shrine maiden day or something?"

I sat down in the hallway, listening to Asahina's frantic cries and Tsuruya's childish laughter. Tsuruya probably didn't care why Asahina was wearing the clothes Tsuruya had supposedly lent to her long-lost sister. Both she and I knew that trying to explain it was pointless. Tsuruya's greatness lay in the fact that she wasn't worried about it. I doubted I would ever reach her level in my lifetime.

I smiled ruefully, just as Haruhi returned with Nagato and Koizumi in tow, the latter carrying the folding table on his back. She strode toward me, proudly rattling the tin full of money, as though she were a fisherman and it was her big haul.

"Why'd you drag Mikuru away? We got booed!"

I'd been afraid she would catch a cold if she were outside in those flimsy clothes any longer, I told her. Besides, it was a waste not to charge at least five hundred yen for the aesthetic appeal of that costume.

"Yeah, good point. I see what you're saying. We've gotta go all out in times like this. People will stop appreciating us, other-wise," Haruhi readily agreed. Perhaps she'd already started the second phase of her plan. "Anyway, Kyon, I was really surprised! Yuki started giving out consolation prizes!" She patted the girl on her slender shoulders. "You know those bargain-size bags of chocolates? The kind with the letters of the alphabet and stuff on 'em? Yuki passed one out to everybody who lost the game! I was really surprised she did that kind of preparation. Yuki, you were really thinking ahead. But it's a good idea. We'll have a consola-tion prize next time we do something like this, and it'll defi-nitely loosen people's wallets!"

I was sure they only wanted to get close to Nagato, but I was

Nagaru Tanigawa

deeply moved by her quick thinking. She'd bought me time that I'd desperately needed.

"..."

Nagato moved slightly, as though indicating that she wanted to get inside the room and start reading. It was an expression only I could read.

Just then, the door opened from the inside.

"Oh, Tsuruya, you're here. What's up with those clothes?"

"Heya, Haru-nyan! I lent these to Mikuru—just comin' to get them back, so I won't get in your way!" Tsuruya draped the coat over her shoulder, putting the remaining clothes in the bag and spinning a shoe around on the tip of her finger. "See ya, Haru-nyan!"

"Sure, see you later, Tsuruya."

After exchanging a high five with Haruhi, Tsuruya disappeared down the hallway, having not even once so much as indicated that anything strange was going on—as though it were a totally ordinary day. I'd never be that good of an actor. She was a person to be reckoned with. The Tsuruya clan would prosper so long as she was around.

"..."

Nagato drifted into the room, artlessly taking a book down from the shelf, opening a folding chair, and immediately sitting down to read.

Watching out of the corner of her eye as I helped Koizumi bring the table in, Haruhi didn't seem to notice that Asahina, in her shrine maiden outfit, was looking a bit nostalgic. "Mikuru, next time you buy tea, go ahead and get the expensive stuff. Our war chest is pretty full now, thanks to you! Be happy, Mikuru! These grades mean I'm promoting you to second lieutenant brigade chief!"

Watching Haruhi sit at the brigade chief's desk looking immensely pleased with herself, I secured a seat at the edge of the table and collapsed on it, exhausted.

274

I was seriously tired. I now understood all too well what it was like to tamper with time in order to make events match up. Even if I'd wanted to blame someone, I'd been the one to do it all, so the responsibility target would be painted squarely on me. Were things always this hard for time travelers? If so, I'd have to be careful not to tell Asahina anything for a while. She was carrying a heavy psychological load, and she might roll into a ball like a pill bug at the slightest prod.

"You could have shared some of that burden with me, you know. Cleaning up after messes is my specialty," said Koizumi quietly enough that only I could hear as he removed the wrapping on a booster pack of trading cards. "I believe I've come to understand a bit of Haruhi's plan."

I looked up to see Koizumi scrutinizing his cards and smiling; our eyes met. "I wonder which hairstyle would go the best with this outfit," I heard Haruhi say; she'd sat Asahina down in a chair and was playing around with her hair. As I watched, Asahina narrowed her eyes like a cat whose fur is being brushed.

"Didn't you say something about Haruhi's behavior not being any different than usual?"

"That's exactly what I mean. Treasure hunting and city patrols are the kinds of things Suzumiya would do. Or rather, she was deliberately trying to appear as though she was simply doing her usual activities. Nobody would've thought you'd actually forgotten Valentine's Day—not even Suzumiya. It's a day every high school boy worries about, whether or not he has someone likely to give him a present. The two consecutive days of patrolling were the embodiment of that. It was designed to make you agonize over whether or not you'd actually get anything."

She could've just put the chocolates in my shoe locker or something. It wasn't only a post office box for time travelers, after all.

"Suzumiya simply hates conventionality. No doubt she thought that wouldn't be very interesting. But toiling to dig up buried treasure makes it that much more rewarding when you finally find it."

Koizumi continued to rearrange the cards in his hand.

"I was very pleased, myself. Were you not?"

What was that, some kind of leading question?

Just as I was trying to think of an effective rebuttal—

"Hey, Kyon and Koizumi! No more private chatter! Break time's over!"

Asahina started at the sudden exclamation, which got both Koizumi's and my attention. Haruhi removed her hands from the chignon into which she'd arranged Asahina's hair.

"Now, it's time for a lecture!" She tapped the whiteboard. "Kyon and Koizumi especially, you guys better listen up."

A strategist's smile flickered across the brigade chief's face, and she spoke like a cram school instructor addressing a group of pleasant but less-than-bright students.

"We're going to discuss activities for the month of March."

I thought about the March calendar. "Oh, like Hinamatsuri?"

Haruhi was silent for a moment. "...Yes, good point. There's that too."

So she'd forgotten about it, I said.

"I remembered it. If you want to enjoy new experiences, it's important to learn from the past, so obviously I'd never forget something like that. So on March third, yes, we'll scatter hina-arare down from the top floor balcony!"

That was the first time I'd heard of that particular Hinamatsuri tradition.

"Be that as it may, there's another March event we can't forget." Haruhi's smile was as brilliant as the heart of the Milky Way galaxy as seen through a powerful telescope. "And today I want you and Koizumi alone to carve that day in your brains."

So what was it that she was so excitedly lecturing us about?

"I'm talking about White Day! March fourteenth! You've got to pay back every single girl who gave you anything on Valentine's Day with a reward thirty times greater!"

Normally she was like a blinkered horse charging madly ahead, so why did she always have to choose the most inconvenient times to turn suddenly conventional? I supposed the "thirty times" figure was the Haruhi inflation factor at work.

"Yuki and Mikuru, you should ask for whatever you want! These two"—Haruhi pointed to Koizumi and me—"will pay you back with anything you ask for. The days of crane spirits repaying their debts are long gone; nowadays humans do it too. And with better stuff than fabric too!"

Haruhi grinned hugely.

"I've thought of many examples of stuff I might want, but I'm still thinking about them. I'll reveal them soon, though. And don't worry; I'll make sure it's something you can get within a month."

She certainly had no compunctions. She'd probably be just as bad as Kaguya-hime in "The Bamboo-Cutter's Tale," who sent all her poor suitors on impossible tasks. I just prayed it wouldn't be something totally impossible, like "finding the kingdom of Atlantis" or "discovering the Fountain of Youth."

"Okay, but we're going to take into account the amount of effort we wasted on all that treasure hunting," I said. By the time I realized my retort was going to backfire, it was too late.

"Of course!" said Haruhi, her eyes shining as though the entire Pleiades was concentrated within them. "I look forward to that. If you're going to give me what I want, I'll go anywhere to get it— even Mars. Right, Mikuru, Yuki? You're with me, aren't you?"

Asahina and Nagato both nodded, though Asahina reluctantly, and Nagato without looking up from her book. At this I could only shrug, along with Koizumi, our timing perfectly in sync.

AFTERWORD

We don't know in advance what we're going to do in the future, but the truth is we often don't even know what we were thinking in the past.

Saying "I don't remember what I was thinking then" might be more accurate than "I don't know," which is why we supposedly make notes—to avoid forgetting. But then there are times when we forget what the note was even talking about. For example—

. . . So that's how I was going to start this afterword. But when I pulled out an old notebook to prove it, the contents were so incomprehensible that it wasn't a question of having forgotten what I meant—it was more like my past self had been receiving mysterious signals and gone into an automatic writing trance. Looking at titles like "The Million Strands of Ginger" or "Pavlov's Tadpole," I found myself totally bewildered; I couldn't even begin to interpret them.

At the time I was no doubt brimming with confidence in the power of my memory, thinking that if I just wrote down those few words, I'd be able to read them later and remember all the related details. Looking back at them now, not only do I not remember what I was thinking about, I don't even care. I'm sure they were stupid ideas, and if by some miracle they were good ones, I'd just be annoyed at having been bested by my past self. So I'd rather not know.

In any case, nowadays when I make notes, I've learned to write down as many details as I can. Of course, it's all well and good to write something down, but it often happens that I forget the plain fact that I ever wrote anything at all. I suppose that's a different problem...

Incidentally, this volume wound up being the longest in the series.

The long winter that began in *The Disappearance* finally ends, and from here on out we'll be getting into spring. I should say that my very favorite time of year is early summer, when you can hear frogs' tranquil voices along with cicadas' busy cries. Just knowing that it won't be cold again for a good long while is enough to make me happy. Plus it's a lot easier to walk over to the corner store in the middle of the night.

All that aside, it's thanks to the support of many people that I've managed to get this far. When I look back, it truly seems like the blink of an eye since the very first volume, which fills me with a combination of surprise and frustration—has the trip been a good one?

Even as I thank you again for your support, I hope that you will enjoy the next volume.

Until we meet again.

THE
INTRIGUES
OF
HARUHI
SUZUMIYA

Illustration by Noizi ITO

SHE BLINKED
IN SURPRISE.

THE SIGHT
OF NAGATO
AND ASAHINA
WENT PRETTY
WELL WITH
THE FOOD.

"EAT."